Captain Jim

Mary Grant Bruce

CAPTAIN JIM

By

MARY GRANT BRUCE

1919

CONTENTS

CHAPTER I

JOHN O'NEILL'S LEGACY

"Queer, isn't it? " Jim said.

"Rather! " said Wally.

They were sitting on little green chairs in Hyde Park. Not far off swirled the traffic of Piccadilly; glancing across to Hyde Park Corner, they could see the great red motor-'buses, meeting, halting, and then rocking away in different directions, hooting as they fled. The roar of London was in their ears.

It was a sunny morning in September. The Park was dotted in every direction with shining perambulators, propelled by smart nurses in uniform, and tenanted by proud little people, fair-haired and rosy, and extremely cheerful. Wally liked the Park babies. He referred to them collectively as "young dukes. "

"They all look so jolly well tubbed, don't they? " he remarked, straying from the subject in hand. "Might be soap advertisements. Look, there's a jolly little duke in that gorgeous white pram, and a bigger sized duke trotting alongside, with a Teddy-bear as big as himself. Awful nice kids. " He smiled at the babies in the way that made it seem ridiculous that he should be grown-up and in uniform.

"They can't both be dukes, " said Jim literally. "Can't grow more than one in a family; at least not at the same time, I believe. "

"Oh, well, it doesn't matter—and anyhow, the one in the pram's a duchess, " returned Wally. "I say, the duke's fallen in love with you, Jim. "

"The duke, " a curly-haired person in a white coat, hesitated on the footpath near the two subalterns, then mustering his courage, came close to Jim and gravely presented him with his Teddy-bear. Jim received the gift as gravely, and shook hands with the small boy, to his great delight.

"Thanks, awfully, " he said. "It's a splendid Teddy, isn't it? "

The nurse, greatly scandalized, swooped down upon her charge, exhorting him to be ashamed, now, and not worry the gentleman. But the "duke" showed such distress when Jim attempted to return the Teddy-bear that the matter had to be adjusted by distracting his attention in the direction of some drilling soldiers, while Wally concealed the toy under the embroidered rug which protected the plump legs of the "duchess" — who submitted with delighted gurgles to being tickled under the chin. They withdrew reluctantly, urged by the still horrified nurse.

"See what it is to be beautiful and have the glad eye! " jeered Wally. "Dukes never give *me* Teddy-bears! "

"It's my look of benevolent age, " Jim said, grinning. "Anyhow, young Wally, if you'll stop beguiling the infant peerage, and attend to business, I'll be glad. We'll have Norah and Dad here presently. "

"I'm all attention, " said his friend. "But there's nothing more to be said than that it *is* rum, is there? And we said that. "

"Norah gave me a letter from poor old O'Neill to show you, " Jim said. "I'll read it, if you like. "

The merriment that was never very far from Wally Meadows' eyes died out as his chum unfolded a sheet of paper, closely written.

"He wrote it in the hotel in Carrignarone, I suppose? " he asked gently.

"Yes; just after dinner on the night of the fight. You see, he was certain he wasn't coming back. Anyhow, this is what he says:

*****

"My Dear Norah, —

"If I am alive after to-night you will not get this letter: it is only to come to you if I shall have 'gone West. ' And please don't worry if I do go West. You see, between you all you have managed almost to make me forget that I am just an apology for a man. I did not think it could be done, but you have done it. Still, now and then I remember, and I know that there will be long years after you have all gone back

2

to that beloved Australia of yours when there will be nothing to keep me from realizing that I am crippled and a hunchback. To-night I have the one chance of my life of living up to the traditions of O'Neills who were fighting men; so if, by good luck, I manage to wing a German or two, and then get in the way of an odd bullet myself, you mustn't grudge my finishing so much more pleasantly than I had ever hoped to do.

"If I do fall, I am leaving you that place of mine in Surrey. I have hardly any one belonging to me, and they have all more money than is good for them. The family estates are entailed, but this is mine to do as I please with. I know you don't need it, but it will be a home for you and your father while Jim and Wally are fighting, if you care for it. And perhaps you will make some use of it that will interest you. I liked the place, as well as I could like any place outside Ireland; and if I can look back—and I am very sure that I shall be able to look back—I shall like to see you all there—you people who brought the sun and light and laughter of Australia into the grey shadows of my life—who never seemed to see that I was different from other men.

"Well, good-bye—and God keep you happy, little mate.

"Your friend,
"John O'Neill. "

*****

Jim folded the letter and put it back in his pocket, and there was a long silence. Each boy was seeing again a strip of Irish beach where a brave man had died proudly.

"Different! " Wall said, at last, with a catch in his voice. "He wasn't different—at least, only in being a jolly sight better than most fellows."

Jim nodded.

"Well, he had his fight, and he did his bit, and, seeing how he felt about things, I'm glad for his sake that he went out, " he said. "Only I'm sorry for us, because it was a pretty big thing to be friends with a man like that. Anyhow, we won't forget him. We wouldn't even without this astonishing legacy of Norah's. "

"Have you any particulars about it? " Wally asked.

"Dad got a letter from O'Neill too—both were sent to his lawyers; he must have posted them himself that evening in Carrignarone. Dad's was only business. The place is really left to him, in trust for Norah, until she comes of age; that's so that there wouldn't be any legal bother about her taking possession of it at once if she wants to. Poor old Norah's just about bowled over. She felt O'Neill's death so awfully, and now this has brought it all back. "

"Yes, it's rough on Norah, " Wally said. "I expect she hates taking the place. "

"She can't bear the idea of it. Dad and I don't much care about it either. "

Wally pondered.

"May I see that letter again? " he asked presently.

Jim Linton took out the letter and handed it to his friend. He filled his pipe leisurely and lit it, while Wally knitted his brows over the sheet of cheap hotel paper. Presently he looked up, a flash of eagerness in his keen brown eyes.

"Well, I think O'Neill left that place to Norah with a purpose, " he said. "I don't believe it's just an ordinary legacy. Of course, it's hers, all right; but don't you think he wanted something done with it? "

"Done with it? "

"Yes. Look here, " Wally put a thin forefinger on the letter. "Look what he says—'Perhaps you will make some use of it that may interest you. ' Don't you think that means something? "

"I believe it might, " Jim said cautiously. "But what? "

Wally hesitated.

4

"Well, he was just mad keen on the War, " he said. "He was always planning what he could do to help, since he couldn't fight, —at least, since he thought he couldn't, " the boy added with a sigh. "I wonder he hadn't used it himself for something in connexion with the War. "

"He couldn't—it's let, " Jim put in quickly. "The lawyers wrote about it to Dad. It's been let for a year, and the lease expires this month—they said O'Neill had refused to renew it. That rather looks as if he had meant to do something with it, doesn't it? "

Wally nodded vigorously.

"I'll bet he did. Now he's left it to Norah to carry on. You see, they told us his own relations weren't up to much. I expect he knew they wouldn't make any use of it except for themselves. Why, it's as clear as mud, Jim! O'Neill knew that Norah didn't actually need the place, and that she and your father wanted to be near you and still help the war themselves. They didn't like working in London—Norah's too much of a kid, and your father says himself he's not trained. Now they've got a perfectly ripping chance! "

"Oh, bless you, Wally! " said a thankful voice behind them.

The boys sprang to their feet. Behind them stood a tall girl with a sun-tanned face and straight grey eyes—eyes that bore marks of tears, of which Norah for once was unashamed. Her brown curls were tied back with a broad black ribbon. She was very slender— "skinny, " Norah would have said—but, despite that she was at what is known as "the awkward age, " no movement of Norah Linton's was ever awkward. She moved with something of the unconcerned grace of a deer. In her blue serge coat and skirt she presented the well-groomed look that was part and parcel of her. She smiled at the two boys, a little tremulously.

"Hallo! " said her brother. "We didn't hear you—where did you spring from? "

"Dad dropped me at the Corner—he had to go on to Harrods, " Norah answered. "I came across the grass, and you two were so busy talking you didn't know I was there. I couldn't help hearing what you said, Wally. "

"Well, I'm glad you did, " Wally answered, "But what do you think yourself, Nor? "

"I was just miserable until I heard you, " Norah said. "It seemed too awful to take Sir John's house—to profit by his death. I couldn't bear it. But of course you're right. I do think I was stupid—I read his letter a dozen times, but I never saw it that way. "

"But you agree with Wally, now? " Jim asked.

"Why, of course—don't you? I suppose I might have had the sense to see his meaning in time, but I could only think of seeming to benefit by his death. However, as long as one member of the family has seen it, it's all right. " She flashed a smile at Wally. "I'm just ever so much happier. It makes it all—different. We were such—" her voice trembled—"such good chums, and now it seems as if he had really trusted us to carry on for him. "

"Of course he did, " Wally said. "He knew jolly well you would make good use of it, and it would help you, too, when Jim was away."

"Jim? " said that gentleman. "Jim? What are you leaving yourself out for? Aren't you coming? Got a Staff job at home? "

"I'm ashamed of you, Wally, " said Norah severely. "Of course, if you don't *want* to belong——! " Whereat Wally Meadows flushed and laughed, and muttered something unintelligible that nevertheless was quite sufficient for his friends.

It was not a thing of yesterday, that friendship. It went back to days of small-boyhood, when Wally, a lonely orphan from Queensland, had been Jim Linton's chum at the Melbourne Grammar School, and had fallen into a habit of spending his holidays at the Linton's big station in the north of Victoria, until it seemed that he was really one of the Billabong family. Years had knitted him and Jim and Norah into a firm triumvirate, mates in the work and play of an Australian cattle-run; watched over by the silent grey man whose existence centred in his motherless son and daughter—with a warm corner in his affections for the lithe, merry Queensland boy, whose loyalty to Billabong and its people had never wavered since his childhood.

Then, just as Jim had outgrown school and was becoming his father's right-hand man on the station, came the world-upheaval of the European War, which had whisked them all to England. Business had, at the moment, summoned Mr. Linton to London; to leave Norah behind was not to be thought of, and as both the boys were wild to enlist, and Wally was too young to be accepted in Australia—though not in England—it seemed that the simplest thing to do was to make the pilgrimage a general one, and let the chums enlist in London. They had joined a famous British regiment, obtaining commissions without difficulty, thanks to cadet training in Australia. But their first experience of war in Flanders had been a short one: they were amongst the first to suffer from the German poison-gas, and a long furlough had resulted.

Mr. Linton and Norah had taken them to Ireland as soon as they were fit to travel; and the bogs and moors of Donegal, coupled with trout-fishing, had gone far to effect a cure. But there, unexpected adventure had awaited them. They had made friends with Sir John O'Neill, the last of an old North of Ireland family: a half-crippled man, eating out his heart against the fate that held him back from an active part in the war. Together they had managed to stumble on an oil-base for German submarines, concealed on the rocky coast; and, luck and boldness favouring them, to trap a U-boat and her crew. It had been a short and triumphant campaign—skilfully engineered by O'Neill; and he alone had paid for the triumph with his life.

John O'Neill had died happily, rejoicing in for once having played the part of a fighting man; but to the Australians his death had been a blow that robbed their victory of all its joy. They mourned for him as for one of themselves, cherishing the memory of the high-souled man whose spirit had outstripped his weak body. Jim and Wally, from exposure on the night of the fight, had suffered a relapse, and throat-trouble had caused their sick-leave to be extended several times. Now, once more fit, they were back in London, expecting to rejoin their regiment immediately.

"So now, " Jim said, "the only question is, what are you going to do with it? "

"I'm going to think hard for a day, " said Norah. "So can you two; and we'll ask Dad, of course. "

"And then Dad will tell you what to do, " said Jim, grinning.

"Yes of course he will. Dad always has splendid ideas, " said Norah, laughing. "But we won't have any decision for a day, because it's a terribly big thing to think of. I wish I was grown up—it must be easier to settle big questions if you haven't got your hair down your back! "

"I don't quite see what your old curly mop has to do with it, but anyhow, you needn't be in a hurry to put it up, " said her brother. "It's awful to be old and responsible, isn't it Wally? " To which Wally responded with feeling, "Beastly! " and endeavoured to look more than nineteen—failing signally.

"Let's go and look at the Row, " Norah said.

"Dad will find us all right, I suppose? " Jim hesitated.

"Why, he couldn't miss you! " said Norah, laughing. "Come on. "

Even when more than a year of War had made uniform a commonplace in London streets, you might have turned to look at Jim and Wally. Jim was immensely tall; his chum little less so; and both were lean and clean-shaven, tanned to a deep bronze, and stamped with a look of resolute keenness. In their eyes was the deep glint that comes to those who have habitually looked across great spaces. The type has become familiar enough in London now, but it generally exists under a slouch hat; and these lads were in British uniform, bearing the badges of a famous marching regiment. At first they had hankered after the cavalry, being much more accustomed to ride than to walk: but as the armies settled down into the Flanders mud it became increasingly apparent that this was not to be a horseman's war, and that therefore, as Wally put it, if they wanted to be in the fun, they had better make up their minds to paddle with the rest. The amount of "fun" had so far been a negligible quantity which caused them some bitterness of spirit. They earnestly hoped to increase it as speedily as might be, and to give the Hun as much inconvenience as they could manage in the process.

They strolled across the grass to the railings, and looked up and down the tan ribbon of Rotten Row. Small boys and girls, on smart ponies and woolly Shetlands, walked or trotted sedately; or occasionally galloped, followed by elderly grooms torn between pride and anxiety. Jim and Wally thought the famous Row an over-rated concern; failing to realize, from its war aspect, the Row of other days, crammed from fence to fence with beautiful horses and well-turned-out riders, and with half the world looking on from the railings. Nowadays the small boys and girls had it chiefly to themselves, and could stray from side to side at their own sweet will. A few ladies were riding, and there was a sprinkling of officers in khaki; obviously on Army horses and out for exercise. Now and then came a wounded man, slowly, on a reliable cob or sturdy pony—bandages visible, or one arm in a sling. A few people sat about, or leaned on the fences, watching; but there was nothing to attract a crowd. Every one looked business-like, purposeful; clothes were plain and useful, with little frippery. The old glitter and splendour of the Row was gone: the London that used to watch it was a London that had forgotten how to play.

Beyond the Row, carriages, drawn by beautiful pairs of horses, high-stepping, with harness flashing in the sunlight, drove up and down. Some contained old ladies and grey-haired men; but nearly all bore a load of wounded soldiers, with sometimes a tired-faced nurse.

"There's that nice old Lady Ellison—the one that used to take Jim and me out when we were in hospital, " Wally said, indicating a carriage with a magnificent pair of bays. "She was an old dear. My word, I'd like to have the driving of those horses—in a good light buggy on the Billabong track! "

"So would I, " Jim assented. "But I'd take those beastly bearing-reins off before I started. "

"Yes, " said Norah eagerly. "Poor darlings, how they must hate them! Jim, I wish we'd struck London when the coaches used to be seen. "

"Rather! " said Jim. "Anstruther used to tell me about them. Coaches bigger than Cobb & Co. 's, and smart as paint, with teams of four so matched you could hardly tell which was which—and educated beyond anything Australians could dream about. There was one man—poor chap, Anstruther said he was drowned in the *Lusitania*— who had a team of four black cobs. I think Anstruther used to dream about them at night; he got poetical and incoherent when he tried to describe 'em. "

"Fancy seeing a dozen or so of those coaches swinging down Piccadilly on a fine morning! " said Wally. "That would be something to tell black Billy about, Norah! "

"He'd only say Plenty! " said Norah, laughing. "Look—there's Dad!"

They turned to meet a tall grey man who came swinging across the grass with a step as light as his son's. David Linton greeted them with a smile.

"I knew I should find you as near as you could get to the horses, " he said. "This place is almost a rest-cure after Harrod's; I never find myself in that amazing shop without wishing I had a bell on my neck, so that I couldn't get lost. And I always take the wrong lift and find myself among garden tools when all I want is collars. "

"Well, they have lifts round every corner: you want a special lift-sense not to take the wrong one, " Norah defended him.

"Yes, and when you ask your way anywhere in one of these fifty-acre London shops they say, 'Through the archway, sir, ' and disappear: and you look round you frantically, and see about seventeen different archways, and there you are, " Wally stated. "So you plunge into them all in turn, and get hopelessly lost. But it's rather fun. "

"I'd like it better if they didn't call me 'Moddam, '" said Norah. "'Shoes, Moddam? Certainly, Moddam; first to the right, second to the left, lift Number fifteen, fifth floor and the attendant will direct you! ' Then you stagger into space, wishing for a wet towel round your head! "

"I could almost believe, " said her father, regarding her gravely, "that you would prefer Cunjee, with one street, one general store, one blacksmith's, and not much else at all. "

"Why, of course I do, " Norah laughed. "At least you can't get lost there, and you haven't got half a day's journey from the oatmeal place to the ribbon department: they'll sell you both at the same counter, and a frying-pan and a new song too! Think of the economy of time and boot-leather! And Mr. Wilkins knows all about you, and talks to you like a nice fat uncle while he wraps up your parcels. And if you're on a young horse you needn't get off at all—all you have to do is to coo-ee, and Mr. Wilkins comes out prepared to sell you all his shop on the footpath. If *that* isn't more convenient than seventeen archways and fifty-seven lifts, then I'd like to know what is! "

"Moddam always had a great turn of eloquence, hadn't she? " murmured Wally, eyeing her with respect. Whereat Norah reddened and laughed, and accused him of sentiments precisely similar to her own.

"I think we're all much the same, " Jim said. "London's all very well for a visit. But just imagine what it would be if we didn't know we were going back to Billabong some day! "

"What a horrible idea! " Norah said. "But we are—when the old War's over, and the Kaiser has retired to St. Helena, and the Huns are busy building up Belgium and France. And you'll both be captains, if you aren't brigadiers, and all Billabong will expect to see you come back in uniform glittering with medals and things. "

"I like their chance! " said Wally firmly.

"Anyhow, we'll all go back; and that's all that matters, " said Norah. Her eyes dwelt wistfully on the two tall lads.

"And meanwhile, " said Jim, "we'll all go down to Fuller's and have morning tea. One thing, young Norah, you won't find a Fuller's in Cunjee! "

"Why would I be trying? " Norah asked cheerfully. "Sure isn't there Brownie at Billabong? "

"Hear, hear! " agreed Wally. "When I think of Brownie's pikelets—"

"Or Brownie's scones, " added Norah. "Or her sponge-cakes. "

"Or Brownie's tea-pot, as large and as brown as herself, " said Mr. Linton—"then London is a desert. But we'll make the best of it for the present. Come along to Fuller's. "

CHAPTER II

THE HOME FOR TIRED PEOPLE

"To begin with, " said Jim—"what's the place like? "

"Eighty acres, with improvements, " answered his father. "And three farms—all let. "

"Daddy, you're like an auctioneer's advertisement, " Norah protested. "Tell us what it is *like*—the house, I mean. "

"We'll run down and see it soon, " said Mr. Linton. "Meanwhile, the lawyers tell me it's a good house, Queen Anne style — —"

"What's that? " queried Jim.

"Oh, gables and things, " said Wally airily. "Go on, sir, please. "

"Standing in well-timbered park lands, " said Mr. Linton, fishing a paper out of his pocket, and reading from it. "Sorry, Norah, but I can't remember all these thrills without the lawyers' letter. Lounge hall, four reception rooms — —"

"Who are you going to receive, Nor? "

"Be quiet, " said Norah, aiming a cushion at the offender. "Not you, if you're not extra polite! "

"Be quiet, all of you, or I will discontinue this penny reading, " said Mr. Linton severely. "Billiard-room, thirteen bedrooms, three baths (h. and c.)— —"

"Hydraulic and condensed, " murmured Wally. Jim sat upon him with silent firmness, and the reading was unchecked.

"Excellent domestic offices, modern drainage, central heating, electric plant, Company's water— —"

"What on earth— —? " said Jim.

"I really don't know, " said his father. "But I suppose it means you can turn taps without fear of a drought, or they wouldn't put it. Grounds including shady old-world gardens, walled kitchen garden, stone-flagged terrace, lily pond, excellent pasture. Squash racquet court. "

"What's that? " asked Norah.

"You play it with pumpkins, " came, muffled, from beneath Jim. "Let me up, Jimmy—I'll be good. "

"That'll be something unusual, " said Jim, rising. "Yes, Dad? "

"Stabling, heated garage, thatched cottage. Fine timber. Two of the farms let on long leases; one lease expires with lease of house. All in excellent order. I think that's about all. So there you are, Norah. And what are you going to do with it? "

It was the next morning, and the treacherous September sunshine had vanished, giving place to a cold, wet drizzle, which blurred the windows of the Lintons' flat in South Kensington. Looking down, nothing was to be seen but a few mackintoshed pedestrians, splashing dismally along the wet, grey street. Across the road the trees in a little, fenced square were already getting shabby, and a few leaves fluttered idly down. The brief, gay English summer had gone; already the grey heralds of the sky sounded the approach of winter, long and cold and gloomy.

"I've been thinking terribly hard, " Norah said. "I don't think I ever lay awake so long in my life. But I can't make up my mind. Of course it must be some way of helping the War. But how? We couldn't make it a hospital, could we? "

"I think not, " said her father. "The hospital idea occurred to me, but I don't think it would do. You see you'd need nurses and a big staff, and doctors; and already that kind of thing is organized. People well established might do it, but not lone Australians like you and me, Norah. "

"How about a convalescent home? "

"Well, the same thing applies, in a less degree. I believe, too, that they are all under Government supervision, and I must admit I've no hankering after that. We wouldn't be able to call our souls our own; and we'd be perpetually irritated by Government under-strappers, interfering with us and giving orders—no, I don't think we could stand it. You and I have always run our own show, haven't we, Norah—that is, until Jim came back to boss us! " He smiled at his tall son.

There was a pause.

"Well, Dad—you always have ideas, " said Norah, in the voice of one who waits patiently.

Mr. Linton hesitated.

"I don't know that I have anything very brilliant now, " he said. "But I was thinking—do you remember Garrett, the fellow you boys used to tell us about? who never cared to get leave because he hadn't any home. "

"Rather! " said the boys. "Fellow from Jamaica. "

"He was an awfully sociable chap, " Wally added, "and he didn't like cities. So London bored him stiff when he was alone. He said the trenches were much more homelike. "

"Well, there must be plenty of people like that, " said Mr. Linton. "Especially, of course, among the Australians. Fellows to whom leave can't mean what it should, for want of a home: and without any ties it's easy for them to get into all sorts of mischief. And they should get all they can out of leave, for the sake of the War, if for nothing else: they need a thorough mental re-fitting, to go back fresh and keen, so that they can give the very best of themselves when the work begins again. "

"So you think of making Sir John's place into a Home for Tired people? " said Norah, excitedly. "Dad, it's a lovely plan! "

"What do you think, Jim? " asked Mr. Linton.

14

"Yes, I think it's a great idea, " Jim said slowly. "Even the little bit of France we had showed us what I told you—that you've got to give your mind a spring-cleaning whenever you can, if you want to keep fit. I suppose if people are a bit older they can stick it better—some of them, at least. But when you're in the line for any time, you sometimes feel you've just *got* to forget things—smells and pain, and—things you see. "

"Well, you'd forget pretty soon at a place like the one you've been reading about, " said Wally. "Do you remember, Jim, how old poor old Garrett used to look? He was always cheery and ragging, and all that sort of thing, but often he used to look like his own grandfather, and his eyes gave you the creeps. And he couldn't sleep. "

"'M! " said Jim. "I remember. If Garrett's still going, will you have him for your first patient, Nor? What will you call them, by the way—guests? patients? cases? "

"Inmates, " grinned Wally.

"Sounds like a lunatic asylum, " rejoined Jim. "How about lodgers? Or patrons? "

"They'll be neither, donkey, " said Norah pleasantly. "Just Tired People, I think. Oh, Dad, I want to begin! "

"You shouldn't call your superiors names, especially when I have more ideas coming to me, " said Jim severely. "Look here—I agree with Dad that you couldn't have a convalescent home, where you'd need nurses and doctors; but I do think you might ask fellows on final sick-leave, like us—who'd been discharged from hospitals, but were not quite fit yet. Chaps not really needing nursing, but not up to much travelling, or to the racket and fuss of an hotel. "

"Yes, " said Wally. "Or chaps who had lost a limb, and were trying to plan out how they were going to do without it. " His young face looked suddenly grave; Norah remembered a saying of his once before—"I don't in the least mind getting killed, but I don't want Fritz to wing me. " She moved a little nearer to him.

"That's a grand idea—yours too, Jimmy, " she said. "Dad, do you think Sir John would be satisfied? "

"If we can carry out our plan as we hope, I think he would, " Mr. Linton said. "We'll find difficulties, of course, and make mistakes, but we'll do our best, Norah. And if we can send back to the Front cheery men, rested and refreshed and keen—well, I think we'll be doing our bit. And after the War? What then? "

"I was thinking about that, too, " said Norah. "And I got a clearer notion than about using it now, I think. Of course, "—she hesitated— "I don't know much about money matters, or if you think I ought to keep the place. You see, you always seem to have enough to give us everything we want, Dad. I won't need to keep it, will I? I don't want to, even if I haven't got much money. "

"I'm not a millionaire, " said David Linton, laughing. "But—no, you won't need an English income, Norah. "

"I'm so glad, " said Norah. "Then when we go back to Billabong, Dad, couldn't we turn it all into a place for partly-disabled soldiers, —where they could work a bit, just as much as they were able to, but they'd be sure of a home and wouldn't have any anxiety. I don't know if it could be made self—self—you know—earning its own living——"

"Self-supporting, " assisted her father.

"Yes, self-supporting, " said Norah gratefully. "Perhaps it could. But they'd all have their pensions to help them. "

"Yes, and it could be put under a partly-disabled officer with a wife and kids that he couldn't support—some poor beggar feeling like committing suicide because he couldn't tell where little Johnny's next pair of boots was coming from! " added Jim. "That's the most ripping idea, Norah! What do you think, Dad? "

"Yes—excellent, " said Mr. Linton. "The details would want a lot of working-out, of course: but there will be plenty of time for that. I would like to make it as nearly self-supporting as possible, so that there would be no idea of charity about it. "

"A kind of colony, " said Wally.

"Yes. It ought to be workable. The land is good, and with poultry-farming, and gardening, and intensive culture, it should pay well enough. We'll get all sorts of expert advice, Norah, and plan the thing thoroughly. "

"And we'll call it 'The O'Neill Colony, ' or something like that, " said Norah, her eyes shining. "I'd like it to carry on Sir John's name, wouldn't you, Dad? "

"Indeed, yes, " said David Linton. "It has some sort of quiet, inoffensive name already, by the way—yes, Homewood. "

"Well, that sounds nice and restful, " said Jim. "Sort of name you'd like to think of in the trenches. When do we go to see it, Dad? "

"The lawyers have written to ask the tenants what day will suit them, " said his father. "They're an old Indian Army officer and his wife, I believe; General Somers. I don't suppose they will raise any objection to our seeing the house. By the way, there is another important thing: there's a motor and some vehicles and horses, and a few cows, that go with the place. O'Neill used to like to have it ready to go to at any time, no matter how unexpectedly. It was only when War work claimed him that he let it to these people. He was unusually well-off for an Irish landowner; it seems that his father made a heap of money on the Stock Exchange. "

"Horses! " said Norah blissfully.

"And a motor. "

"That will be handy for bringing the Tired People from the station, " said she. "Horses that one could ride, I wonder, Daddy? "

"I shouldn't be surprised, " said her father, laughing. "Anyhow, I daresay you will ride them. "

"I'll try, " said Norah modestly. "It sounds too good to be true. Can I run the fowls, Daddy? I'd like that job. "

"Yes, you can be poultry-expert, " said Mr. Linton. "As for me, I shall control the pigs. "

"You won't be allowed to, " said Wally. "You'll find a cold, proud steward, or bailiff, or head-keeper or something, who would die of apoplexy if either of you did anything so lowering. You may be allowed to ride, Norah, but it won't be an Australian scurry—you'll have to be awfully prim and proper, and have a groom trotting behind you. With a top-hat. " He beamed upon her cheerfully.

"Me! " said Norah, aghast. "Wally, don't talk of such horrible things. It's rubbish, isn't it, Dad? "

"Grooms and top-hats don't seem to be included in the catalogue, " said Mr. Linton, studying it.

"Bless you, that's not necessary, " said Jim. "I mean, you needn't get too bucked because they're not. Public opinion will force you to get them. Probably Nor will have to ride in a top-hat, too. "

"Never! " said Norah firmly. "Unless you promise to do it too, Jimmy. "

"My King and Country have called me, " said Jim, with unction. "Therefore I shall accompany you in uniform—and watch you trying to keep the top-hat on. It will be ever so cheery. "

"You won't, " said Norah. "You'll be in the mud in Flanders——" and then broke off, and changed the subject laboriously. There were few subjects that did not furnish more or less fun to the Linton family; but Norah never could manage to joke successfully about even the Flanders mud, which appeared to be a matter for humorous recollection to Jim and Wally. Whenever the thought of their return to that dim and terrible region that had swallowed up so many crossed her vision, something caught at her heart and made her breath come unevenly. She knew they must go: she would not have had it otherwise, even had it been certain that they would never come back to her. But that they should not—so alive, so splendid in their laughing strength—the agony of the thought haunted her dreams, no matter how she strove to put it from her by day.

Jim saw the shadow in her eyes and came to her rescue. There was never a moment when Jim and Norah failed to understand each other.

"You'll want a good deal of organization about that place, Dad, " he said. "I suppose you'll try to grow things—vegetables and crops? "

"I've been trying to look ahead, " said Mr. Linton. "This is only the second year of the War, and I've never thought it would be a short business. It doesn't seem to me that England realizes war at all, so far; everything goes on just the same—not only 'business as usual, ' but other things too: pleasure, luxuries, eating, clothes; everything as usual. I reckon that conscription is bound to come, and before the Hun gets put in his place nearly every able-bodied man in these islands will be forced to help in the job. "

"I think you're about right, " Jim said.

"Well, then, other things will happen when the men go. Food will get scarcer—the enemy will sink more and more ships; everything that the shops and the farmers sell will get dearer and dearer, and many things will cease to exist altogether. You'll find that coal will run short; and live stock will get scarce because people won't be able to get imported food stuffs that they depend on now. Oh, it's my idea that there are tight times coming for the people of England. And that, of course, means a good deal of anxiety in planning a Home for Tired People. Tired People must be well fed and kept warm. "

"Can't we do it, Daddy? " queried Norah, distressed.

"We're going to try, my girl. But I'm looking ahead. One farm comes in with the house, you know. I think we had better get a man to run that with us on the shares system, and we'll grow every bit of food for the house that we can. We'll have plenty of good cows, plenty of fowls, vegetables, fruit; we'll grow potatoes wherever we can put them in, and we'll make thorough provision for storing food that will keep. "

"Eggs—in water glass, " said Norah. "And I'll make tons of jam and bottle tons of fruit and vegetables. "

"Yes. We'll find out how to preserve lots of things that we know nothing about now. I don't in the least imagine that if real shortage came private people would be allowed to store food; but a house run for a war purpose might be different. Anyhow, there's no shortage yet, so there's no harm in beginning as soon as we can. Of course we can't do very much before we grow things—and that won't be until next year. "

"There's marmalade, " said Norah wisely. "And apple jam—and we'll dry apples. And if the hens are good there may be eggs to save."

"Hens get discouraged in an English winter, and I'm sure I don't blame them, " said Jim, laughing. "Never mind, Nor, they'll buck up in the spring. "

"Then there's the question of labour, " said Mr. Linton. "I'm inclined to employ only men who wouldn't be conscripted: partially-disabled soldiers or sailors who could still work, or men with other physical drawbacks. Lots of men whose hearts are too weak to go 'over the top' from the trenches could drive a plough quite well. Then, if conscription does come, we shall be safe. "

"I'll like to do it, too, " said Norah. "It would be jolly to help them. "

"Of course, it will cut both ways, " Mr. Linton said. "There should be no difficulty in getting men of the kind—poor lads, there are plenty of disabled ones. I'm inclined to think that the question of women servants will be more difficult. "

"Well, I can cook a bit, " said Norah—"thanks to Brownie. "

"My dear child, " said her father, slightly irritated—"you've no idea of what a fairly big English house means, apart from housekeeping and managing. We shall need a really good housekeeper as well as a cook; and goodness knows how many maids under her. You see the thing has got to be done very thoroughly. If it were just you and the boys and me you'd cook our eggs and bacon and keep us quite comfortable. But it will be quite another matter when we fill up all those rooms with Tired People. "

"I suppose so, " said Norah meekly. "But I can be useful, Daddy. "

He patted her shoulder.

"Of course you can, mate. I'm only afraid you'll have too much to do. I must say I wish Brownie were here instead of in Australia. "

"Dear old Brownie, wouldn't she love it all! " said Norah, her eyes tender at the thought of the old woman who had been nurse and mother, and mainspring of the Billabong house, since Norah's own mother had laid her baby in her kind arms and closed tired eyes so many years ago. "Wouldn't she love fixing the house! And how she'd hate cooking with coal instead of wood! Only nothing would make Brownie bad-tempered. "

"Not even Wal and I, " said Jim. "And I'll bet we were trying enough to damage a saint's patience. However, as we can't have Brownie, I suppose you'll advertise for some one else, Dad? "

"Oh, I suppose so—but sufficient unto the day is the evil thereof, " returned Mr. Linton. "I've thought of nothing but this inheritance of Norah's all day, and I'm arriving at the conclusion that it's going to be an inheritance of something very like hard work! "

"Well, that's all right, 'cause there shouldn't be any loafers in war-time, " Norah said. She looked out of the window. "The rain is stopping; come along, everybody, and we'll go down Regent Street on a 'bus. " To do which Norah always maintained was the finest thing in London.

They went down to see Norah's inheritance two days later. A quick train from London dropped them at a tiny station, where the stationmaster, a grizzled man apparently given over to the care of nasturtiums, directed them to Homewood. A walk of a mile along a wide white road brought them to big iron gates, standing open, beside a tiny lodge with diamond-paned windows set in lattice-work, under overhanging eaves; and all smothered with ivy out of which sparrows fluttered busily. The lodgekeeper, a neat woman, looked at the party curiously: no doubt the news of their coming had spread.

From the lodge the drive to the house wound through the park—a wide stretch of green, with noble trees, oak, beech and elm; not towering like Norah's native gum-trees, but flinging wide arms as though to embrace as much as possible of the beauty of the landscape. Bracken, beginning to turn gold, fringed the edge of the gravelled track. A few sheep and cows were to be seen, across the grass.

Captain Jim

"Nice-looking sheep, " said Mr. Linton.

"Yes, but you wouldn't call it over-stocked, " was Jim's comment. Jim was not used to English parks. He was apt to think of any grass as "feed, " in terms of so many head per acre.

The drive, well-gravelled and smoothly rolled, took them on, sauntering slowly, until it turned in a great sweep round a lawn, ending under a stone porch flung out from the front of the house. A wide porch, almost a verandah; to the delighted eyes of the Australians, who considered verandah-less houses a curious English custom, verging on lunacy. Near the house it was shut in with glass, and furnished with a few lounge chairs and a table or two.

"That's a jolly place! " Jim said quickly.

The house itself was long and rambling, and covered with ivy. There were big windows—it seemed planned to catch all the sunlight that could possibly be tempted into it. The lawn ended in a terrace with a stone balustrade, where one could sit and look across the park and to woods beyond it—now turning a little yellow in the sunlight, and soon to glow with orange and flame-colour and bronze, when the early frosts should have painted the dying leaves. From the lawn, to right and left, ran shrubberies and flower-beds, with winding grass walks.

"Why, it's lovely! " Norah breathed. She slipped a hand into her father's arm.

Jim rang the bell. A severe butler appeared, and explained that General and Mrs. Somers had gone out for the day, and had begged that Mr. Linton and his party would make themselves at home and explore the house and grounds thoroughly: an arrangement which considerably relieved the minds of the Australians, who had rather dreaded the prospect of "poking about" the house under the eyes of its tenants. The butler stiffened respectfully at the sight of the boys' uniforms. It appeared presently that he had been a mess-sergeant in days gone by, and now regarded himself as the personal property of the General.

"Very sorry they are to leave the 'ouse, too, sir, " said the butler. "A nice place, but too big for them. "

"Haven't they any children? " Norah asked.

"Only the Captain, miss, and he's in Mesopotamia, which is an 'orrible 'ole for any gentleman to be stuck in, " said the butler with a fine contempt for Mesopotamia and all its works. "And the mistress is tired of 'ousekeeping, so they're going to live in one of them there family 'otels, as they call them. " The butler sighed, and then, as if conscious of having lapsed from correct behaviour, stiffened to rigidity and became merely butler once more. "Will you see the 'ouse now, sir? "

They entered a wide hall in which was a fireplace that drew an exclamation from Norah, since she had not seen so large a one since she left Billabong. This was built to take logs four feet long, to hold which massive iron dogs stood in readiness. Big leather armchairs and couches and tables strewn with magazines and papers, together with a faint fragrance of tobacco in the air, gave to the hall a comforting sense of use. The drawing-room, on the other hand, was chillingly splendid and formal, and looked as though no one had ever sat in the brocaded chairs: and the great dining room was almost as forbidding. The butler intimated that the General and his wife preferred the morning-room, which proved to be a cheery place, facing south and west, with a great window-recess filled with flowering plants.

"This is jolly, " Jim said. "But so would the other rooms be, if they weren't so awfully empty. They only want people in them. "

"Tired people, " Norah said.

"Yes, " Wally put in. "I'm blessed if I think they would stay tired for long, here. "

There was a long billiard-room, with a ghostly table shrouded in dust-sheets; and upstairs, a range of bedrooms of all shapes and sizes, but all bright and cheerful, and looking out upon different aspects of park and woodland. Nothing was out of order; everything was plain, but care and taste were evident in each detail. Then, down a back staircase, they penetrated to outer regions where the corner of Norah's soul that Brownie had made housewifely rejoiced over a big, bright kitchen with pantries and larders and sculleries of the most modern type. The cook, who looked severe, was reading the *Daily*

Mail in the servants' hall; here and there they had glimpses of smart maids, irreproachably clad, who seemed of a race apart from either the cheery, friendly housemaids of Donegal, or Sarah and Mary of Billabong, who disliked caps, but had not the slightest objection to helping to put out a bush-fire or break in a young colt. Norah tried to picture the Homewood maids at either task, and failed signally.

From the house they wandered out to visit well-appointed stables with room for a dozen horses, and a garage where a big touring car stood—Norah found herself quite unable to realize that it belonged to her! But in the stables were living things that came and nuzzled softly in her hand with inquiring noses that were evidently accustomed to gifts of sugar and apples, and Norah felt suddenly, for the first time, at home. There were two good cobs, and a hunter with a beautiful lean head and splendid shoulders; a Welsh pony designed for a roomy tub-cart in the coach house; and a good old stager able for anything from carrying a nervous rider to drawing a light plough. The cobs, the groom explained, were equally good in saddle or harness; and there was another pony, temporarily on a visit to a vet., which Sir John had liked to ride. "But of course Killaloe was Sir John's favourite, " he added, stroking the hunter's soft brown muzzle. "There wasn't no one could show them two the way in a big run. "

They tore themselves with difficulty from the stables, and, still guided by the butler, who seemed to think he must not let them out of his sight, wandered through the grounds. Thatched cottage, orchard, and walled garden, rosery, with a pergola still covered with late blooms, lawns and shrubberies. There was nothing very grand, but all was exquisitely kept; and a kind of still peace brooded over the beauty of the whole, and made War and its shadows seem very far away. The farms, well-tilled and prosperous-looking, were at the western side of the park: Mr. Linton and Jim talked with the tenant whose lease was expiring while Norah and Wally sat on an old oak log and chatted to the butler, who told them tales of India, and asked questions about Australia, being quite unable to realize any difference between the natives of the two countries. "All niggers, I calls them, " said the butler loftily.

"That seems a decent fellow, " said Mr. Linton, as they walked back across the park. "Hawkins, the tenant-farmer, I mean. Has he made a success of his place, do you know? "

"'Awkins 'as an excellent name, sir, " replied the butler. "A good, steady man, and a rare farmer. The General thinks 'ighly of 'im. 'E's sorry enough that 'is lease is up, 'Awkins is. "

"I think of renewing it, under slightly different conditions, " Mr. Linton observed. "I don't wish to turn the man out, if he will grow what I want. "

"Well, that's good news, " said the butler heartily. "I'm sure 'Awkins'll do anything you may ask 'im to, sir. " A sudden dull flush came into his cheeks, and he looked for a moment half-eagerly at Mr. Linton, as if about to speak. He checked himself, however, and they returned to the house, where, by the General's orders, coffee and sandwiches awaited the visitors in the morning-room. The butler flitted about them, seeing to their comfort unobtrusively.

"If I may make so bold as to ask, sir, " he said presently, "you'll be coming to live here shortly? "

"As soon as General Somers leaves, " Mr. Linton answered.

The man dropped his voice, standing rigidly to attention.

"I suppose, sir, " he said wistfully, "you would not be needing a butler? "

"A butler—why. I hadn't thought of such a thing, " said Mr. Linton, laughing. "There are not very many of you in Australia, you know. "

"But indeed, sir, you'll need one, in a place like this, " said the ex-sergeant, growing bold. "Every one 'as them—and if you would be so kind as to consider if I'd do, sir? I know the place, and the General 'ud give me a good record. I've been under him these fifteen years, but he doesn't need me after he leaves here. "

"Well——" said Mr. Linton thoughtfully. "But we shan't be a small family—we mean to fill this place up with officers needing rest. We're coming here to work, not to play. "

"Officers! " said the ex-sergeant joyfully. "But where'd you get any one to 'elp you better, sir? Lookin' after officers 'as been my job this many a year. And I'd serve you faithful, sir. "

Captain Jim

Norah slipped her hand into her father's arm.

"We really would need him, I believe, Daddy, " she whispered.

"You would, indeed, miss, " said the butler gratefully. "I could valet the young gentlemen, and if there's any special attention needed, I could give it. I'd do my very utmost, miss. I'm old to go out looking for a new place at my time of life. And if you've once been in the Army, you like to stay as near it as you can. "

"Well, we'll see, " Mr. Linton said guardedly. "I'll probably write to General Somers about you. " At which the butler, forgetting his butlerhood, came smartly to attention—and then became covered with confusion and concealed himself as well as he could behind a coffee-pot.

"You might do much worse, " Jim remarked, on their way to the station. "He looks a smart man—and though this place is glorious, it's going to take a bit of running. Keep him for a bit, at any rate, Dad. "

"I think it might be as well, " Mr. Linton answered. He turned at a bend in the drive, to look back at Homewood, standing calm and peaceful in its clustering trees. "Well, Norah, what do you think of your property? "

"I'm quite unable to believe it's mine, " said Norah, laughing. "But I suppose that will come in time. However, there's one thing quite certain, Dad—you and I will have to get very busy! "

CHAPTER III

OF LONDON AND OTHER MATTERS

Jim and Wally dropped lightly from the footboard of a swift motor-'bus, dodged through the traffic, and swung quickly down a quiet side-street. They stopped before a stone house, where, from a window above, Norah watched their eager faces as Jim fitted his latchkey and opened the door. She turned back into the room with a little sigh.

"There they are, Dad. And they're passed fit—I know. "

David Linton looked up from the elbow-splint he was making.

"Well, it had to come, mate, " he said.

"Yes, I know. But I hoped it wouldn't! " said poor Norah inconsistently.

"You wouldn't like them not to go, " said her father. And then cheery footsteps clattered up the stairs, and the boys burst in.

"Passed! " shouted Jim. "Fit as fiddles! "

"When? " Norah asked.

"This day week. So we'll have nice time to settle you into Homewood and try those horses, won't we? "

"Yes, rather! " said Norah. "Were they quite satisfied with your arm, Wally? "

"Yes, they say it's a lovely arm, " said that gentleman modestly. "I always knew it, but it's nice to have other people agreeing with me! And they say our lungs are beautiful too; not a trace of gas left. And—oh, you tell them, Jim! "

"And we're not to go out yet, " said Jim, grinning widely. "Special Lewis-gun course at Aldershot first, and after that a bombing course.

27

So there you are. " He broke off, his utterance hindered by the fact that Norah had suddenly hugged him very hard, while David Linton, jumping up, caught Wally's hand.

"Not the Front, my dear boys! "

"Well, not yet, " said Wally, pumping the hand, and finding Norah's searching for his free one. "It's pretty decent, isn't it? because every one knows there will be plenty of war at the Front yet. "

"Plenty indeed, " said Mr. Linton.

"I say, buck up, old chap, " said Jim, patting Norah's shoulder very hard. "One would think we were booked for the trenches to-night! "

"I wouldn't have made an ass of myself if you had been, " said Norah, shaking back her curls and mopping her eyes defiantly. "I was prepared for that, and then you struck me all of a heap! Oh, Jimmy, I am glad! I'd like to hug the War Office! "

"You're the first person I ever heard with such sentiments, " returned her brother. "Most people want to heave bombs at it. However, they've treated us decently, and no mistake. You see, ever since June we've kept bothering them to go out, and then getting throat-trouble and having to cave in again; and now that we really are all right I suppose they think they'll make sure of us. So that's that. "

"I would have been awfully wild if they hadn't passed us, " Wally said. "But since they have, and they'll put us to work, I don't weep a bit at being kept back for awhile. Lots of chaps seem to think being at the Front is heavenly, but I'm blessed if I can see it that way. We didn't have very much time there, certainly, but there were only three ingredients in what we did have—mud, barbed wire, and gas."

"Yes, and it's not much of a mixture, " said Jim. "All the same, it's got to be taken if necessary. Still, I'm not sorry it's postponed for a bit; there will be heaps of war yet, and meanwhile we're just learning the trade. " He straightened his great shoulders. "I never felt so horribly young and ignorant as when I found grown-up men in my charge in France. "

28

"Poor old Jimmy always did take his responsibilities heavily, " said Wally, laughing.

Mr. Linton looked at his big son, remembering a certain letter from his commanding officer which had caused him and Norah to glow with pride; remembering, also, how the men on Billabong Station had worked under "Master Jim. " But he knew that soldiering had always been a serious business to his boy. Personal danger had never entered into Jim's mind; but the danger of ignorant handling of his men had been a tremendous thing to him. Even without "mud, barbed-wire, and gas" Jim was never likely to enjoy war in the light-hearted way in which Wally would certainly take it under more pleasant conditions.

"Well—we've a week then, boys, " he said cheerfully, "and no anxieties immediately before us except the new cook-ladies. "

"Well, goodness knows they are enough, " Norah said fervently.

"Anything more settled? " Jim asked.

"I have an ecstatic letter from Allenby. " Allenby was the ex-sergeant. "He seems in a condition of trembling joy at the prospect of being our butler; and, what is more to the point, he says he has a niece whom he can recommend as a housemaid. So I have told him to instal her before we get to Homewood on Thursday. Hawkins has written a three-volume list of things he will require for the farm, but I haven't had time to study it yet. And Norah has had letters from nineteen registry-offices, all asking for a deposit! "

The boys roared.

"That makes seventy-one, doesn't it, Nor? " Wally asked.

"Something like it, " Norah admitted ruefully. "And the beauty of it is, not one of them will guarantee so much as a kitchenmaid. They say sadly that 'in the present crisis' it's difficult to supply servants. They don't seem to think there's any difficulty about paying them deposit-fees. "

"That phrase, 'in the present crisis, ' is the backbone of business to-day, " Mr. Linton said. "If a shop can't sell you anything, or if they mislay your property, or sell your purchase to some one else, or keep your repairs six months and then lose them, or send in your account with a lot of items you never ordered or received, they simply wave 'the present crisis' at you, and all is well. "

"Yes, but they don't regard it as any excuse if you pay too little, or don't pay at all, " Jim said.

"Of course not—that wouldn't be business, my son, " said Wally, laughing. "The one department the Crisis doesn't hit is the one that sends out bills. " He turned to Norah. "What about the cook-lady, Nor? "

"She's safe, " said Norah, sighing with relief. "There's an awfully elegant letter from her, saying she'll come. "

"Oh, that's good business! " Jim said. For a fortnight Norah had had the unforgettable experience of sitting in registry-offices, attempting to engage a staff for Homewood. She had always been escorted by one or more of her male belongings, and their extreme ignorance of how to conduct the business had been plain to the meanest intelligence. The ex-sergeant, whose spirit of meekness in proposing himself had been in extraordinary contrast to the condescending truculence of other candidates, had been thankfully retained. There had at times seemed a danger that instead of butler he might awake to find himself maid-of-all-work, since not one of the applicants came up to even Norah's limited standard. Finally, however, Mr. Linton had refused to enter any more registry-offices or to let Norah enter them, describing them, in good set terms as abominable holes; and judicious advertising had secured them a housekeeper who seemed promising, and a cook who insisted far more on the fact that she was a lady than on any ability to prepare meals. The family, while not enthusiastic, was hopeful.

"I hope she's all right, " Norah said doubtfully. "I suppose we can't expect much—they all tell you that nearly every servant in England has 'gone into munitions, ' which always sounds as though she'd get fired out of a trench-mortar presently. "

"Some of those we saw might be benefited by the process, " said Mr. Linton, shuddering at memories of registry-offices.

"Well, what about the rest? —haven't you got to get a kitchenmaid and some more housemaids or things? " queried Jim vaguely.

"I'm not going to try here, " said Mr. Linton firmly. "Life is too short; I'd sooner be my own kitchenmaid than let Norah into one of those offices again. Allenby's niece will have to double a few parts at first, and I've written to Ireland—to Mrs. Moroney—to see if she can find us two or three nice country girls. I believe she'll be able to do it. Meanwhile we'll throw care to the winds. I've told Allenby to order in all necessary stores, so that we can be sure of getting something to eat when we go down; beyond that, I decline to worry, or let Norah worry, about anything. "

"Then let's go out and play, " cried Norah, jumping up.

"Right! " said the boys. "Where? "

"Oh, anywhere—we'll settle as we go! " said Norah airily. She fled for her hat and coat.

So they went to the Tower of London—a place little known to the English, but of which Australians never tire—and spent a blissful afternoon in the Armoury, examining every variety of weapons and armament, from Crusaders' chain-mail to twentieth-century rifles. There is no place so full of old stories and of history—history that suddenly becomes quite a different matter from something you learn by the half-page out of an extremely dull book at school. This is history alive, and the dim old Tower becomes peopled with gay and gallant figures clad in shining armour, bent on knightly adventures. There you see mail shirts of woven links that slip like silken mesh through the fingers, yet could withstand the deadliest thrust of a dagger; maces with spiked heads, that only a mighty man could swing; swords such as that with which Coeur-de-Lion could slice through such a mace as though it were no more than a carrot— sinuous blades that Saladin loved, that would sever a down cushion flung in the air. Daggers and poignards, too, of every age, needle-pointed yet viciously strong, with exquisitely inlaid hilts and fine-lined blades; long rapiers that brought visions of gallants with curls and lace stocks and silken hose, as ready to fight as to dance or to make a poem to a fair lady's eyebrow. Helmets of every age, with visors behind which the knights of old had looked grimly as they charged down the lists at "gentle and joyous passages of arms. "

Horse-armour of amazing weight—"I always pictured those old knights prancing out on a thirteen-stone hack, but you'd want a Suffolk Punch to carry that ironmongery! " said Wally. So through room after room, each full of brave ghosts of the past, looking benevolently at the tall boy-soldiers from the New World; until at length came closing-time, and they went out reluctantly, across the flagged yard where poor young Anne Boleyn laid her gentle head on the block; where the ravens hop and caw to-day as their ancestors did in the sixteenth century when she walked across from her grim prison that still bears on its wall a scrawled "Anne. " A dull little prison-room, it must have been, after the glitter and pomp of castles and palaces—with only the rugged walls of the Tower Yard to look upon from the tiny window.

"And she must have had such a jolly good time at first, " said Wally. "Old Henry VIII was very keen on her, wasn't he? And then she was only his second wife—by the time he'd had six they must have begun to feel themselves rather two-a-penny! "

They found a 'bus that took them by devious ways through the City; the part of London that many Londoners never see, since it is another world from the world of Bond Street and Oxford Street, with their newness and their glittering shops. But to the queer folk who come from overseas, it is the real London, and they wander in its narrow streets and link fingers with the past. Old names look down from the smoke-grimed walls: Black Friars and White Friars, Bread Street, St. Martin's Lane, Leadenhall Street, Temple Bar: the hurrying crowd of to-day fades, and instead come ghosts of armed men and of leather-jerkined 'prentices, less ready to work than to fight; of gallants with ruffs, and fierce sailor-men of the days of Queen Bess, home from the Spanish Main with ships laden with gold, swaggering up from the Docks to spend their prize-money as quickly as they earned it. Visions of dark nights, with link-boys running beside chair-bearers, carrying exquisite ladies to routs and masques: of foot-pads, slinking into dark alleys and doorways as the watch comes tramping down the street. Visions of the press-gang, hunting stout lads, into every tavern, whisking them from their hiding-places and off to the ships: to disappear with never a word of farewell until, years later, bronzed and tarred and strange of speech, they returned to astounded families who had long mourned them as dead. Visions of Queen Bess, with her haughty face and her red hair, riding through the City that adored her, her white palfrey stepping daintily through the cheering crowd: and great gentlemen beside her—Raleigh, Essex, Howard. They all wander together through the grey streets where the centuries-old buildings tower overhead: all blending together, a formless jumble of the Past, and yet very much alive: and it does not seem to matter in the least that you look down upon them from a rattling motor-'bus that leaves pools of oil where perchance lay the puddle over which Raleigh flung his cloak lest his queen's slipper should be soiled. Very soon we shall look down on the City from airships while conductors come and stamp our tickets with a bell-punch: but the old City will be unchanged, and it will be only we who look upon it who will pass like shadows from its face.

The Australians left their 'bus in Fleet Street, and dived down a narrow lane to a low doorway with the sign of the *Cheshire Cheese*— the old inn with sanded floor and bare oak benches and tables, where Dr. Johnson and his followers used to meet, to dine and afterwards to smoke long churchwarden pipes and talk, as Wally said, "such amazing fine language that it made you feel a little light-headed. " It is to be feared that the Australians had not any great enthusiasm for Dr. Johnson. They had paid a visit of inspection to the room upstairs where the great man used to take his ease, but not one of them had felt any desire to sit in his big armchair.

"You don't understand what a chance you're scorning, " Mr. Linton had said, laughing, as his family turned from the seat of honour. "Why, good Americans die happy if they can only say they have sat in Dr. Johnson's chair! "

"*I* think he was an ill-mannered old man! " quoth Norah, with her nose tilted. Which seemed to end the matter, so far as they were concerned.

But if the Billabong family took no interest in Dr. Johnson, they had a deep affection for the old inn itself. They loved its dim rooms with their blackened oak, and it was a never-ending delight to watch the medley of people who came there for meals: actors, artists, literary folk, famous and otherwise; Americans, foreigners, Colonials; politicians, fighting men of both Services, busy City men: for everybody comes, sooner or later, to the old *Cheshire Cheese*. Being people of plain tastes they liked the solid, honest meals—especially since increasing War-prices were already inducing hotels and restaurants everywhere to disguise a tablespoonful of hashed oddments under an elegant French name and sell it for as much money as a dinner for a hungry man. Norah used to fight shy of the famous "lark-pudding" until it was whispered to her that what was not good beef steaks in the dish was nothing more than pigeon or possibly even sparrow! after which she enjoyed it, and afterwards pilgrimaged to the kitchen to see the great blue bowls, as big as a wash-hand basin, in which the puddings have been made since Dr. Johnson's time, and the great copper in which they are boiled all night. Legend says that any one who can eat three helpings of lark-pudding is presented with all that remains: but no one has ever heard of a hero able to manage his third plateful!

Best of all the Billabong folk loved the great cellars under the inn, which were once the cloisters of an old monastery: where there are unexpected steps, and dim archways, and winding paths where it is very easy to imagine that you see bare-footed friars with brown habits and rope girdles pacing slowly along. There they bought quaint brown jars and mustard-pots of the kind that are used, and have always been used, on the tables above. But best of all were the great oaken beams above them, solid as England itself, but blackened and charred by the Great Fire of 1666. Norah used to touch the burned surface gently, wondering if it was not a dream—if the hand on the broken charcoal were really her own, more used to Bosun's bridle on the wide plains of Billabong!

There were not many people in the room as they came in this evening, for it was early; dinner, indeed, was scarcely ready, and a few customers sat about, reading evening papers and discussing the war news. In one corner were an officer and a lady; and at sight of the former Jim and Wally saluted and broke into joyful smiles. The officer jumped up and greeted them warmly.

"Hullo, boys! " he said. "I'm delighted to see you. Fit again? —you look it! "

"Dad, this is Major Hunt, " Jim said, dragging his father forward. "You remember, of our regiment. And my sister, sir. I say, I'm awfully glad to see you! "

"Come and meet my wife, " said Major Hunt. "Stella, here are the two young Australians that used to make my life a burden! "

Everybody shook hands indiscriminately, and presently they joined forces round a big table, while Jim and Wally poured out questions concerning the regiment and every one in it.

"Most of them are going strong, " Major Hunt said—"we have a good few casualties, of course, but we haven't lost many officers—most of them have come back. I think all your immediate chums are still in France. But I've been out of it myself for two months—stopped a bit shrapnel with my hand, and it won't get better. " He indicated a bandaged left hand as he spoke, and they realized that his face was worn, and deeply lined with pain. "It's stupid, " he said, and laughed. "But when are you coming back? We've plenty of work for you. "

They told him, eagerly.

"Well, you might just as well learn all you can before you go out, " Major Hunt said. "The war's not going to finish this winter, or the next. Indeed, I wouldn't swear that my six-year-old son, who is drilling hard, won't have time to be in at the finish! " At which Mrs. Hunt shuddered and said, "Don't be so horrible, Douglas! " She was a slight, pretty woman, cheery and pleasant, and she made them all laugh by her stories of work in a canteen.

"All the soldiers used to look upon us as just part of the furniture, " she said. "They used to rush in, in a break between parades, and give their orders in a terrible hurry. As for saying "Please—well——"

"You ought to have straightened them up, " said Major Hunt, with a good-tempered growl.

"Ah, poor boys, they hadn't time! The Irish regiments were better, but then it isn't any trouble for an Irishman to be polite; it comes to him naturally. But those stolid English country lads can't say things easily. " She laughed. "I remember a young lance-corporal who used often to come to our house to see my maid. He was terribly shy, and if I chanced to go into the kitchen he always bolted like a rabbit into the scullery. The really terrible thing was that sometimes I had to go on to the scullery myself, and run him to earth among the saucepans, when he would positively shake with terror. I used to wonder how he ever summoned up courage to speak to Susan, let alone to face the foe when he went to France! "

"That's the sort that gets the V. C. without thinking about it, " said Major Hunt, laughing.

"I was very busy in the Canteen one morning—it was a cold, wet day, and the men rushed us for hot drinks whenever they had a moment. Presently a warrior dashed up to the counter, banged down his penny and said 'Coffee! ' in a voice of thunder. I looked up and caught his eye as I was turning to run for the coffee—and it was my lance-corporal! "

"What did you do? "

"We just gibbered at each other across the counter for a moment, I believe—and I never saw a face so horror-stricken! Then he turned and fled, leaving his penny behind him. Poor boy—I gave it to Susan to return to him. "

"Didn't you ever make friends with any of them, Mrs. Hunt? " Norah asked.

"Oh yes! when we had time, or when they had. But often one was on the rush for every minute of our four-hour shifts. "

"Jolly good of you, " said Jim.

"Good gracious, no! It was a very poor sort of war-work, but busy mothers with only one maid couldn't manage more. And I loved it, especially in Cork: the Irish boys were dears, and so keen. I had a great respect for those boys. The lads who enlisted in England had all their chums doing the same thing, and everybody patted them on the back and said how noble they were, and gave them parties and speeches and presents. But the Irish boys enlisted, very often, dead against the wishes of their own people, and against their priest—and you've got to live in Ireland to know what *that* means. "

"The wonder to me was, always, the number of Irishmen who did enlist, " said Major Hunt. "And aren't they fighters! "

"They must be great, " Jim said. "You should hear our fellows talk about the Dublins and the Munsters in Gallipoli. " His face clouded: it was a grievous matter to Jim that he had not been with those other

36

Australian boys who had already made the name of Anzac ring through the world.

"Yes, you must be very proud of your country, " Mrs. Hunt said, with her charming smile. "I tell my husband that we must emigrate there after the war. It must be a great place in which to bring up children, judging by all the Australians one sees. "

"Possibly—but a man with a damaged hand isn't wanted there, " Major Hunt said curtly.

"Oh, you'll be all right long before we want to go out, " was his wife's cheerful response. But there was a shadow in her eyes.

Wally did not notice any shadow. He had hero-worshipped Major Hunt in his first days of soldiering, when that much-enduring officer, a Mons veteran with the D. S.O. to his credit, had been chiefly responsible for the training of newly-joined subalterns: and Major Hunt, in his turn, had liked the two Australian boys, who, whatever their faults of carelessness or ignorance, were never anything but keen. Now, in his delight at meeting his senior officer again, Wally chattered away like a magpie, asking questions, telling Irish fishing-stories, and other stories of adventures in Ireland, hazarding wild opinions about the war, and generally manifesting a cheerful disregard of the fact that the tired man opposite him was not a subaltern as irresponsible as himself. Somehow, the weariness died out of Major Hunt's eyes. He began to joke in his turn, and to tell queer yarns of the trenches: and presently, indeed, the whole party seemed to be infected by the same spirit, so that the old walls of the *Cheshire Cheese* echoed laughter that must have been exceedingly discouraging to the ghost of Dr. Johnson, if, as is said, that unamiable maker of dictionaries haunts his ancient tavern.

"Well, you've made us awfully cheerful, " said Major Hunt, when dinner was over, and they were dawdling over coffee. "Stella and I were feeling rather down on our luck, I believe, when you appeared, and now we've forgotten all about it. Do you always behave like this, Miss Linton? "

"No, I have to be very sedate, or I'd never keep my big family in order, " said Norah, laughing. "You've no idea what a responsibility they are. "

"Haven't I? " said he. "You forget I have a houseful of my own. "

"Tell me about them, " Norah asked. "Do you keep them in order? "

"We say we do, for the sake of discipline, but I'm not too sure about it, " said Mrs. Hunt. "As a matter of fact, I am very strict, but Douglas undoes all my good work. Is it really true that he is strict in the regiment, Mr. Jim? "

Jim and Wally shuddered.

"I'd find it easier to tell you if he wasn't here, " Jim said. "There are awful memories, aren't there, Wal? "

"Rather! " said Wally feelingly. "Do you remember the day I didn't salute on parade? "

"I believe your mangled remains were carried off the barrack-square, " said Jim, with a twinkle. "I expect I should have been one of the fatigue-part, only that was the day I was improperly dressed! "

"What, you didn't come on parade in a bath-towel, did you? " his father asked.

"No, but I had a shoulder-strap undone—it's nearly as bad, isn't it, sir? " Jim grinned at Major Hunt.

"If I could remember the barrack-square frown, at the moment, I would assume it, " said that officer, laughing. "Never mind, I'll deal with you both when we all get back. "

"You haven't told me about the family, " Norah persisted. "The family you are strict with, I mean, " she added kindly.

"You have no more respect for a field-officer than your brother has, " said he.

"Whisper! " said Mrs. Hunt. "He was only a subaltern himself before the war! "

Her husband eyed her severely.

"You'll get put under arrest if you make statements liable to excite indiscipline among the troops! " he said. "Don't listen to her, Miss Linton, and I'll tell you about the family she spoils. There's Geoffrey, who is six, and Alison, who's five—at least I think she's five, isn't she, Stella? "

"Much you know of your babies! " said his wife, with a fine scorn. "Alison won't be five for two months. "

"Hasn't she a passion for detail! " said her husband admiringly. "Well, five-ish, Miss Linton. And finally there's a two-year-old named Michael. And when they all get going together they make rather more noise than a regiment. But they're rather jolly, and I hope you'll come and see them. "

"Oh, do, " said Mrs. Hunt. "Geoff would just love to hear about Australia. He told me the other day that when he grows up he means to go out there and be a kangaroo! "

"I suppose you know you must never check a child's natural ambitions! " Mr. Linton told her gravely.

"Was that your plan? " she laughed.

"Oh, my pair hadn't any ambitions beyond sitting on horses perpetually and pursuing cattle! " said Mr. Linton. "That was very useful to me, so I certainly didn't check it. "

"H'm! " said Jim, regarding him inquiringly. "I wonder how your theory would have lasted, Dad, if I'd grown my hair long and taken to painting? "

"That wouldn't have been a natural ambition at all, so I should have been able to deal with it with a clear conscience, " said his father, laughing. "In any case, the matter could safely have been left to Norah—she would have been more than equal to it. "

"I trust so, " said Norah pleasantly. "*You* with long hair, Jimmy! "

"It's amazing—and painful—to see the number of fellows who take long hair into khaki with them, " said Major Hunt. "The old Army custom was to get your hair cut over the comb for home service and under the comb for active service. Jolly good rule, too. But the subaltern of the New Army goes into the trenches with locks like a musician's. At least, too many of him does. "

"Never could understand any one caring for the bother of long hair, " said Jim, running his hand over his dark, close-cropped poll. "I say, isn't it time we made a move, if we're going to a show? " He looked half-shyly at Mrs. Hunt. "Won't you and the Major come with us? It's been so jolly meeting you. "

"Good idea! " said Mr. Linton, cutting across Mrs. Hunt's protest. "Do come—I know Norah is longing to be asked to meet the family, and that will give you time to fix it up. " He over-ruled any further objections by the simple process of ignoring them, whereupon the Hunts wisely gave up manufacturing any more: and presently they had discovered two taxis, Norah and her father taking Mrs. Hunt in the first, leaving the three soldiers to follow in the second. They slid off through the traffic of Fleet Street.

"We really shouldn't let you take possession of us like this, " said Mrs. Hunt a little helplessly. "But it has been so lovely to see Douglas cheerful again. He has not laughed so much for months. "

"You are anxious about his hand? " David Linton asked.

"Yes, very. He has had several kinds of treatment for it, but it doesn't seem to get better; and the pain is wearing. The doctors say his best chance is a thorough change, as well as treatment, but we can't manage it—the three babies are expensive atoms. Now there is a probability of another operation to his hand, and he has been so depressed about it, that I dragged him out to dinner in the hope of cheering him up. But I don't think I should have succeeded if we hadn't met you. "

"It was great luck for us, " Norah said. "The boys have always told us so much of Major Hunt. He was ever so good to them. "

"He told me about them, too, " said Mrs. Hunt. "He liked them because he said he never succeeded in boring them! "

"Why, you couldn't bore Jim and Wally! " said Norah, laughing. Then a great idea fell upon her, and she grew silent, leaving the conversation to her companions as the taxi whirred on its swift way through the crowded streets until they drew up before the theatre.

In the vestibule she found her father close to her and endeavoured to convey many things to him by squeezing his arm very hard among the crowd, succeeding in so much that Mr. Linton knew perfectly well that Norah was the victim of a new idea—and was quite content to wait to be told what it was. But there was no chance of that until the evening was over, and they had bade farewell to the Hunts, arranging to have tea with them next day: after which a taxi bore them to the Kensington flat, and they gathered in the sitting-room while Norah brewed coffee over a spirit-lamp.

"I'm jolly glad we met the Hunts, " Jim said. "But isn't it cruel luck for a man like that to be kept back by a damaged hand! "

"Rough on Mrs. Hunt, too, " Wally remarked. "She looked about as seedy as he did. "

"Daddy——! " said Norah eagerly.

David Linton laughed.

"Yes, I knew you had one, " he said, "Out with it—I'll listen. "

"They're Tired People, " said Norah: and waited.

"Yes, they're certainly tired enough, " said her father. "But the children, Norah? I don't think we could possibly take in little children, considering the other weary inmates. "

"No, I thought that too, " Norah answered eagerly. "But don't you remember the cottage, Daddy? Why shouldn't they have it? "

"By Jove! " said Jim. "That jolly little thatched place? "

"Yes—it has several rooms. They could let their own house, and then they'd save heaps of money. It would get them right out of London; and Mrs. Hunt told me that London is the very worst place for him— the doctors said so. "

41

"That is certainly an idea, " Mr. Linton said. "It's near enough to London for Hunt to run up for his treatment. We could see that they were comfortable. " He smiled at Norah, whose flushed face was dimly visible through the steam of the coffee. "I think it would be rather a good way to begin our job, Norah. "

"It would be so nice that it doesn't feel like any sort of work! " said Norah.

"I think you may find a chance of work; they have three small children, and not much money, " said her father prophetically.

"I say, I hope the Major would agree, " Jim put in. "I know he's horribly proud. "

"We'll kidnap the babies, and then they'll just have to come, " Norah laughed.

"Picture Mr. Linton, " said Wally happily, "carrying on the good work by stalking through London with three kids sticking out of his pockets—followed by Norah, armed with feeding-bottles! "

"Wounded officer and wife hard in pursuit armed with shot guns! " supplemented Jim. "I like your pacifist ideas of running a home for Tired People, I must say! "

"Why, they would forget that they had ever been tired! " said Norah. "I think it's rather a brilliant notion—there certainly wouldn't be another convalescent home in England run on the same lines. But you're not good on matters of detail—people don't have feeding-bottles for babies of that age. "

"I'm not well up in babies, " said Wally. "Nice people, but I like somebody else to manage 'em. I thought bottles were pretty safe until they were about seven! "

"Well, we'll talk it over with the Hunts to-morrow—the cottage, not the bottles, " Mr. Linton said. "Meanwhile, it's bed-time, so good-night, everybody. " He dispersed the assembly by the simple process of switching off the electric light—smiling to himself as Jim and Norah two-stepped, singing, down the tiny corridor in the darkness.

But the mid-day post brought a worried little note from Mrs. Hunt, putting off the party. Her husband had had a bad report on his hand that morning, and was going into hospital for an immediate operation. She hoped to fix a day later on—the note was a little incoherent. Norah had a sudden vision of the three small Hunts "who made rather more noise than a regiment" rampaging round the harassed mother as she tried to write.

"Perhaps it's as well—we'll study the cottage, and make sure that it's all right for them, " said her father. "Then we'll kidnap them. Meanwhile we'll go and send them a big hamper of fruit, and put some sweets in for the babies. " A plan which was so completely after Norah's heart that she quite forgot her disappointment.

CHAPTER IV

SETTLING IN

They bade good-bye to the flat early next morning and went down to Homewood through a dense fog that rolled up almost to the carriage windows like masses of white wool. At the station the closed carriage waited for them, with the brown cobs pawing the ground impatiently. General Somers' chauffeur had gone with his master, and so far they had not succeeded in finding a substitute, but the groom and coachman, who were also gardeners in their spare time, considered themselves part and parcel of the place, and had no idea of changing their home.

"The cart for the luggage will be here presently, sir, " Jones, the old coachman, told Mr. Linton. So they left a bewildering assortment of suit-cases and trunks piled up on the platform in the care of an ancient porter, and packed themselves into the carriage. Norah was wont to say that the only vehicle capable of accommodating her three long men-folk comfortably was an omnibus. The fog was lifting as they rolled smoothly up the long avenue; and just as they came within sight of the house a gleam of pale sunlight found its way through the misty clouds and lingered on the ivy-clad gables. The front door was flung wide to welcome them: on the steps hovered the ex-sergeant, wearing a discreet smile. Behind him fluttered a print dress and a white apron, presumably worn by his niece.

"I say, Norah, don't you feel like the Queen of Sheba entering her ancestral halls? " whispered Wally wickedly, as they mounted the steps.

"If she felt simply horrible, then I do! " returned Norah. "I suppose I'll get used to it in time, but at present I want a hollow log to crawl into! "

Allenby greeted them respectfully.

"We did not know what rooms you would like, sir, " he said. "They are all practically ready, of course. My niece, miss, thought you might prefer the blue bedroom. Her name is Sarah, miss. "

"We don't want the best rooms—the sunniest, I mean, " Norah said. "They must be for the Tired People, mustn't they, Dad? "

"Well, there are no Tired People, except ourselves, at present, " said her father, laughing. "So if you have a fancy for any room, you had better take it, don't you think? "

"Well, we'll tour round, and see, " said Norah diplomatically, with mental visions of the sudden "turning-out" of rooms should weary guests arrive. "It might be better to settle down from the first as we mean to be. "

"A lady has come, miss, " said Allenby. "I understood her to say she was the cook, but perhaps I made a mistake? " He paused, questioningly, his face comically puzzled.

"Oh—Miss de Lisle? "

"Yes, miss. "

"Oh, yes, she's the cook, " said Norah. "And the housekeeper—Mrs. Atkins? "

"No one else has arrived, miss. "

"Well, I expect she'll come, " said Norah. "At least she promised. "

"Miss de Lisle, miss, asked for her kitchenmaid. "

"There isn't one, at present, " said Norah, feeling a little desperate.

"Oh! " said Allenby, looking blank. "I—I am afraid, miss, that the lady expects one. "

"Well, she can't have one until one comes, " said Mr. Linton. "Cheer up, Norah, I'll talk to Miss de Lisle. "

"I'll be the kitchenmaid, if necessary, " said Wally cheerfully. "What does one do? "

Allenby shuddered visibly.

"My niece, I am sure, will do all she can, sir, " he said. His gaze dwelt on Wally's uniform; it was easy to see him quailing in spirit before the vision of an officer with a kitchen mop. "Perhaps, miss, if you would like to see the rooms? "

They trooped upstairs, the silent house suddenly waking to life with the quick footsteps and cheery voices. The big front bedrooms were at once put aside for future guests. Norah fell in love with, and promptly appropriated, a little room that appeared to have been tucked into a corner by the architect, as an afterthought. It was curiously shaped, with a quaint little nook for the bed, and had a big window furnished with a low cushioned seat, wide enough for any one to curl up with a book. Mr. Linton and the boys selected rooms principally remarkable for bareness. Jim had a lively hatred for furniture; they left him discussing with Allenby the question of removing a spindle-legged writing table. Mr. Linton and Norah went downstairs, with sinking hearts, to encounter Miss de Lisle.

On the way appeared Sarah; very clean and starched as to dress, very pink and shiny as to complexion. Her hair was strained back from her forehead so tightly it appeared to be pulling her eyes up.

"Oh, Sarah, " said Mr. Linton, pausing.

"Yes, sir, " said Sarah meekly.

"You may be required to help the cook for a few days until we—er— until the staff is complete, " said her employer. "Your uncle tells me you will have no objection. "

"It being understood, sir, as it is only tempory, " said Sarah firmly.

"Oh, quite, " said Mr. Linton hurriedly.

"And of course I will help you with the housework, Sarah, " put in Norah.

Sarah looked more wooden than before.

"Thank you, miss, I'm sure, " she returned.

They went on.

"Doesn't she make you feel a worm! " said Norah.

"This is a terrible business, Norah! " said Mr. Linton fervently. "I didn't guess what Brownie was saving me from, all these years. "

They found Miss de Lisle in the kitchen, where an enormous range glowed like a fiery furnace, in which respect Miss de Lisle rather resembled it. She was a tall, stout woman, dressed in an overall several sizes too small for her. The overall was rose-coloured, and Miss de Lisle was many shades deeper in hue. She accepted their greetings without enthusiasm, and plunged at once into a catalogue of grievances.

"The butler tells me there is no kitchenmaid, " she boomed wrathfully. "And I had not expected such an antiquated range. Nor could I possibly manage with these saucepans"—sweeping a scornful hand towards an array which seemed to the hapless Lintons to err only on the side of magnificence. "There will be a number of necessary items. And where am I to sit? You will hardly expect me to herd with the servants. "

"It would be rough on them! " rose to Norah's lips. But she prudently kept the reflection to herself.

"To sit? " echoed Mr. Linton. "Why, I really hadn't thought of it. " His brow cleared. "Oh—there is the housekeeper's room. "

"And who is the housekeeper? Is she a lady? "

"She hasn't said so, yet, " said Mr. Linton. It was evident that he considered this a point in the absent housekeeper's favour. Miss de Lisle flamed anew.

"I cannot sit with your housekeeper, " she averred. "You must remember, Mr. Linton, that I told you when engaging with you, that I expected special treatment. "

"And *you* must remember, " said Mr. Linton, with sudden firmness, "that we ourselves have not been half an hour in the house, and that we must have time to make arrangements. As for what you require, we will see into that later. "

Miss de Lisle sniffed.

"It's not what I am accustomed to, " she said. "However, I will wait. And the kitchenmaid? "

"I can't make a kitchenmaid out of nothing, " said Mr. Linton gloomily. "I hope to hear of one in a day or two; I have written to Ireland. "

"To Ireland! " ejaculated Miss de Lisle in accents of horror. "My dear sir, do you know what Irish maids are like? "

"They're the nicest maids I know, " said Norah, speaking for the first time. "And so kind and obliging. "

"H'm, " sniffed the cook-lady. "But you are not sure of obtaining even one of these treasures? "

"Well, we'll all help, " said Norah. "Sarah will give you a hand until we get settled, and my brother and Mr. Meadows and I can do anything. There can't be such an awful lot of work! " She stopped. Miss de Lisle was regarding her with an eye in which horror and amazement were mingled.

"But we don't *do* such things in England! " she gasped. "Your brother! And the other officer! In my kitchen, may I ask? "

"Well, one moment you seem afraid of too much work, and the next, of too much help, " said Norah, laughing. "You'd find them very useful. "

"I trust that I have never been afraid of work, " said Miss de Lisle severely. "But I have my position to consider. There are duties which belong to it, and other duties which do not. My province is cooking. Cooking. And nothing else. Who, I ask, is to keep my kitchen clean?"

"Me, if necessary, " said a voice in which Allenby the butler was clearly merged in Allenby the sergeant. "Begging your pardon, sir. "

He was deferential again—save for the eye with which he glared upon Miss de Lisle. "I think, perhaps, between me and Sarah and—er—this lady, we can arrange matters for the present without troubling you or Miss Linton. "

"Do, " said his employer thankfully. He beat a retreat, followed by Norah—rather to Norah's disappointment. She was beginning to feel warlike, and hankered for the battle, with Allenby ranged on her side.

"I'm going to love Allenby, " she said with conviction, as they gained the outer regions.

"He's a trump! " said her father. "But isn't that a terrible woman, Norah! "

"Here's another, anyhow, " said Norah with a wild inclination to giggle.

A dismal cab halted at a side entrance, and the driver was struggling with a stout iron trunk. The passenger, a tall, angular woman, was standing in the doorway.

"The housekeeper! " breathed Mr. Linton faintly. "Do you feel equal to her, Norah? " He fled, with disgraceful weakness, to the billiard-room.

"Good morning, " Norah said, advancing.

"Good morning, " returned the newcomer, with severity. "I have rung three times. "

"Oh—we're a little shorthanded, " said Norah, and began to giggle hopelessly, to her own dismay. Her world seemed suddenly full of important upper servants, with no one to wait on them. It was rather terrible, but beyond doubt it was very funny—to an Australian mind.

The housekeeper gazed at her with a sort of cold anger.

"I'm afraid I don't know which is your room, " Norah said, recovering under that fish-like glare. "You see, we've only just come. I'll send Allenby. " She hurried off, meeting the butler in the passage.

"Oh, Allenby, " she said; "it's the housekeeper. And her trunk. Allenby, what does a housekeeper do? She won't clean the kitchen for Miss de Lisle, will she? "

"I'm afraid not, miss, " said Allenby. His manner grew confidential; had he not been so correct a butler, Norah felt that he might have patted her head. "Now look, miss, " he said. "You just leave them women to me; I'll fix them. And don't you worry. "

"Oh, thank you, Allenby, " said Norah gratefully. She followed in her father's wake, leaving the butler to advance upon the wrathful figure that yet blocked the side doorway.

In the billiard-room all her men-folk were gathered, looking guilty.

"It's awful to see you all huddling together here out of the storm! " said Norah, laughing. "Isn't it all terrible! Do you think we'll ever settle down, Daddy? "

"Indeed, I wouldn't be too certain, " responded Mr. Linton gloomily. "How did you get on, Norah? Was she anything like Miss de Lisle? That's an appalling woman! She ought to stand for Parliament! "

"She's not like Miss de Lisle, but I'm not sure that she's any nicer, " said Norah. "She's very skinny and vinegarish. I say, Daddy, aren't we going to have a wild time! "

"Well, if she and the cook-lady get going the encounter should be worth seeing, " remarked Jim. "Talk about the Kilkenny cats! "

"I only hope it will come off before we go, " said Wally gleefully. "We haven't had much war yet, have we, Jim? I think we deserve to see a little. "

"I should much prefer it in some one else's house, " said Mr. Linton with haste. "But it's bound to come, I should think, and then I shall be called in as referee. Well, Australia was never like this. Still, there are compensations. "

He went out, returning in a moment with a battered hat of soft grey felt.

"Now you'll be happy! " said Norah, laughing.

"I am, " responded her father. He put on the hat with tender care. "I haven't been so comfortable since I was in Ireland. It's one of the horrors of war that David Linton of Billabong has worn a stiff bowler hat for nearly a year! "

"Never mind, no one in Australia would believe it unless they saw it photographed! " said Jim soothingly. "And it hasn't had to be a top-hat, so you really haven't had to bear the worst. "

"That is certainly something, " said his father. "In the dim future I suppose you and Norah may get married; but I warn you here and now that you needn't expect me to appear in a top-hat. However, there's no need to face these problems yet, thank goodness. Suppose we leave the kitchen to fight it out alone, and go and inspect the cottage? "

It nestled at the far side of a belt of shrubbery: a cheery, thatched place, with wide casement windows that looked out on a trim stretch of grass. At one side there was actually a little verandah! a sight so unusual in England that the Australians could scarcely believe their eyes. Certainly it was only a very tiny verandah.

Within, all was bright and cheery and simple. The cottage had been used as a "barracks" when the sons of a former owner had brought home boy friends. Two rooms were fitted with bunks built against the wall, as in a ship's cabin: there was a little dining-room, plainly furnished, and a big sitting-room that took up the whole width of the building, and had casement windows on three sides. There was a roomy kitchen, from which a ladder-like staircase ascended to big attics, one of which was fitted as a bedroom.

"It's no end of a jolly place, " was Jim's verdict. "I don't know that I wouldn't rather live here than in your mansion, Norah; but I suppose it wouldn't do. "

"I think it would be rather nice, " Norah said. "But you can't, because we want it for the Hunts. And it will be splendid for them, won't it, Dad? "

"Yes, I think it will do very well, " said Mr. Linton. "We'll get the housekeeper to come down and make sure that it has enough pots and pans and working outfit generally. "

"And then we'll go up to London and kidnap Mrs. Hunt and the babies, " said Norah, pirouetting gently. "Now, shall we go and see the horses? "

They spent a blissful half-hour in the stables, and arranged to ride in the afternoon—the old coachman was plainly delighted at the absence of a chauffeur, and displayed his treasures with a pride to which he had long been a stranger.

"The 'orses 'aven't 'ad enough to do since Sir John used to come, " he said. "The General didn't care for them—an infantry gent he must have been—and it was always the motor for 'im. We exercised 'em, of course, but it ain't the same to the 'orses, and don't they know it! "

"Of course they do. " Norah caressed Killaloe's lean head.

"You'll hunt him, sir, won't you, this season? " asked Jones anxiously. "The meets ain't what they was, of course, but there's a few goes out still. The Master's a lady—Mrs. Ainslie; her husband's in France. He's 'ad the 'ounds these five years. "

"Oh, we'll hunt, won't we, Dad? " Norah's face glowed as she lifted it.

"Rather! " said Jim. "Of course you will. What about the other horses, Jones? Can they jump? "

"To tell you the truth, sir, " said Jones happily, "there's not one of them that can't. Even the cobs ain't too bad; and the black pony that's at the vet. 's, 'e's a flyer. 'E'll be 'ome to-morrow; the vet. sent me word yesterday that 'is shoulder's all right. Strained it a bit, 'e did. Of course they ain't made hunters, like Killaloe; but they're quick and clever, and once you know the country, and the short cuts, and the gaps, you can generally manage to see most of a run. " He sighed ecstatically. "Eh, but it'll be like old times to get ready again on a hunting morning! "

The gong sounded from the house, and they bade the stables a reluctant good-bye. Lunch waited in the morning-room; there was a pleasant sparkle of silver and glass on a little table in the window. And there was no doubt that Miss de Lisle could cook.

"If her temper were as good as her pastry, I should say we had found a treasure, " said Mr. Linton, looking at the fragments which remained of a superlative apple-pie. "Let's hope that Mrs. Moroney will discover a kitchenmaid or two, and that they will induce her to overlook our other shortcomings. "

"I'm afraid we'll never be genteel enough for her, " said Norah, shaking her curly head. "And the other servants will all hate her because she thinks they aren't fit for her to speak to. If she only knew how much nicer Allenby is! "

"Or Brownie, " said Wally loyally. "Brownie could beat that pie with one hand tied behind her. "

Allenby entered—sympathy on every line of his face.

"The 'ousekeeper—Mrs. Atkins—would like to see you, sir. Or Miss Linton. And so would Miss de Lisle. "

But Miss de Lisle was on his heels, breathing threatenings and slaughter.

"There must be some arrangement made as to my instructions, " she boomed. "Your housekeeper evidently does not understand my position. She has had the impertinence to address me as 'Cook. ' Cook! " She paused for breath, glaring.

"But, good gracious, isn't it your profession? " asked Mr. Linton.

Miss de Lisle fairly choked with wrath. Wally's voice fell like oil on a stormy sea.

"If I could make a pie like that I'd *expect* to be called 'Cook, '" said he. "It's—it's a regular poem of a pie! " Whereat Jim choked in his turn, and endeavoured, with signal lack of success, to turn his emotion into a sneeze.

Miss de Lisle's lowering countenance cleared somewhat. She looked at Wally in a manner that was almost kindly.

"War-time cookery is a makeshift, not an art, " she said. "Before the war I could have shown you what cooking could be. "

"That pie wasn't a makeshift, " persisted Wally. "It was a dream. I say, Miss de Lisle, can you make pikelets? "

"Yes, of course, " said the cook-lady. "Do you like them? "

"I'd go into a trap for a pikelet, " said Wally, warming to his task. "Oh, Norah, do ask Miss de Lisle if she'll make some for tea! "

"Oh, do! " pleaded Norah. As a matter of stern fact, Norah preferred bread-and-butter to pikelets, but the human beam in the cook-lady's eye was not to be neglected. "We haven't had any for ages. " She cast about for further encouragement for the beam. "Miss de Lisle, I suppose you have a very special cookery-book? "

"I make my own recipes, " said the cook-lady with pride. "But for the war I should have brought out my book. "

"By Jove, you don't say so! " said Jim. "I say, Norah, you'll have to get that when it comes out. "

"Rather! " said Norah. "I wonder would it bother you awfully to show me some day how to make meringues? I never can get them right. "

"We'll see, " said Miss de Lisle graciously. "And would you really like pikelets for tea? "

"Please—if it wouldn't be too much trouble. "

"Very well. " Jim held the door open for the cook-lady as she marched out. Suddenly she paused.

"You will see the housekeeper, Mr. Linton? "

"Oh, certainly! " said David Linton hastily. The door closed; behind it they could hear a tread, heavy and martial, dying away.

"A fearsome woman! " said Mr. Linton. "Wally, you deserve a medal! But are we always to lick the ground under the cook's feet in this fashion? "

"Oh, she'll find her level, " said Jim. "But you'd better tell Mrs. Atkins not to offend her again. Talk to her like a father, Dad—say she and Miss de Lisle are here to run the house, not to bother you and Norah. "

"It's excellent in theory, " said his father sadly, "but in practice I find my tongue cleaving to the roof of my mouth when these militant females tackle me. And if you saw Mrs. Atkins you would realize how difficult it would be for me to regard her as a daughter. But I'll do my best. "

Mrs. Atkins, admitted by the sympathetic Allenby, proved less fierce than the cook-lady, although by no stretch of imagination could she have been called pleasant.

"I have never worked with a cook as considered herself a lady, " she remarked. "It makes all very difficult, and no kitchen-maid, and am I in authority or am I not? And such airs, turning up her nose at being called Cook. Which if she is the cook, why not be called so? And going off to her bedroom with her dinner, no one downstairs being good enough to eat with her. I must say it isn't what I'm used to, and me lived with the first families. *Quite* the first. " Mrs. Atkins ceased her weary monologue and gazed on the family with conscious virtue. She was dressed in dull black silk, and looked overwhelmingly respectable.

"Oh, well, you must put up with things as they are, " said Mr. Linton vaguely. "Miss de Lisle expects a few unusual things, but apparently there is no doubt that she can do her work. I hope to have more maids in a few days; if not" —a brilliant idea striking him—"I must send you up to London to find us some, Mrs. Atkins. "

"I shall be delighted, sir, " replied the housekeeper primly. "And do I understand that the cook is to have a separate sitting-room? "

"Oh, for goodness' sake, ask Allenby! " ejaculated her employer. "It will have to be managed somewhere, or we shall have no cook! "

CHAPTER V

HOW THE COOK-LADY FOUND HER LEVEL

Two days later, the morning mail brought relief—not too soon, for there was evidence that the battle between the housekeeper and the cook-lady could not be much longer delayed, and Sarah was going about with a face of wooden agony that gave Norah a chilly feeling whenever she encountered her. Allenby alone retained any cheerfulness; and much of that was due to ancient military discipline. Therefore Mrs. Moroney's letter was hailed with acclamation. "Two maids she can recommend, bless her heart! " said Mr. Linton. "She doesn't label their particular activities, but says they'll be willing to do anything at all. "

"That's the kind I like, " said Norah thankfully.

"And their names are Bride Kelly and Katty O'Gorman; doesn't that bring Killard and brown bogs back to you? And—oh, by Jove! "

"What is it? " demanded his family, in unison.

"This is what it is. 'I don't know would your honour remember Con Hegarty, that was shofer to Sir John at Rathcullen, and a decent boy with one leg and he after coming back from the war. He have no job since Sir John died, and he bid me tell you he'd be proud to drive a car for you, and to be with ye all. And if he have only one leg itself he's as handy as any one with two or more. Sir John had him with him at Homewood, and he knows the car that's there, and 'tis the way if you had a job for him he could take the two girls over when he went, and he used to travelling the world. ' That's all, I think, " Mr. Linton ended.

"What luck! " Jim ejaculated. "We couldn't have a better chauffeur. "

"I wonder we never thought of Con, " said his father. "A nice boy; I'd like to have him. "

"So would I, " added Norah. "When will you get them, Dad? "

"I'll write at once and send a cheque for their fares, " said her father. "I'll tell them to send me a telegram when they start. " He rose to leave the room. "What are you going to do this morning, children? "

"We're all turning out the cottage, " Norah answered promptly. "I haven't told Sarah; she disapproves of me so painfully if I do any work, and hurts my feelings by always doing it over again, if possible. At the same time, she looks so unhappy about working at all, and sighs so often, that I don't feel equal to telling her that the cottage has to be done. So Jim and Wally have nobly volunteered to help me. "

"Don't knock yourself up, " said her father. "Will you want me? "

"No—unless you like to come as a guest and sit still and do nothing. My two housemaids and I can easily finish off that little job. There's not really a great deal to do, " Norah added; "the place is very clean. Only one likes to have everything extra nice when Tired People come. "

"Well, I'm not coming to sit still and do nothing, " said her father firmly, "so I'll stay at home and write letters. " He watched them from the terrace a little later, racing across the lawn, and smiled a little. It was so unlikely that this long-legged family of his would ever really grow up.

The house was very quiet that morning. Mrs. Atkins and Miss de Lisle having quarrelled over the question of dinner, had retreated, the one to the housekeeper's room, the other to the kitchen. Sarah went about her duties sourly. Allenby was Sarah's uncle, and, as such, felt some duty to her, which he considered he had discharged in getting her a good place; beyond that, Sarah frankly bored him, and he saw no reason to let her regard him as anything else than a butler. "Bad for discipline, too! " he reflected. Therefore Allenby was lonely. He read the *Daily Mail* in the seclusion of his pantry, and then, strolling through the hall, with a watchful eye alert lest a speck of dust should have escaped Sarah, he saw his master cross the garden and strike across the park in the direction of Hawkins' farm. Every one else was out, Allenby knew not where. An impulse for fresh air fell upon him, and he sauntered towards the shrubbery.

Voices and laughter came to him from the cottage. He pushed through the shrubs and found himself near a window; and, peeping through, received a severe shock to his well-trained nerves. Norah, enveloped in a huge apron, was energetically polishing the kitchen tins; the boys, in their shirt-sleeves, were equally busy, Wally scrubbing the sink with Monkey soap, and Jim blackleading the stove. It was very clear that work was no new thing to any of the trio. Allenby gasped with horror.

"Officers, too! " he ejaculated. "What's the world coming to, I wonder! " He hesitated a moment, and then walked round to the back door.

"May I come in, please, miss? "

"Oh, come in, Allenby, " Norah said, a little confused. "We're busy, you see. Did you want anything? "

"No, miss, thank you. But really, miss—I could 'ave got a woman from the village for you, to do all this. Or Sarah. "

"Sarah has quite enough to do, " said Norah.

"Indeed, Sarah's not killed with work, " said that damsel's uncle. "I don't like to see you soilin' your 'ands, miss. Nor the gentlemen. "

"The gentlemen are all right, " said Wally cheerfully. "Look at this sink, now, Allenby; did you ever see anything better? "

"It's—it's not right, " murmured Allenby unhappily. He threw off his black coat suddenly, and advanced upon Jim. "If you please, sir, I'll finish that stove. "

"That you won't, " said Jim. "Thanks all the same, Allenby, but I'm getting used to it now. " He laughed. "Besides, don't you forget that you're a butler? "

"I can't forget that you're an officer, sir, " said Allenby, wretchedly. "It's not right: think of the regiment. And Miss Norah. Won't you let me 'elp sir? "

Captain Jim

"You can clean the paint, Allenby, " said Norah, taking pity on his distressed face. "But there's really no need to keep you. "

"If you'd only not mind telling any of them at the 'ouse what I was doing, " said the butler anxiously. "It 'ud undermine me position. There's that Miss de Lisle, now—she looks down on everybody enough without knowin' I was doin' any job like this. "

"She shall never know, " said Jim tragically, waving a blacklead brush. "Now I'm off to do the dining-room grate. If you're deadly anxious to work, Allenby, you could wash this floor—couldn't he, Norah? "

"Thanks very much, sir, " said Allenby gratefully, "I'll leave this place all right—just shut the door, sir, and don't you bother about it any more. "

"However did you dare, Jim? " breathed Norah, as the cleaning party moved towards the dining-room. "Do you think a butler ever washed a floor before? "

"Can't say, " said Jim easily. "I'm regarding him more as a sergeant than a butler, for the moment—not that I can remember seeing a sergeant wash a floor, either. But he seemed anxious to help, so why not let him? It won't hurt him; he's getting disgracefully fat. And there's plenty to do. "

"Heaps, " said Wally cheerily. "Where's that floor-polish, Nor? These boards want a rub. What are you going to do? "

"Polish brass, " said Norah, beginning on a window-catch. "When I grow up I think I'll be an architect, and then I'll make the sort of house that women will care to live in. "

"What sort's that? " asked Jim.

"I don't know what the outside will be like. But it won't have any brass to keep clean, or any skirting-boards with pretty tops to catch dust, or any corners in the rooms. Brownie and I used to talk about it. All the cupboards will be built in, so's no dust can get under them, and the windows will have some patent dodge to open inwards

60

when they want cleaning. And there'll be built-in washstands in every room, with taps and plugs——"

"Brass taps? " queried Wally.

"Certainly not. "

"What then? "

"Oh—something. Something that doesn't need to be kept pretty. And then there will be heaps of cupboard-room and heaps of shelf-room—only all the shelves will be narrow, so that nothing can be put behind anything else. "

"Whatever do you mean? " asked Jim.

"She means dead mice—you know they get behind bottles of jam, " said Wally kindly. "Go on, Nor, you talk like a book. "

"Well, dead mice are as good as anything, " said Norah lucidly. "There won't be any room for their corpses on *my* shelves. And I'll have some arrangement for supplying hot water through the house that doesn't depend on keeping a huge kitchen fire alight. "

"That's a good notion, " said Jim, sitting back on his heels, blacklead brush in hand. "I think I'll go architecting with you, Nor. We'll go in for all sorts of electric dodges; plugs in all the rooms to fix to vacuum cleaners you can work with one hand—most of 'em want two men and a boy; and electric washing-machines, and cookers, and fans and all kinds of things. And everybody will be using them, so electricity will have to be cheap. "

"I really couldn't help listening to you, " said a deep voice in the doorway.

Every one jumped. It was Miss de Lisle, in her skimpy red overall—rather more flushed than usual, and a little embarrassed.

"I hope you don't mind, " she said. "I heard voices—and I didn't think any one lived here. I knocked, but you were all so busy you didn't hear me. "

"So busy talking, you mean, " laughed Wally. "Terrible chatterboxes, Jim and Norah; they never get any work done. " A blacklead brush hurtled across the room: he caught it neatly and returned it to the owner.

"But you're working terribly hard, " said the cook-lady, in bewilderment. "Is any one going to live here? "

Norah explained briefly. Miss de Lisle listened with interest, nodding her head from time to time.

"It's a beautiful idea, " she said at length. "Fancy now, you rescuing those poor little children and their father and mother! It makes me feel quite sentimental. Most cooks are sentimental, you know: it's such a—a warm occupation, " she added vaguely. "When I'm cooking something that requires particular care I always find myself crooning a love song! " At which Wally collapsed into such a hopeless giggle that Jim and Norah, in little better case themselves, looked at him in horror, expecting to see him annihilated. To their relief, Miss de Lisle grinned cheerfully.

"Oh, yes, you may laugh! " she said—whereupon they all did. "I know I don't look sentimental. Perhaps it's just as well; nobody would want a cook with golden hair and languishing blue eyes. And I do cook so much better than I sing! Now I'm going to help. What can I do? "

"Indeed, you're not, " said Norah. "Thanks ever so, Miss de Lisle, but we can manage quite well. "

"Now, you're thinking of what I said the other day, " said Miss de Lisle disgustedly. "I know I did say my province was cooking, and nothing else. But if you knew the places I've struck. Dear me, there was one place where the footman chucked me under the chin! "

It was too much for the others. They sat down on the floor and shrieked in unison.

"Yes, I know it's funny, " said Miss de Lisle. "I howled myself, after it was all over. But I don't think the footman ever chucked any one under the chin again. I settled him! " There was a reminiscent gleam in her eye: Norah felt a flash of sympathy for the hapless footman.

"Then there was another house—that was a duke's—where the butler expected me to walk out with him. That's the worst of it: if you behave like a human being you get that sort of thing, and if you don't you're a pig, and treated accordingly. " She looked at them whimsically. "Please don't think me a pig! " she said. "I—I shall never forget how you held the door open for me, Mr. Jim! "

"Oh, I say, don't! " protested the unhappy Jim, turning scarlet.

"Now you're afraid I'm going to be sentimental, but I'm not. I'm going to polish the boards in the passage, and then you can give me another job. Lunch is cold to-day: I've done all the cooking. Now, please don't—" as Norah began to protest. "Dear me, if you only knew how nice it is to speak to some one again! " She swooped upon Wally's tin of floor-polish, scooped half of its contents into the lid with a hair-pin, commandeered two cloths from a basketful of cleaning matters, and strode off. From the passage came a steady pounding that spoke of as much "elbow-grease" as polish being applied.

"Did you ever! " said Jim weakly.

"Never, " said Wally. "I say, I think she's a good sort. "

"So do I. But who'd have thought it! "

"Poor old soul! " said Norah. "She must be most horribly dull. But after our first day I wouldn't have dared to make a remark to her unless she'd condescended to address me first. "

"I should think you wouldn't, " said Wally. "But she's really quite human when she tucks her claws in. "

"Oh, my aunt! " said Jim, chuckling. "I'd give a month's pay to have seen the footman chuck her under the chin! " They fell into convulsions of silent laughter.

From the passage, as they regained composure, came a broken melody, punctuated by the dull pounding on the floor. Miss de Lisle, on her knees, had become sentimental, and warbled as she rubbed.

"'I do not ask for the heart of thy heart. '"

"Why wouldn't you? " murmured Wally, with a rapt expression. "Any one who can make pikelets like you— —"

"Be quiet, Wally, " grinned Jim. "She'll hear you. "

"Not she—she's too happy. Listen. "

> "'All that I a-a-sk for is all that may be,
> All that thou ca-a-a-rest to give unto me!
> I do not ask'"— —

Crash! Bang! Splash!

"Heavens, what's happened! " exclaimed Jim.

They rushed out. At the end of the passage Miss de Lisle and the irreproachable Allenby struggled in a heap—in an ever-widening pool of water that came from an overturned bucket lying a yard away. The family rushed to the rescue. Allenby got to his feet as they arrived, and dragged up the drenched cook-lady. He was pale with apprehension.

"I—I—do beg your pardon, mum! " he gasped. "I 'adn't an idea in me 'ead there was any one there, least of all you on your knees. I just come backin' out with the bucket! "

"I say, Miss de Lisle, are you hurt? " Jim asked anxiously.

"Not a bit, which is queer, considering Allenby's weight! " returned Miss de Lisle. "But it's—it's just t-too funny, isn't it! " She broke into a shout of laughter, and the others, who had, indeed, been choking with repressed feeling, followed suit. Allenby, after a gallant attempt to preserve the correct demeanour of a butler, unchanged by any circumstance, suddenly bolted into the kitchen like a rabbit. They heard strange sounds from the direction of the sink.

"But, I say, you're drenched! " said Jim, when every one felt a little better.

Miss de Lisle glanced at her stained and dripping overall.

"Well, a little. I'll take this off, " she said, suiting the action to the word, and appearing in a white blouse and grey skirt which suited her very much better than the roseate garment. "But my floor! And I had it so beautifully polished! " she raised her voice. "Allenby! What are you going to do about this floor? "

"Indeed, mum, I've made a pretty mess of it, " said Allenby, reappearing.

"You have, indeed, " said she.

"But I never expected to find you 'ere a-polishin', " said the bewildered ex-sergeant.

"And I certainly never expected to find the butler scrubbing! " retorted Miss de Lisle; at which Allenby's jam dropped, and he cast an appealing glance at Jim.

"This is a working-bee, " said Jim promptly. "We're all in it, and no one else knows anything about it. "

"Not Mrs. Atkins, I hope, sir, " said Allenby.

"Certainly not. As for Sarah, she's out of it altogether. "

Allenby sighed, a relieved butler.

"I'll see to the floor, sir, " he said. "It's up to me, isn't it? And polish it after. I can easy slip down 'ere for a couple of hours after lunch, when you're all out ridin'. "

"Then I really had better fly, " said Miss de Lisle. "I am pretty wet, and there's lunch to think about. " She looked at them in friendly fashion. "Thank you all very much, " she said—and was gone, with a kind of elephantine swiftness.

The family returned to the dining-room, leaving Allenby to grapple with the swamp in the passage.

"Don't we have cheery adventures when we clean house! " said Wally happily. "I wouldn't have missed this morning for anything. "

"No—it *has* been merry and bright, " Jim agreed. "And isn't the cook-lady a surprise-packet! I say, Nor, do you think you'd find a human side to Mrs. Atkins if we let Allenby fall over her with a bucket of water? "

"'Fraid not, " said Norah.

"You can't find what doesn't exist, " said Wally wisely. "Mrs. Atkins is only a walking cruet—sort of mixture of salt and vinegar. "

They told the story to Mr. Linton over the luncheon-table, after Allenby had withdrawn. Nevertheless, the butler, listening from his pantry to the shouts of laughter from the morning-room, had a fairly good idea of the subject under discussion, and became rather pink.

"It's lovely in another way, " Norah finished. "For you see, I thought Miss de Lisle wasn't human, but I was all wrong. She's rather a dear when you come to know her. "

"Yes, " said her father thoughtfully. "But you'll have to be careful, Norah; you mustn't make any distinctions between her and Mrs. Atkins. It doesn't matter if Miss de Lisle's pedigree is full of dukes and bishops—Mrs. Atkins is the upper servant, and she'll resent it if you put Miss de Lisle on a different footing to herself. "

"Yes, I see, " said Norah, nodding. "I'll do my best, Dad. "

Miss de Lisle, however, played the game. She did not encounter Norah often, and when she did it was in Mrs. Atkins' presence: and on these occasions she maintained an attitude of impersonal politeness which made it hard to realize that she and the butler had indeed bathed together on the floor of the cottage. She found various matters in her little sitting-room: an easy-chair, a flowering pot-plant, a pile of books that bore Norah's name—or Jim's; but she made no sign of having received them except that Norah found on her table at night a twisted note in a masculine hand that said "Thank you. —C. de L. " As for Mrs. Atkins, she made her silent way about the house, sour and watchful, her green eyes rather resembling those of a cat, and her step as stealthy. Norah tried hard to talk to her on other matters than housekeeping, but found her so stolidly unresponsive that at last she gave up the attempt. Life, as she said to Wally, was too short to woo a cruet-stand!

Captain Jim

The week flew by swiftly, every moment busy with work and plans for the Tired People to come. Mrs. Atkins, it was plain, did not like the scheme. She mentioned that it would make a great deal of work, and how did Norah expect servants in these days to put up with unexpected people coming at all sorts of hours?

"But, " said Norah, "that's what the house is *for*. My father and I would not want a houseful of servants if we didn't mean to have a houseful of people. What would we do with you all? " At which Mrs. Atkins sniffed, and replied haughtily that she had been in a place where there was only one lady, and *she* kept eleven servants.

"More shame for her, " said Norah. "Anyhow, we explained it all to you when we engaged you, Mrs. Atkins. If we weren't going to have people here we should still be living in London, in a flat. And if the servants won't do their work, we shall just have to get others who will. " Which was a terrible effort of firmness for poor Norah, who inwardly hoped that Mrs. Atkins did not realize that she was shaking in her shoes!

"Easier said than done, in war-time, " said the housekeeper morosely. "Servants don't grow on gooseberry-bushes now, and what they don't expect——! Well, *I* don't know what the world's coming to. " But Norah, feeling unequal to more, fled, and, being discovered by Wally and Jim with her head in her hands over an account-book, was promptly taken out on Killaloe—the boys riding the cobs, which they untruthfully persisted that they preferred.

Then came Tuesday morning: with early breakfast, and the boys once more in khaki, and Jones, in the carriage, keeping the browns moving in the chill air. Not such a hard parting as others they had known since for the present there was no anxiety: but from the days when Jim used to leave Billabong for his Melbourne boarding-school, good-bye morning had been a difficult one for the Lintons. They joked through it in their usual way: it was part of the family creed to keep the flag flying.

"Well, you may have us back at any time as your first Tired People, " said Wally, his keen face looking as though it never could grow weary. "Machine-gun courses must be very fatiguing, don't you think, Jim? "

"Poor dears! " said Norah feelingly. "We'll have a special beef-tea diet for you, and bath-chairs. Will they send you in an ambulance? "

"Very likely, and then you'll be sorry you were so disrespectful, won't she, Mr. Linton? "

"I'm afraid you can't count on it, " said that gentleman, laughing. "Norah's bump of respect isn't highly developed, even for me. You'll write soon, Jim, and tell us how you get on—and what your next movements are. "

"Rather, " answered Jim. "Don't let the lady of the house wear off all her curls over the accounts, will you, Dad? I'd hate to see her bald! "

"I'll keep an eye on her, " said his father. "Now, boys; it's time you were off. "

They shook hands with Allenby, to his secret gratification. He closed the carriage door upon them, and stood back at attention, as they drove off. From an upper window—unseen, unfortunately—a figure in a red overall leaned, waving a handkerchief.

The train was late, and they all stamped about the platform—it was a frosty morning.

"Buck up, old kiddie, " said Jim. "We'll be home in no time. And look after Dad. "

"Yes—rather! " said Norah. "Send me all your socks when they want darning—which is every week. "

"Right. " They looked at each other with the blank feeling of having nothing to say that comes on station platforms or on the decks of ships before the final bell rings. Then the train came in sight, the elderly porter, expectant of a tip, bustled mightily with suit-cases and kit-bags, and presently they were gone. The two brown faces hung out of the carriage-window until the train disappeared round a curve.

Norah and her father looked at each other.

Captain Jim

"Well, my girl, " said he. "Now I suppose we had better begin our job. "

They went out to the carriage. Just as they were getting in, the ancient porter hurried after them.

"There's some people come by that train for you, sir. "

The Lintons turned. A thin man, with sad Irish eyes, was limping out of the station. Behind him came two girls.

"Why, it's Con! " Norah cried.

"It is, miss, " said the chauffeur. "And the gerrls I have with me—Bridie and Katty. "

"But you didn't write, " Mr. Linton said.

"Well, indeed, I was that rushed, an' we gettin' off, " said Con. "But I give Patsy Burke the money and towld him to send the wire. But 'tis the way with Patsy he'll likely think it'll do in a day or two as well as any time. " And as a matter of fact, the telegram duly arrived three days later—by which time the new arrivals had shaken down, and there seemed some prospect of domestic peace in the Home for Tired People.

CHAPTER VI

KIDNAPPING

Mrs. Hunt came slowly down the steps of a Park Lane mansion, now used as an officers' hospital. She was tired and dispirited; her steps dragged as she made her way towards Piccadilly. Beneath her veil her pretty face showed white, with lines of anxiety deepening it.

An officer, hurrying by, stopped and came eagerly to speak to her.

"How are you, Mrs. Hunt? And how's the Major? "

"Not very well, " said Mrs. Hunt, answering the second part of the question. "The operation was more successful than any he has had yet, but there has been a good deal of pain, and he doesn't seem to pick up strength. The doctors say that his hand now depends a good deal upon his general health: he ought to live in the country, forget that there's a war on, and get thoroughly fit. " She sighed. "It's so easy for doctors to prescribe these little things. "

"Yes—they all do it, " said the other—a captain in Major Hunt's regiment. "May I go to see him, do you think? "

"Oh, do, " Mrs. Hunt answered. "It will cheer him up; and anything that will do that is good. He's terribly depressed, poor old boy. " She said good-bye, and went on wearily.

It was a warm afternoon for October. Norah Linton and her father had come up to London by an early train, and, after much shopping, had lunched at a little French restaurant in Soho, where they ate queer dishes and talked exceedingly bad French to the pretty waitress. It was four o'clock when they found themselves at the door of a dingy building in Bloomsbury.

"Floor 3, the Hunts' flat, Daddy, " said Norah, consulting a note-book. "I suppose there is a lift. "

There was a lift, but it was out of order; a grimy card, tucked into the lattice of the doorway, proclaimed the fact. So they mounted flight after flight of stairs, and finally halted before a doorway bearing Major Hunt's card. A slatternly maid answered their ring.

"Mrs. Hunt's out, " she said curtly. "Gorn to see the Mijor. "

"Oh—will she be long? "

"Don't think so—she's gen'lly home about half-past four. Will yer wait? "

Norah looked at her father.

"Oh yes, we'll wait, " he said. They followed the girl into a narrow passage, close and airless, and smelling of Irish stew. Sounds of warfare came from behind a closed door: a child began to cry loudly, and a boy's voice was heard, angry and tired.

The maid ushered the visitors into a dingy little drawing-room. Norah stopped her as she was departing.

"Could I see the children? "

The girl hesitated.

"They're a bit untidy, " she said sullenly. "I ain't had no time to clean 'em up. There ain't no one to take them for a walk to-day. "

"Oh, never mind how untidy they are, " said Norah hastily. "Do send them in. "

"Oh, all right, " said the girl. "You'll tell the missus it was you arsked for 'em, won't yer? "

"Yes, of course. "

She went out, and the Lintons looked at each other, and then at the hopeless little room. The furniture was black horsehair, very shiny and hard and slippery; there was a gimcrack bamboo overmantel, with much speckled glass, and the pictures were of the kind peculiar to London lodging-houses, apt to promote indigestion in the beholder. There was one little window, looking out upon a blank courtyard and a dirty little side-street, where children played and fought incessantly, and stray curs nosed the rubbish in the gutters in the hope of finding food. There was nothing green to be seen, nothing clean, nothing pleasant.

"Oh, poor kiddies! " said Norah, under her breath.

The door opened and they came in; not shyly—the London child is seldom shy—but frankly curious, and in the case of the elder two, with suspicion. Three white-faced mites, as children well may be who have spent a London summer in a Bloomsbury square, where the very pavements sweat tar, and the breathless, sticky heat is as cruel by night as by day. A boy of six, straight and well-grown, with dark hair and eyes, who held by the hand a small toddling person with damp rings of golden hair: behind them a slender little girl, a little too shadowy for a mother's heart to be easy; with big brown eyes peeping elfishly from a cloud of brown curls.

The boy spoke sullenly.

"Eva told us to come in, " he said.

"We wanted you to take care of us, " said Norah. "You see, your mother isn't here. "

"But we can't have tea, " said the boy. "Eva says she isn't cleaned up yet, and besides, there's no milk, and very likely Mother'll forget the cakes, she said. "

"But we don't want tea, " said Norah. "We had a big lunch, not so long ago. And besides, we've got something nicer than tea. It's in his pocket. " She nodded at her father, who suddenly smiled in the way that made every child love him, and, fishing in his pocket drew out a square white box—at sight of which the baby said delightedly, "Choc! " and a kind of incredulous wonder, rather pitiful to see, came into the eyes of Geoffrey and his sister.

"There's a very difficult red ribbon on this, " said Mr. Linton, fumbling with it. "I can't undo it. " He smiled at little Alison. "You show me how. "

She was across the room in a flash, the baby at her heels, while Geoffrey made a slow step or two, and then stopped again.

"But you don't undone it 'tall, " she said. "It sticks on top. You breaks this paper"—pointing to the seal—"and then it undones himself. "

"You're quite right, " said Mr. Linton, as the lid came off. "So it does. How did you know? "

"We did have lots of boxes when we lived with the wegiment, " said the small girl; "but now the wegiment's in Fwance, and Daddy doesn't have enough pennies for chocs. " Her busy fingers tossed aside tissue paper and silver wrapping, until the brown rows of sweets were revealed. Then she put her hands by her sides.

"Is we to have some? "

"Oh, you poor little soul! " said David Linton hurriedly, and caught her up on his knee. He held the box in front of her.

"Now, which sort do you think is best for weeshy boys like that? " he asked, indicating the baby, who was making silent dives in the direction of the box. "And which do you like? —and Geoffrey? "

"Michael likes these. " She fished one out carefully, and Michael fell upon it, sitting on the carpet that he might devour it at his ease. "And Geoff and me—oh, we likes any 'tall. "

"Then you shall have any at all. " He held out his free hand. "Come on, Geoff. " And the boy, who had hesitated, digging one foot into the carpet, suddenly capitulated and came.

"Are you an officer? " he asked presently.

"No, I'm too old, " said David Linton. "But I have a big son who is one—and another boy too. "

"What's their regiment? "

"The same as your father's. "

"Truly? " A sparkle came into the boy's eyes. "I'm going to be in it some day. "

"Of course you will—and Michael too, I suppose. And then you'll fight the Germans—that is, if there are any left. "

"Daddy says there won't be. But I keep hoping there'll be just a few for me and Michael. '

"Alison wants some too, " said that lady. "Wants to kill vem wiv my wevolver. "

"A nice young fire-eater, you are, " said Mr. Linton, laughing.

"Girls can't kill Germans, silly, " said Geoffrey scornfully. "They have to stop at home and make bandages. " To which his sister replied calmly, "Shan't: I'm going to kill forty 'leven, " with an air of finality which seemed to end the discussion. Norah checked any further warlike reflections by finding a new layer of sweets as attractive as those on top, and the three heads clustered over the box in a pleasant anxiety of selection.

The carriages on the Tube railway had been very stuffy that afternoon. Mrs. Hunt emerged thankfully from the crowded lift which shot up the passengers from underground. She came with slow step into the dusty street. The flat was not far away: that was one comfort. But she sighed impatiently as she entered the building, to be confronted with the "Not Working" legend on the lift.

"Little wretch! " she said, alluding to the absent lift-boy. "I'm sure he's only playing pitch-and-toss round the corner. " She toiled up the three long flights of stairs—her dainty soul revolting at their unswept dinginess. Stella Hunt had been brought up in a big house on a wind-swept Cumberland fell, and there was no day in crowded Bloomsbury when she did not long for the clean open spaces of her girlhood.

She let herself into the flat with her latch-key. Voices came to her from the sitting-room, with a gurgle of laughter from little Michael. She frowned.

"Eva should not have let the children in there, " she thought anxiously. "They may do some damage. " She opened the door hurriedly.

No one noticed her for a moment, David Linton, with Alison on one knee and Geoffrey on the other, was deep in a story of kangaroo-hunting. On the floor sat Norah, with Michael tucked into her lap, his face blissful as she told on his fat fingers the tale of the little pigs who went to market. The box of chocolates was on the table, its scarlet ribbon making a bright spot of colour in the drab room. The mother looked for a minute in silence, something of the weariness dying out of her eyes.

Then Geoffrey looked up and saw her—a slight figure, holding a paper bag.

"Hallo! " he said. "I'm glad you didn't forget the cakes, 'cause we've got people to tea! "

Mr. Linton placed his burden on the hearthrug, and got up.

"How are you, Mrs. Hunt? I hope you don't mind our taking possession like this. We wanted to get acquainted. "

"I could wish they were cleaner, " said Mrs. Hunt, laughing, as she shook hands. "I've seldom seen three grubbier people. Geoff, dear, couldn't Eva have washed your face? "

"She said she hadn't time, " said Geoffrey easily. "We tried to wash Michael, but he only got more streaky. "

"Oh, please don't mind, Mrs. Hunt, " Norah pleaded. "They've been such darlings! "

"I'm afraid I don't mind at all, " said Mrs. Hunt, sitting down thankfully. "I've been picturing my poor babies tired to death of not being out—and then to come home and find them in the seventh heaven——" She broke off, her lip quivering a little.

"You're just as tired as you can be, " said Norah. "Now you're going to rest, and Geoff will show me how to get tea. "

"Oh, I couldn't let you into that awful little kitchen, " said Mrs. Hunt hastily. "And besides—I'm awfully sorry—I don't believe the milkman has been yet. "

"I could go to the milk-shop round the corner with a jug, " said Geoffrey anxiously. "Do let's, Mother. "

"Is there one? " Norah asked. "Now, Mrs. Hunt, do rest—make her put her feet up on the sofa, Dad. And Geoff and I will go for milk, and I'll ask Eva to make tea. Can she? "

"Oh, of course she *can*" said Mrs. Hunt, ceasing to argue the point. "But she's never fit to be seen. "

"That doesn't matter, " said David Linton masterfully. "We've seen her once, and survived the shock. Just put your feet up, and tell me all about your husband—Norah will see to things. "

Eva, however, was found to have risen to the situation. She had used soap and water with surprising effect, and now bloomed in a fresh cap and an apron that had plainly done duty a good many times, but, being turned inside out, still presented a decent front to the world. She scorned help in preparing tea, but graciously permitted Norah to wash the three children and brush their hair, and indicated where clean overalls might be found. Then, escorted by all three, Norah sallied forth, jug in hand, and found, not only the milk-shop, but another where cakes and scones so clamoured to be bought that they all returned laden with paper bags. Eva had made a huge plate of buttered toast; so that the meal which presently made its appearance on the big table in the drawing-room might well have justified the query as to whether indeed a war were in progress.

Mrs. Hunt laughed, rather mirthlessly.

"I suppose I ought to protest—but I'm too tired, " she said. "And it is very nice to be taken care of again. Michael, you should have bread-and-butter first. "

"Vere isn't any, " said Alison with triumph.

Norah was tucking a feeder under Michael's fat chin.

"Now he's my boy for a bit—not yours at all, Mrs. Hunt, " she said, laughing. "Forget them all: I'm going to be head nurse. " And Mrs. Hunt lay back thankfully, and submitted to be waited on, while the shouts of laughter from the tea-table smoothed away a few more lines from her face, and made even Eva, feasting on unaccustomed cakes in the kitchen, smile grimly and murmur, "Lor, ain't they 'avin' a time! "

Not until tea was over, and the children busy with picture books that had come mysteriously from another of his pockets, did David Linton unfold his plan: and then he did it somewhat nervously.

"We want to take you all out of this, Mrs. Hunt, " he said. "There's a little cottage—a jolly little thatched place—close to our house that is simply clamouring to have you all come and live in it. I think it will hold you all comfortably. Will you come? "

Mrs. Hunt flushed.

"Don't talk to poor Bloomsbury people of such heavenly things as thatched cottages, " she said. "We have this horrible abode on a long lease, and I don't see any chance of leaving it. "

"Oh, never mind the lease—we'll sub-let it for you, " said Mr. Linton. He told her briefly of John O'Neill's bequest to Norah.

"I want you to put it out of your head that you're accepting the slightest favour, " he went on. "We feel that we only hold the place in trust; the cottage is there, empty, and indeed it is you who will be doing us the favour by coming to live in it. "

"Oh—I couldn't, " she said breathlessly.

"Just think of it, Mrs. Hunt! " Norah knelt down by the hard little horsehair sofa. "There's a big lawn in front, and a summer-house where the babies could play, and a big empty attic for them on wet days, and heaps of fresh milk, and you could keep chickens; and the sitting-room catches all the sun, and when Major Hunt comes out of the hospital it would be so quiet and peaceful. He could lie out under the trees on fine days on a rush lounge; and there are jolly woods for him to walk in. " The poor wife caught her breath. "And he'd be such tremendous company for Dad, and I know you'd help me when I got into difficulties with my cook-lady. There's a little stream, and a tiny lake, and ——"

"When is we goin', Muvver? "

The question was Alison's, put with calm certainty. She and Geoffrey had stolen near, and were listening with eager faces.

"Oh, my darling, I'm afraid we can't, " said Mrs. Hunt tremulously.

"But the big girl says we can. When is we going? "

"Oh, Mother! " said Geoffrey, very low. "Away from—*here*! " He caught her hand. "Oh, say we're going, Mother—darling! "

"Of course she'll say it, " David Linton said. "The only question is, how soon can you be ready? "

"Douglas is terribly proud, " Mrs. Hunt said. "I am afraid I couldn't be proud. But he will never accept a favour. I know it would be no use to ask him. "

"Then we won't ask him, " said David Linton calmly. "When does he leave the hospital? "

"This day week, if he is well enough. "

"Then we'll have you comfortably installed long before that. We won't tell him a thing about it: on the day he's to come out I'll go for him in the motor and whisk him down to Homewood before he realizes where he's going. Now, be sensible, Mrs. Hunt"—as she tried to speak. "You know what his state is—how anxious you are: you told me all about it just now. Can you, in justice to him, refuse to come? —can you face bringing him back here? "

Geoffrey suddenly burst into sobs.

"Oh, don't Mother! " he choked. "You know how he hates it. And— trees, and grass, and woods, and ——" He hid his face on her arm.

"An' tsickens, " said Alison. "An' ackits to play in. "

"You're in a hopeless minority, you see, Mrs. Hunt, " said Mr. Linton. "You'll have to give in. "

Mrs. Hunt put her arms round the two children who were pressing against her in their eagerness: whereupon Michael raised a wrathful howl and flung himself bodily upon them, ejaculating: "Wants to be hugged, too! " Over the three heads the mother looked up at her visitors.

"Yes, I give in, " she said. "I'm not brave enough not to. But I don't know what Douglas will say. "

"I'll attend to Douglas, " said Mr. Linton cheerfully. "Now, how soon can you come? " He frowned severely. "There's to be no question of house-cleaning here—I'll put in people to do that. You'll have your husband to nurse next week, and I won't have you tiring yourself out beforehand. So you have only to pack. "

"Look, Mrs. Hunt, " Norah was flushed with another brilliant idea. "Let us take the babies down to-day—I'm sure they will come with me. Then you and Eva will have nothing to do but pack up your things. "

"Oh, I couldn't——" Mrs. Hunt began.

"Ah yes, you could. " She turned to the children. "Geoff, will you all come with my Daddy and me and get the cottage ready for Mother?"

Geoffrey hesitated.

"Would you come soon, Mother? "

"I—I believe if I had nothing else to do I could leave the flat to-morrow, " Mrs. Hunt said, submitting. "Would you all be happy, Geoff? —and very good? "

"Yes, if you'd hurry up and come. You'll be a good kid, Alison, won't you? "

"'Ess, " said Alison. "Will I see tsickens? "

"Ever so many, " Norah said. "And Michael will be a darling: and we'll all sleep together in one big room, and have pillow-fights! "

"You had certainly better come soon, before your family's manners become ruined, Mrs. Hunt, " said Mr. Linton, laughing. "Then you can really manage to get away to-morrow? Very well—I'll call for you about five, if that will do. "

"Yes; that will give me time to see Douglas first. "

"But you won't tell him anything? "

"Oh, no: he would only worry. Of course, Mr. Linton, I shall be able to get up to see him every day? "

"We're less than an hour by rail, " he told her. "And the trains are good. Now I think you had better pack up those youngsters, and I'll get a taxi. "

Norah helped to pack the little clothes, trying hard to remember instructions as to food and insistence on good manners.

"Oh, I know you'll spoil them, " said Mrs. Hunt resignedly. "Poor mites, they could do with a bit of spoiling: they have had a dreary year. But I think they will be good: they have been away with my sister sometimes, and she gives them a good character. "

The children said good-bye to their mother gaily enough: the ride in the motor was sufficient excitement to smooth out any momentary dismay at parting. Only Geoffrey sat up very straight, with his lips tightly pressed together. He leaned from the window—Norah gripping his coat anxiously.

"You'll be true-certain to come to-morrow, Mother? "

"I promise, " she said. "Good-bye, old son. "

"Mother always keeps her promises, so it's all right, " he said, leaning back with a little smile. Alison had no worries. She sang "Hi, diddle, diddle! " loud and clear, as they rushed through the crowded streets. When a block in the traffic came, people on 'buses looked down, smiling involuntarily at the piping voice coming from the recesses of the taxi. As for Michael, he sat on Norah's knee and sucked his thumb in complete content.

Jones met them at the end of the little journey. His lips involuntarily shaped themselves to a whistle of amazement as the party filed out of the station, though to the credit of his training be it recorded that no sound came. Geoffrey caught his breath with delight at the sight of the brown cobs.

"Oh-h! Are they yours? "

"Yes—aren't they dears? " responded Norah.

The boy caught her hand.

"Oh—could I *possibly* sit in front and look at them? "

Norah laughed.

"Could he, Jones? Would you take care of him? "

"'E'd be as safe as in a cradle, Miss Norah, " said Jones delightedly. "Come on up, sir, and I'll show you 'ow to drive. " Mr. Linton swung him up, smiling at the transfigured little face. Norah had already got her charges into the carriage: a porter stowed away their trunk, and the horses trotted off through the dusk.

"I didn't ever want to get out, " Geoffrey confided to Norah, as they went up the steps to the open door of Homewood. "That kind man let me hold the end of the reins. And he says he'll show me more horses to-morrow. "

"There's a pony too—we'll teach you to ride it, " said Mr. Linton. Whereat Geoffrey gasped with joy and became speechless.

"Well—have you got them all tucked up? " asked Mr. Linton, when Norah joined him in the morning-room an hour later.

"Oh, yes; they were so tired, poor mites. Bride helped me to bathe them, and we fed them all on bread and milk—with lots of cream. Michael demanded "Mummy, " but he was too sleepy to worry much. But; Dad—Geoff wants you badly to say 'good-night. ' He says his own Daddy always says it to him when he's in bed. Would you mind? "

"Right, " said her father. He went upstairs, with Norah at his heels, and tiptoed into the big room where two of his three small guests were already sleeping soundly. He looked very tall as he stood beside the little bed in the corner. Geoff's bright eyes peeped up at him.

"It was awful good of you to come, " he said sleepily. "Daddy does. He says, 'Good night, old chap, and God bless you. '"

"Good night, old chap, and God bless you, " said David Linton gravely. He held the small hand a moment in his own, and then, stooping, brushed his forehead with his lips.

"God bless you, " said Geoff's drowsy voice. "I'm going—going to ride the pony . .. to-morrow. " His words trailed off in sleep.

CHAPTER VII

THE THATCHED COTTAGE

But for the narrow white beds, you would hardly have thought that the big room was a hospital ward. In days before all the world was caught into a whirlpool of war it had been a ballroom. A famous painter had made the vaulted ceiling an exquisite thing of palest blush-roses and laughing Cupids, tumbling among vine-leaves and tendrils. The white walls bore long panels of the same design. There were no fittings for light visible: when darkness fell, the touch of a button flooded the room with a soft glow, coming from some unseen source in the carved cornice. The shining floor bore heavy Persian rugs, and there were tables heaped with books and magazines; and the nurses who flitted in and out were all dainty and good to look at. All about the room were splendid palms in pots; from giants twenty feet high, to lesser ones the graceful leaves of which could just catch the eye of a tired man in bed—fresh from the grim ugliness of the trenches. It was the palms you saw as you came in—not the beds here and there among them.

A good many of the patients were up this afternoon, for this was a ward for semi-convalescents. Not all were fully dressed: they moved about in dressing-gowns, or lay on the sofas, or played games at the little tables. One man was in uniform: Major Hunt, who sat in a big chair near his bed, and from time to time cast impatient glances at the door.

"Wish we weren't going to lose you, Major, " said a tall man in a purple dressing-gown, who came up the ward with wonderful swiftness, considering that he was on crutches. "But I expect you're keen to go. "

"Oh, yes; though I'll miss this place. " Major Hunt cast an appreciative glance down the beautiful room. "It has been great luck to be here; there are not many hospitals like this in England. But—well, even if home is only a beastly little flat in Bloomsbury it *is* home, and I shall be glad to get back to my wife and the youngsters. I miss the kids horribly. "

"Yes, one does, " said the other.

"I daresay I'll find them something of a crowd on wet days, when they can't get out, " said Major Hunt, laughing. "The flat is small, and my wretched nerves are all on edge. But I want them badly, for all that. And it's rough on my wife to be so much alone. She has led a kind of wandering life since war broke out—sometimes we've been able to have the kids with us, but not always. " He stretched himself wearily. "Gad! how glad I'll be when the Boche is hammered and we're able to have a decent home again! "

"We're all like that, " said the other man. "I've seen my youngsters twice in the last year. "

"Yes, you're worse off than I am, " said Major Hunt. He looked impatiently towards the door, fidgeting. "I wish Stella would come."

But when a nurse brought him a summons presently, and he said good-bye to the ward and went eagerly down to the ground-floor (in an electric lift worked by an earl's daughter in a very neat uniform), it was not his wife who awaited him in a little white-and-gold sitting-room, but a very tall man, looking slightly apologetic.

"Your wife is perfectly well, " said David Linton, checking the quick inquiry that rose to the soldier's lips. "But I persuaded her to give me the job of calling for you to-day: our car is rather more comfortable than a taxi, and the doctor thought it would be a good thing for you to have a little run first. "

Major Hunt tried not to look disappointed, and failed signally.

"It's awfully good of you, " he said courteously. "But I don't believe I'm up to much yet—and I'm rather keen on getting home. If you wouldn't mind going there direct. "

David Linton cast an appealing look at the nurse, who had accompanied her patient. She rose to the occasion promptly.

"Now, Major Hunt, " she protested. "Doctor's orders! You promised to take all the exercise you could, and a run in the car would be the very thing for you. "

"Oh, very well. " Major Hunt's voice was resigned. David Linton leaned towards him.

"I'll make it as short as I can, " he said confidentially. They said good-bye, and emerged into Park Lane, where the big blue motor waited.

"Afraid you must think me horribly rude, " said the soldier, as they started. "Fact is, I'm very anxious to see my youngsters: I don't know why, but Stella wouldn't bring them to the hospital to see me this last week. But it's certainly jolly to be out again. " He leaned back, enjoying the comfort of the swift car. "I suppose—" he hesitated—"it would be altogether too much trouble to go round by the flat and pick up my wife and Geoff. They would love a run. "

"Oh! Ah! The flat—yes, the flat! " said David Linton, a little wildly. "I'm afraid—that is, we should be too early. Mrs. Hunt would not expect us so soon, and she—er—she meant to be out, with all the children. Shopping. Fatted calf for the prodigal's return, don't you know. Awfully sorry. "

"Oh, it's quite all right, " said Major Hunt, looking rather amazed. "Only she doesn't generally take them all out. But of course it doesn't matter. "

"I'll tell you what, " said his host, regaining his composure. "We'll take all of you out to-morrow—Mrs. Hunt and the three youngsters as well as yourself. The car will hold all. "

Major Hunt thanked him, rather wearily. They sped on, leaving the outskirts of London behind them. Up and down long, suburban roads, beyond the trail of motor-'buses, until the open country gleamed before them. The soldier took a long breath of the sweet air.

"Gad, it's good to see fields again! " he said. Presently he glanced at the watch on his wrist.

"Nearly time to turn, don't you think? " he said. "I don't want Stella to be waiting long. "

"Very soon, " said Mr. Linton. "Just a little more country air. The chauffeur has his orders: I won't keep you much longer. "

He racked his brains anxiously for a moment, and then plunged into a story of Australia—a story in which bushrangers, blacks and bushfires mingled so amazingly that it was impossible not to listen to it. Having once secured his hapless guest's attention, he managed to leave the agony of invention and to slide gracefully to cattle-mustering, about which it was not necessary to invent anything. Major Hunt became interested, and asked a few questions; and they were deep in a comparison of the ways of handling cattle on an Australian run and a Texan ranch, when the car suddenly turned in at a pair of big iron gates and whirled up a drive fringed with trees. Major Hunt broke off in the middle of a sentence.

"Hallo! Where are we going? "

"I have to stop at a house here for an instant, " said Mr. Linton. "Just a moment; I won't keep you. "

Major Hunt frowned. He was tired; the car was wonderfully comfortable, but the rush through the keen air was wearying to a semi-invalid, and he was conscious of a feeling of suppressed irritation. He wanted to be home. The thought of the hard little sofa in the London flat suddenly became tempting—he could lie there and talk to the children, and watch Stella moving about. Now they were miles into the country—long miles that must be covered again before he was back in Bloomsbury. He bit his lips to restrain words that might not seem courteous.

"I should really be very grateful if— —"

He stopped. The car had turned into a side-avenue—he caught a glimpse of a big, many-gabled house away to the right. Then they turned a corner, and the car came to a standstill with her bonnet almost poking into a great clump of rhododendrons. There was a thatched cottage beside them. And round the corner tore a small boy in a sailor suit, with his face alight with a very ecstasy of welcome.

"Daddy! Oh, Daddy! "

"Geoff! " said Major Hunt amazedly. "But how? —I don't understand. "

There were other people coming round the corner: his wife, tall and slender, with her eyes shining; behind her, Norah Linton, with Alison trotting beside her, and Michael perched on one shoulder. At sight of his father Michael drummed with his heels to Norah's great discomfort, and uttered shrill squeaks of joy.

"Come on, " said Geoffrey breathlessly, tugging at the door. "Come on! they're all here. "

"Come on, Hunt, " said David Linton, jumping out. "Let me help you—mind your hand. "

"I suppose I'll wake up in a moment, " said Major Hunt, getting out slowly. "At present, it's a nice dream. I don't understand anything. How are you, Miss Linton? "

"You don't need to wake up, " said his wife, in a voice that shook a little. Her brave eyes were misty. "Only, you're home. "

"It's the loveliest home, Daddy! " Geoff's hand was in his father's, pulling him on.

"There's tsickens! " said Alison in a high pipe. "An' a ackit wiv toys."

"She means an attic, " said Geoffrey scornfully. "Come on, Daddy. We've got such heaps to show you. "

Somehow they found themselves indoors. Norah and her father had disappeared; they were all together, father, mother, and babies, in a big room flooded with sunlight: a room covered with a thick red matting with heavy rugs on it; a room with big easy-chairs and gate-legged tables, and a wide couch heaped with bright cushions, drawn close to an open casement. There was a fire of logs, crackling cheerily in the wide fireplace: there were their own belongings—photographs, books, his own pipe-rack and tobacco-jar: there were flowers everywhere, smiling a greeting. Tea-cups and silver sparkled on a white-cloth; a copper kettle bubbled over a spirit-lamp. And there were his own people clinging round him, welcoming, holding him wherever little hands could grasp: the babies fresh, clean, even rosy; his wife's face, no longer tired. And there was no Bloomsbury anywhere.

Major Hunt sat down on the sofa, disentangled Michael from his leg, and lifted him with his good arm.

"It isn't a dream, really, I suppose, Stella? " he said. "I won't wake up presently? I don't want to. "

"No; it's just a blessed reality, " she told him, smiling. "Hang up Daddy's cap, Geoff: steady, Alison, darling—mind his hand. Don't worry about anything, Douglas—only—you're home. "

"I don't even want to ask questions, " said her husband, in the same dazed voice. "I find one has no curiosity, when one suddenly gets to heaven. We won't be going away from heaven, though, will we? "

"No—we're permanent residents, " she told him, laughing. "Now get quite comfy; we'll all have tea together. "

"Tea's is lovely here, " confided Alison to him. "They's cweam—an' cakes, *evewy* day. An' the tsickens make weal eggs, in nesses! "

"And I can ride. A pony, Daddy! " Geoffrey's voice was quivering with pride. He stood by the couch, an erect little figure.

"Why, he's grown—ever so much! " said Major Hunt. "They've all grown; you too, my little fat Michael. I left white-faced babies in that beastly flat. And you too——" She bent over him. "Your dear eyes have forgotten the old War! " he said, very low.

There was a heavy knock at the door. Entered Eva, resplendent in a butterfly cap and an apron so stiffly starched that it stood away resentfully from her figure. By no stretch of imagination could Eva ever have been called shy; but she had a certain amount of awe for her master, and found speech in his presence a little difficult. But on this occasion it was evident that she felt that something was demanded of her. She put her burden of buttered toast on a trivet in the fender, and said breathlessly:

"'Ope I see yer well, sir. And *ain't* this a nice s'prise! "

"Thank you, Eva—yes, " said Major Hunt.

Whereat, the handmaiden withdrew, her heavy tread retreating to the kitchen to the accompaniment of song.

Captain Jim

"Ow—Ow—*Ow*, it's a lovely War! "

"I didn't know her for a moment, " Major Hunt said, laughing. "You see, she never had less than six smuts on her face in Bloomsbury. She's transformed, like all of you in this wonderful dream. "

"Tea isn't a dream, " said his wife. She made it in the silver tea-pot, and they all fluttered about him, persuading him to eat: and made his tea a matter of some difficulty, since all three children insisted on getting as close to him as possible, and he had but one good hand. He did not mind. Once, as his wife brought him a refilled cup, she saw him lean his face down until it rested for a moment on the gold rings of Michael's hair.

It was with some anxiety that Norah and her father went to call on their guest next morning.

"What will we do if he's stiff-necked and proud, Dad? " Norah asked. "I simply couldn't part with those babies now! "

"Let's hope he won't be, " said her father. "But if the worst comes to worst, we could let him pay us a little rent for the place—we could give the money to the Red Cross, of course. "

"'M! " said Norah, wrinkling her nose expressively. "That would be horrid—it would spoil all the idea of the place. "

But they found Major Hunt surprisingly meek.

"I daresay that if you had propounded the idea to me at first I should have said 'No' flatly, " he admitted. "But I haven't the heart to disturb them all now—and, frankly, I'm too thankful. If you'll let me pay you rent— —"

"Certainly not! " said Mr. Linton, looking astonished and indignant. "We don't run our place on those lines. Just put it out of your head that we have anything to do with it. You're taking nothing from us— only from a man who died very cheerfully because he was able to do five minutes' work towards helping the War. He's helping it still if his money makes it easier for fellows like you; and I believe, wherever he is, he knows and is glad. "

"But there are others who may need it more, " said Hunt weakly.

"If there are, I haven't met them yet, " Mr. Linton responded. He glanced out of the window. "Look there now, Hunt! "

Norah had slipped away, leaving the men to talk. Now she came riding up the broad gravel path across the lawn, on the black pony: leading the fat Welsh pony, with Geoffrey on his back. The small boy sat very straight, with his hands well down. His flushed little face sought anxiously for his father's at the window.

Major Hunt uttered a delighted exclamation.

"I didn't know my urchin was so advanced, " he said. "Well done, old son! " He scanned him keenly. "He doesn't sit too badly, Mr. Linton. "

"He's not likely to do so, with Norah as his teacher. But Norah says he doesn't need much teaching, and that he has naturally good hands. She's proud of him. I think, " said Mr. Linton, laughing, "that they have visions of hunting together this winter! "

"I must go out and see him, " said the father, catching up his cap. Mr. Linton watched him cross the lawn with quick strides: and turned, to find Mrs. Hunt at his elbow.

"Well—he doesn't look much like an invalid, Madam! " he said, smiling.

"He's not like the same man, " she said, with grateful eyes. "He slept well, and ate a huge breakfast: even the hand is less painful. And he's so cheery. Oh, I'm so thankful to you for kidnapping us! "

"Indeed, it's you that we have to thank, " he told her. "You gave us our first chance of beginning our job. "

CHAPTER VIII
ASSORTED GUESTS

"I beg your pardon—is this Homewood? "

Norah, practising long putts at a hole on the far side of the terrace, turned with a start. The questioner was in uniform, bearing a captain's three stars. He was a short, strongly-built young man, with a square, determined face.

"Yes, this is Homewood, " she answered. "Did you—have you come to see my father? "

"I wrote to him last week, " the officer said—"from France. It's Miss Linton, isn't it? I'm in your brother's regiment. My name is Garrett. "

"Oh—I've heard Jim speak of you ever so many times, " she cried. She put out her hand, and felt it taken in a close grasp. "But we haven't had your letter. Dad would have told me if one had come. "

Captain Garrett frowned.

"What a nuisance! " he ejaculated. "Letters from the front are apt to take their time, but I did think a week would have been long enough. I wrote directly I knew my leave was coming. You see—your brother told me——" He stopped awkwardly.

Intelligence suddenly dawned upon Norah.

"Why, you're a Tired Person! " she exclaimed, beaming.

"Not at all, I assure you, " replied he, looking a trifle amazed. Norah laughed.

"I don't mean quite that, " she said—"at least I'll explain presently. But you *have* come to stay, haven't you? "

"Well—your brother was good enough to——" He paused again.

"Yes, of course. Jim told you we wanted you to come. This is the Home for Tired People, you see; we want to get as many of you as we can and make you fit. And you're our very first in the house, which will make it horribly dull for you. "

"Indeed, it won't, " said Garrett gallantly.

"Well, we'll do our best for you. I'm so very sorry you weren't met. Did you leave your luggage at the station? "

"Yes. You're quite sure it's convenient to have me, Miss Linton? I could easily go back to London. "

"Good gracious, no! " said Norah. "Why, you're a godsend! We weren't justifying our name. But you *will* be dull to-day, because Dad has gone to London, and there's only me. " Norah's grammar was never her strong point. "And little Geoff Hunt was coming to lunch with me. Will it bore you very much to have a small boy here?"

"Rather not! " said Garrett. "I like them—got some young brothers of my own in Jamaica. "

"Well, that's all right. Now come in, and Allenby will show you your room. The car will bring your things up when it goes to meet Dad. "

Norah had often rehearsed in her own mind what she would do when the first Tired Person came. The rooms were all ready—"in assorted sizes, " Allenby said. Norah had awful visions of eight or ten guests arriving together, and in her own mind characterized the business of allotting them to their rooms as a nasty bit of drafting. But the first guest had tactfully come alone, and there was no doubt that he deserved the blue room—a delightful little corner room looking south and west, with dainty blue hangings and wall-paper, and a big couch that beckoned temptingly to a tired man. Captain Garrett had had fourteen months in France without a break. He had spent the previous night in the leave-train, only pausing in London for a hasty "clean-up. " The lavender-scented blue room was like a glimpse of Heaven to him. He did not want to leave it—only that downstairs Jim Linton's sister awaited him, and it appeared that the said sister was a very jolly girl, with a smile like her brother's cheerful grin, and a mop of brown curls framing a decidedly attractive face. Bob Garrett decided that there were better things than even the blue room, and, having thankfully accepted Allenby's offer of a hot tub, presently emerged from the house, much improved in appearance.

This time Norah was not alone. A small boy was with her, who greeted the newcomer with coolness, and then suddenly fell upon him excitedly, recognizing the badge on his collar.

"You're in Daddy's regiment! " he exclaimed.

"Am I? " Garrett smiled at him. "Who is Daddy? "

"He's Major Hunt, " said Geoff; and had the satisfaction of seeing the new officer become as eager as he could have wished.

"By Jove! Truly, Miss Linton? —does Major Hunt live here? I'd give something to see him. "

"He lives just round the corner of that bush, " said Norah, laughing. She indicated a big rhododendron. "Is he at home, Geoff? "

"No—he's gone to London, " Geoff answered. "But he'll be back for tea. "

"Then we'll go and call on Mrs. Hunt and ask her if we may come to tea, " Norah said. They strolled off, Geoff capering about them.

"I don't know Mrs. Hunt, " Garrett said. "You see I only joined the regiment when war broke out—I had done a good bit of training, so they gave me a commission among the first. I didn't see such a lot of the Major, for he was doing special work in Ireland for awhile; but he was a regular brick to me. We're all awfully sick about his being smashed up. "

"But he's going to get better, " Norah said cheerfully. "He's ever so much better now. "

They came out in front of the cottage, and discovered Mrs. Hunt playing hide-and-seek with Alison and Michael—with Alison much worried by Michael's complete inattention to anything in the shape of a rule. Michael, indeed, declined to be hid, and played on a steady line of his own, which consisted in toddling after his mother whenever she was in sight, and catching her with shrill squeaks of joy. It was perfectly satisfactory to him, but somewhat harassing to a stickler for detail.

Mrs. Hunt greeted Garrett warmly.

"Douglas has often talked about you—you're from Jamaica, aren't you? " she said. "He will be so delighted that you have come. Yes, of course you must come to tea, Norah. I'd ask you to lunch, only I'm perfectly certain there isn't enough to eat! And Geoff would be so disgusted at being done out of his lunch with you, which makes me think it's not really your society he wants, but the fearful joy of Allenby behind his chair. "

"I don't see why you should try to depress me, " Norah laughed. "Well, we'll all go for a ride after lunch, and get back in time for tea, if you'll put up with me in a splashed habit—the roads are very muddy. You ride, I suppose, Captain Garrett? "

"Oh, yes, thanks, " Garrett answered. "It's the only fun I've had in France since the battalion went back into billets: a benevolent gunner used to lend me a horse—both of us devoutly hoping that I wouldn't be caught riding it. "

"Was it a nice horse? " Geoffrey demanded.

"Well, you wouldn't call it perfect, old chap. I think it was suffering from shell-shock: anyhow, it had nerves. It used to shake all over when it saw a Staff-officer! " He grinned. "Or perhaps I did. On duty, that horse was as steady as old Time: but when it was alone, it jumped out of its skin at anything and everything. However, it was great exercise to ride it! "

"We'll give him Killaloe this afternoon, Geoff, " said Norah. "Come on, and we'll show him the stables now. "

They bade *au revoir* to Mrs. Hunt and sauntered towards the stables. On the way appeared a form in a print frock, with flying cap and apron-strings.

Captain Jim

"Did you want me, Katty? " Norah asked.

"There's a tallygrum after coming, miss, on a bicycle. And the boy's waiting. "

Norah knitted her brows over the sheet of flimsy paper.

"There's no answer, Katty, tell the boy. " She turned to Garrett, laughing. "You're not going to be our only guest for long. Dad says he's bringing two people down to-night—Colonel and Mrs. West. Isn't it exciting! I'll have to leave you to Geoff while I go and talk to the housekeeper. Geoff, show Captain Garrett all the horses—Jones is at the stables. "

"Right! " said Geoffrey, bursting with importance. "Come along, Captain Garrett. I'll let you pat my pony, if you like! "

Mrs. Atkins looked depressed at Norah's information.

"Dear me! And dinner ordered for three! " she said sourly. "It makes a difference. And of course I really had not reckoned on more than you and Mr. Linton. "

"I can telephone for anything you want, " said Norah meekly.

"The fish will not be sufficient, " said the housekeeper. "And other things likewise. I must talk to the cook. It would be so much easier if one knew earlier in the day. And rooms to get ready, of course? "

"The big pink room with the dressing-room, " Norah said.

"Oh, I suppose the maids can find time. Those Irish maids have no idea of regular ways: I found Bride helping to catch a fowl this morning when she should have been polishing the floor. Now, I must throw them out of routine again. "

Norah suppressed a smile. She had been a spectator of the spirited chase after the truant hen, ending with the appearance of Mrs. Atkins, full of cold wrath; and she had heard Bride's comment afterwards. "Is it her, with her ould routheen? Yerra, that one wouldn't put a hand to a hin, and it eshcapin'! "

"Yes, " said Mrs. Atkins. "Extraordinary ways. Very untrained, I must say. "

"But you find that they do their work, don't they? " Norah asked.

"Oh, after a fashion, " said the housekeeper, with a sniff—unwilling to admit that Bride and Katty got through more work in two hours than Sarah in a morning, were never unwilling, and accepted any and every job with the utmost cheerfulness. "Their ways aren't my ways. Very well, Miss Linton. I'll speak to the cook. "

Feeling somewhat battered, Norah escaped. In the hall she met Katty, who jumped—and then broke into a smile of relief.

"I thought 'twas the Ould Thing hersilf, " she explained. "She'd ate the face off me if she found me here again—'tis only yesterday she was explaining to me that a kitchenmaid has no business in the hall, at all. But Bridie was tellin' me ye've the grandest ould head of an Irish elk here, and I thought I'd risk her, to get a sight of it. "

"It's over there, " Norah said, pointing to a mighty pair of horns on the wall behind the girl. Katty looked at it in silence.

"It's quare to think of the days when them great things walked the plains of Ireland, " she said at length. "Thank you, miss: it done me good to see it. "

"How are you getting on, Katty? " Norah asked.

"Yerra, the best in the world, " said Katty cheerfully. "Miss de Lisle's that kind to me—I'll be the great cook some day, if I kape on watchin' her. She's not like the fine English cooks I've heard of, that 'ud no more let you see how they made so much as a pudding than they'd fly over the moon. 'Tis Bridie has the bad luck, to be housemaid. "

Norah knew why, and sighed. There were moments when her housekeeper seemed a burden too great to be borne.

"But Mr. Allenby's very pleasant with her, and she says wance you find out that Sarah isn't made of wood she's not so bad. She found that out when she let fly a pillow at her, and they bedmaking, " said

Katty, with a joyous twinkle. "'Tis herself had great courage to do that same, hadn't she, now, miss? "

"She had, indeed, " Norah said, laughing. The spectacle of the stiff Sarah, overwhelmed with a sudden pillow, was indeed staggering.

"And then, haven't we Con to cheer us up if we get lonely? " said Katty. "And Misther Jones and the groom—they're very friendly. And the money we'll have to send home! But you'd be wishful for Ireland, no matter how happy you'd be. "

The telephone bell rang sharply, and Norah ran to answer it. It was Jim.

"That you, Nor? " said his deep voice. "Good—I'm in a hurry. I say, can you take in a Tired Person to-night? "

Norah gasped.

"Oh, certainly! " she said, grimly. "Who is it, Jimmy? Not you or Wally? "

"No such luck, " said her brother. "It's a chap I met last night; he's just out of a convalescent home, and a bit down on his luck. " His voice died away in a complicated jumble of whir and buzz, the bell rang frantically, and Norah, like thousands of other people, murmured her opinion of the telephone and all its works.

"Are you there? " she asked.

"B-z-z-z-z-z! " said the telephone.

Norah waited a little, anxiously debating whether it would be more prudent to ring up herself and demand the last speaker, or to keep quiet and trust to Jim to regain his connexion. Finally, she decided to ring: and was just about to put down the receiver when Jim's voice said, "Are you there? " in her ear sharply, and once more collapsed into a whir. She waited again, in dead silence. At last she rang. Nothing happened, so she rang again.

"Number, please? " said a bored voice.

"Some one was speaking to me—you've cut me off, " said Norah frantically.

"I've been trying to get you for the last ten minutes. You shouldn't have rung off, " said the voice coldly. "Wait, please. "

Norah swallowed her feelings and waited.

"Hallo! Hallo! Hallo! —oh, *is* that you, Norah? " said Jim, his tone crisp with feeling. "Isn't this an unspeakable machine! And I'm due in three minutes—I must fly. Sure you can have Hardress? He'll get to you by the 6.45. Are you all well? Yes, we're all right. Sorry, I'll get told off horribly if I'm late. Good-bye. "

Norah hung up the receiver, and stood pondering. She wished the telephone had not chosen to behave so abominably; only the day before Wally had rung her up and had spent quite half an hour in talking cheerful nonsense, without any hindrance at all. Norah wished she knew a little more about her new "case"; if he were very weak—if special food were needed. It was very provoking. Also, there was Mrs. Atkins to be faced—not a prospect to be put off, since, like taking Gregory's Powder, the more you looked at it the worse it got. Norah stiffened her shoulders and marched off to the housekeeper's room.

"Oh, Mrs. Atkins, " she said pleasantly, "there's another officer coming this evening. "

Mrs. Atkins turned, cold surprise in her voice.

"Indeed, miss. And will that be all, do you think? "

"I really don't know, " said Norah recklessly. "That depends on my father, you see. "

"Oh. May I ask which room is to be prepared? "

"The one next Captain Garrett's, please. I can do it, if the maids are too busy. "

Mrs. Atkins froze yet more.

"I should very much rather you did not, miss, thank you, " she said.

"Just as you like, " said Norah. "Con can take a message for anything you want; he is going to the station. "

"Thank you, miss, I have already telephoned for larger supplies, " said the housekeeper. The conversation seemed to have ended, so Norah departed.

"What did she ever come for? " she asked herself desperately. "If she didn't want to housekeep, why does she go out as a housekeeper? " Turning a corner she met the butler.

"Oh, Allenby, " she said. "We'll have quite a houseful to-night! " She told him of the expected arrivals, half expecting to see his face fall. Allenby, on the contrary, beamed.

"It'll be almost like waiting in Mess! " he said. "When you're used to officers, miss, you can't get on very well without them. " He looked in a fatherly fashion at Norah's anxious face. "All the arrangements made, I suppose, miss? "

"Oh, yes, I think they're all right, " said Norah, feeling anything but confident. "Allenby—I don't know much about managing things; do you think it's too much for the house? "

"No, miss, it isn't, " Allenby said firmly. "Just you leave it all to me, and don't worry. Nature made some people bad-tempered, and they can't 'elp it. I'll see that things are all right; and as for dinner, all that worries Miss de Lisle, as a rule, is, that she ain't got enough cooking to do! "

He bent the same fatherly glance on her that evening as she came into the hall when the hoot of the motor told that her father and his consignment of Tired People were arriving. Norah had managed to forget her troubles during the afternoon. A long ride had been followed by a very cheerful tea at Mrs. Hunt's, from which she and Garrett had returned only in time for Norah to slip into a white frock and race downstairs to meet her guests. She hoped, vaguely, that she looked less nervous than she felt.

The hall door opened, letting in a breath of the cold night air.

"Ah, Norah—this is my daughter, Mrs. West, " she heard her father's voice; and then she was greeting a stout lady and a grey-haired officer.

"Dear me! " said the lady. "I expected some one grown up. How brave! Fancy you, only—what is it—a flapper! And don't you hate us all very much? *I* should, I'm sure! "

Over her shoulder Norah caught a glimpse of her father's face, set in grim lines. She checked a sudden wild desire to laugh, and murmured something civil.

"Our hostess, Algernon, " said the stout lady, and Norah shook hands with Colonel West, who was short and stout and pompous, and said explosively, "Haw! Delighted! Cold night, what? "—which had the effect of making his hostess absolutely speechless. Somehow with the assistance of Allenby and Sarah, the newcomers were "drafted" to their rooms, and Norah and her father sought cover in the morning-room.

"You look worn, Daddy, " said his daughter, regarding him critically.

"I feel it, " said David Linton. He sank into an armchair and felt hurriedly for his pipe. "Haven't had a chance of a smoke for hours. They're a little trying, I think, Norah. "

"Where did you get them? " Norah asked, perching on the arm of his chair, and dropping a kiss on the top of his head.

"From the hospital where the boys were. Colonel West has been ill there. Brain-fever, Mrs. West says, but he doesn't look like it. Anyhow, they're hard up, I believe; their home is broken up and they have five or six children at school, and a boy in Gallipoli. They seemed very glad to come. "

"Well, that's all right, " said Norah practically. "We can't expect to have every one as nice as the Hunts. But they're not the only ones, Dad: Captain Garrett is here, and Jim is sending some one called Hardress by the 6.45—unfortunately the telephone didn't allow Jim to mention what he is! I hope he isn't a brigadier. "

100

"I don't see Jim hob-nobbing to any extent with brigadiers, " said her father. "I say, this is rather a shock. Four in a day! "

"Yes, business is looking up, " said Norah, laughing. "Captain Garrett is a dear—and he can ride, Dad. I had him out on Killaloe. I'm a little uneasy about the Hardress person, because he's just out of a convalescent home, and Jim seemed worried about him. But the telephone went mad, and Jim was in a hurry, so I didn't get any details. "

"Oh, well, we'll look after him. How is the household staff standing the invasion? "

"Every one's very happy except Mrs. Atkins, and she is plunged in woe. Even Sarah seems interested. I haven't dared to look at Miss de Lisle, but Allenby says she is cheerful. "

"Has Mrs. Atkins been unpleasant? "

"Well, " said Norah, and laughed, "you wouldn't call her exactly a bright spot in the house. But she has seen to things, so that is all that counts. "

"I won't have that woman worry you, " said Mr. Linton firmly.

"I won't have *you* worried about anything, " said Norah. "Don't think about Mrs. Atkins, or you won't enjoy your tea. And here's Allenby. "

"Tea! " said Mr. Linton, as the butler entered, bearing a little tray. "I thought I was too late for such a luxury—but I must say I'm glad of it. "

"I sent some upstairs, sir, " said Allenby, placing a little table near his master. "Just a little toast, sir, it being so late. And if you please, miss, Miss de Lisle would be glad if you could spare a moment in the kitchen. "

The cook-lady, redder than ever, was mixing a mysterious compound in a bowl. Katty, hugely important, darted hither and thither. A variety of savoury smells filled the air.

"I just wanted to tell you, " said Miss de Lisle confidentially, "that I'm making a special *souffle* of my own, and Allenby will put it in front of you. Promise me"—she leaned forward earnestly—"to use a thin spoon to help it, and slide it in edgeways as gently as—as if you were stroking a baby! It's just a *perfect* thing—I wouldn't sleep to-night if you used a heavy spoon and plunged it in as if it was a suet-pudding! "

"I won't forget, " Norah promised her, resisting a wild desire to laugh.

"That's a dear, " said the cook-lady, disregarding the relations of employer and employed, in the heat of professional enthusiasm. "And you'll help it as quickly as possible, won't you? It will be put on the table after all the other sweets. Every second will be of importance! " She sighed. "A *souffle* never gets a fair chance. It ought, of course, to be put on a table beside the kitchen-range, and cut within two seconds of leaving the oven. With a *hot* spoon! " She sighed tragically.

"We'll do our best for it, " Norah promised her. "I'm sure it will be lovely. Shall I come and tell you how it looked, afterwards? "

Miss de Lisle beamed.

"Now, that would be very kind of you, " she said. "It's so seldom that any one realizes what these things mean to the cook. A *souffle* like this is an inspiration—like a sonata to a musician. But no one ever dreams of the cook; and the most you can expect from a butler is, 'Oh, it cut very nice, ma'am, I'm sure. Very nice! '" She made a despairing gesture. "But some people would call Chopin 'very nice'!"

"Miss de Lisle, " said Norah earnestly, "some day when we haven't any guests and Dad goes to London, we'll give every one else a holiday and you and I will have lunch here together. And we'll have that *souffle*, and eat it beside the range! "

For a moment Miss de Lisle had no words.

"Well! " she said at length explosively. "And I was so horrible to you at first! " To Norah's amazement and dismay a large tear trickled down one cheek, and her mouth quivered like a child's. "Dear me, how foolish I am, " said the poor cook-lady, rubbing her face with her overall, and thereby streaking it most curiously with flour. "Thank you very much, my dear. Even if we never manage it, I won't forget that you said it! "

Norah found herself patting the stalwart shoulder.

"Indeed, we'll manage it, " she said. "Now, don't you worry about anything but that lovely *souffle*. "

"Oh, the *souffle* is assured now, " said Miss de Lisle, beating her mixture scientifically. "Now I shall have beautiful thoughts to put into it! You have no idea what that means. Now, if I sat here mixing, and thought of, say, Mrs. Atkins, it would probably be as heavy as lead! " She sighed. "I believe, Miss Linton, I could teach you something of the real poetry of cooking. I'm sure you have the right sort of soul! "

Norah looked embarrassed.

"Jim says I've no soul beyond mustering cattle, " she said, laughing. "We'll prove him wrong, some day, Miss de Lisle, shall we? Now I must go: the motor will be back presently. " She turned, suddenly conscious of a baleful glance.

"Oh! —Mrs. Atkins! " she said feebly.

"I came, " said Mrs. Atkins stonily, "to see if any help was needed in the kitchen. Perhaps, as you are here, miss, you would be so good as to ask the cook? "

"Oh—nothing, thank you, " said Miss de Lisle airily, over her shoulder. Mrs. Atkins sniffed, and withdrew.

"That's done it, hasn't it? " said the cook-lady. "Well, don't worry, my dear; I'll see you through anything. "

A white-capped head peeped in.

"'Tis yersilf has all the luck of the place, Katty O'Gorman! " said Bride enviously. "An' that Sarah won't give me so much as a look-in, above: if it was to turn down the beds, itself, it's as much as she'll do to let me. Could I give you a hand here at all, Miss de Lisle? God help us, there's Miss Norah! "

"If 'tis the way you'd but let her baste the turkey for a minyit, she'd go upstairs reshted in hersilf, " said Katty in a loud whisper. "The creature's destroyed with bein' out of all the fun. "

"Oh, come in—if you're not afraid of Mrs. Atkins, " said Miss de Lisle. Norah had a vision of Bride, ecstatically grasping a basting-ladle, as she made her own escape.

Allenby was just shutting the hall-door as she turned the corner. A tall man in a big military greatcoat was shaking hands with her father.

"Here's Captain Hardress, Norah. "

Norah found herself looking up into a face that at the first glance she thought one of the ugliest she had ever seen. Then the newcomer smiled, and suddenly the ugliness seemed to vanish.

"It's too bad to take you by storm this way. But your brother wouldn't hear of anything else. "

"Of course not, " said Mr. Linton. "My daughter was rather afraid you might be a brigadier. She loses her nerve at the idea of pouring tea for anything above a colonel. "

"Indeed, a colonel's bad enough, " said Norah ruefully. "I'm accustomed to people with one or two stars: even three are rather alarming! " She shot a glance at his shoulder, laughing.

"I'm sure you're not half as alarmed as I was at coming, " said Captain Hardress. "I've been so long in hospital that I've almost forgotten how to speak to any one except doctors and nurses. " His face, that lit up so completely when he smiled, relapsed into gloom.

"Well, you mustn't stand here, " Norah said. "Please tell me if you'd like dinner in your room, or if you'd rather come down. " She had a sudden vision of Mrs. West's shrill voice, and decided that she might be tiring to this man with the gaunt, sad face.

Hardress hesitated.

"I think you'd better stay upstairs, " said David Linton. "Just for to-night—till you feel rested. I'll come and smoke a pipe with you after dinner, if I may. "

"I should like that awfully, " said Hardress. "Well, if you're sure it would not be too much trouble, Miss Linton——? "

"It's not a scrap of trouble, " she said. "Allenby will show you the way. See that Captain Hardress has a good fire, Allenby—and take some papers and magazines up. " She looked sadly after the tall figure as it limped away. He was not much older than Jim, but his face held a world of bitter experience.

"You mustn't let the Tired People make you unhappy, mate, " said her father. He put his arm round her as they went into the drawing-room to await their guests. "Remember, they wouldn't be here if they didn't need help of some sort. "

"I won't be stupid, " said Norah. "But he has such a sorry face, Dad, when he doesn't smile. "

"Then our job is to keep him smiling, " said David Linton practically.

There came a high-pitched voice in the hall, and Mrs. West swept in, her husband following at her heels. To Norah's inexperienced eyes, she was more gorgeous than the Queen of Sheba, in a dress of sequins that glittered and flashed with every movement. Sarah, who had assisted in her toilette, reported to the kitchen that she didn't take much stock in a dress that was moulting its sequins for all the world like an old hen; but Norah saw no deficiencies, and was greatly impressed by her guest's magnificence. She was also rather overcome by her eloquence, which had the effect of making her feel speechless. Not that that greatly mattered, as Mrs. West never noticed whether any one else happened to speak or remain silent, so long as they did not happen to drown her own voice.

"Such a lovely room! " she twittered. "*So* comfortable. And I feel sure there is an exquisite view. And a fire in one's bedroom—in wartime! Dear me, I feel I ought to protest, only I haven't sufficient moral courage; and those pine logs are *too* delicious. Perhaps you are burning your own timber? —ah, I thought so. That makes it easier for me to refrain from prodding up my moral courage—ha, ha! "

Norah hunted for a reply, and failed to find one.

"And you are actually Australians! " Mrs. West ran on. "*So* interesting! I always do think that Australians are so original—so quaintly original. It must be the wild life you lead. So unlike dear, quiet little England. Bushrangers, and savage natives, and gold-mining. How I should like to see it all! "

"Oh, you would find other attractions as well, Mrs. West, " Mr. Linton told her. "The 'wild life in savage places' phase of Australian history is rather a back number. "

"Oh, quite—quite, " agreed his guest. "We stay-at-homes know so little of the other side of the world. But we are not aloof—not uninterested. We recognize the fascination of it all. The glamour—yes, the glamour. Gordon's poems bring it all before one, do they not? Such a true Australian! You must be very proud of him. "

"We are—but he wasn't an Australian, " said Mr. Linton. The lady sailed on, unheeding.

"Yes. The voice of the native-born. And your splendid soldiers, too! —I assure you I thrill whenever I meet one of the dear fellows in the street in London. So tall and stern under their great slouch-hats. Outposts of Empire, that is what I say to myself. Outposts here, in the heart of our dear little Surrey! Linking the ends of the earth, as it were. The strangeness of it all! "

Garrett, who had made an unobtrusive entrance some little time before, and had been enjoying himself hugely in the background, now came up to the group on the hearthrug and was duly introduced.

"Lately from France, did you say? " asked Mrs. West. "Yesterday! Fancy! Like coming from one world into another, is it not, Captain

Garrett? To be only yesterday 'mid the thunder of shot and shell out yonder; and to-night in — — "

"In dear little Surrey, " said Garrett innocently.

"Quite. Such a peaceful county — war seems so remote. You must tell me some of your experiences to-morrow. "

"Oh, I never have any, " said Garrett hastily.

"Now, now! " She shook a playful forefinger at him. "I was a mother to my husband's regiment, Captain Garrett, I assure you. Quite. I used to say to all our subalterns, 'Now, remember that this house is open to you at any time. ' I felt that they were so far from their own homes. 'Bring your troubles to me, ' I would say, 'and let us straighten them out together. '"

"And did they? " Garrett asked.

"They understood me. They knew I wanted to help them. And my husband encouraged them to come. "

"Takes some encouragin', the subaltern of the present day, unless it's to tennis and two-step, " said Colonel West.

"But such dear boys! I felt their mothers would have been so glad. And our regiment had quite a name for nice subalterns. There is something so delightful about a subaltern — so care-free. "

"By Jove, yes! " said Colonel West. "Doesn't care for anything on earth — not even the adjutant! "

"Now, Algernon — — " But at that moment dinner was announced, and the rest of the sentence was lost — which was an unusual fate for any remark of Mrs. West's.

It was Norah's first experience as hostess at her father's dinner-table — since, in this connexion, Billabong did not seem to count. No one could ever have been nervous at Billabong. Besides, there was no butler there: here, Allenby, gravely irreproachable, with Sarah and Bride as attendant sprites, seemed to intensify the solemnity of everything. However, no one seemed to notice anything unusual, and conversation flowed apace. Colonel West did not want to talk: such cooking as Miss de Lisle's appeared to him to deserve the compliment of silence, and he ate in an abstraction that left Garrett free to talk to Norah; while Mrs. West overwhelmed Mr. Linton with a steady flow of eloquence that began with the soup and lasted until dessert. Then Norah and Mrs. West withdrew leaving the men to smoke.

"My dear, your cook's a poem, " said Mrs. West, as they returned to the drawing-room. "*Such* a dinner! That *souffle*—well, words fail me!"

"I'm so glad you liked it, " Norah said.

"It melted in the mouth. And I watched you help it; your face was so anxious—you insinuated the spoon with such an expression—I couldn't describe it——"

Norah burst out laughing.

"I could, " she said. "The cook was so anxious about that *souffle*, and she said to do it justice it should be helped with a hot spoon. So I told Allenby to stand the spoon in a jug of boiling water, and give it to me at the very last moment. He was holding it in the napkin he had for drying it, I suppose, and he didn't know that the handle was nearly red-hot. But I did, when I took it up! "

"My dear child! " exclaimed Mrs. West. "So your expression was due to agony! "

"Something like it, " Norah laughed. "It was just all I could do to hold it. But the *souffle was* worth it, wasn't it? I must tell Miss de Lisle. "

"Miss de Lisle? Your cook? "

"Yes—it sounds well, doesn't it? " said Norah. "She's a dear, too. "

"She is certainly a treasure, " said Mrs. West. "Since the regiment went out I have been living in horrible boarding-houses, where they half-starve you, and what they do give you to eat is so murdered in the cooking that you can hardly swallow it. Economical for the management, but not very good for the guests. But one must take things as they come, in this horrible war. " She paused, the forced smile fading from her lips. Somehow Norah felt that she was sorry for her: she looked suddenly old, and worn and tired.

"Come and sit in this big chair, Mrs. West, " she said. "You must have had a long day. "

"Well, quite, " said Mrs. West. "You see, I went to take my husband from the hospital at twelve o'clock, and then I found that your father had made this delightful arrangement for us. It seemed too good to be true. So I had to send Algernon to his club, and I rushed back to my boarding-house and packed my things: and then I had to do some shopping, and meet them at the station. And of course I never could get a taxi when I wanted one. I really think I am a little tired. This seems the kind of house where it doesn't matter to admit it. "

"Of course not—isn't it a Home for Tired People? " Norah laughed. Sarah entered with coffee, and she fussed gently about her guest, settling her cushions and bringing her cup to her side with cream and sugar.

"It's very delightful to be taken care of, " said Mrs. West, with a sigh. The affected, jerky manner dropped from her, and she became more natural. "My children are all boys: I often have been sorry that one was not a girl. A daughter must be a great comfort. Have you any sisters, my dear? "

"No. Just one brother—he's in Captain Garrett's regiment. "

"And you will go back to Australia after the war? "

"Oh, yes. We couldn't possibly stay away from Australia, " Norah said, wide-eyed. "You see, it's home. "

"And England has not made you care any less for it? "

"Goodness, no! " Norah said warmly. "It's all very well in its way, but it simply can't hold a candle to Australia! "

"But why? "

Norah hesitated.

"It's a bit hard to say, " she answered at length. "Life is more comfortable here, in some ways: more luxuries and conveniences of living, I mean. And England is beautiful, and it's full of history, and we all love it for that. But it isn't our own country. The people are different—more reserved, and stiffer. But it isn't even that. I don't know, " said Norah, getting tangled—"I think it's the air, and the space, and the freedom that we're used to, and we miss them all the time. And the jolly country life— —"

"But English country life is jolly. "

"I think we'd get tired of it, " said Norah. "It seems to us all play: and in Australia, we work. Even if you go out for a ride there, most likely there is a job hanging to it—to bring in cattle, or count them, or see that a fence is all right, or to bring home the mail. Every one is busy, and the life all round is interesting. I don't think I explain at all well; I expect the real explanation is just that the love for one's own country is in one's bones! "

"Quite! " said Mrs. West. "Quite! " But she said the ridiculous word as though for once she understood, and there was a comfortable little silence between them for a few minutes. Then the men came in, and the evening went by quickly enough with games and music. Captain Garrett proved to be the possessor of a very fair tenor, together with a knack of vamping not unmelodious accompaniments. The cheery songs floated out into the hall, where Bride and Katty crouched behind a screen, torn between delight and nervousness.

"If the Ould Thing was to come she'd have the hair torn off of us, " breathed Katty. "But 'tis worth the rishk. Blessed Hour, haven't he the lovely voice? "

"He have—but I'd rather listen to Miss Norah, " said Bride loyally. "'Tisn't the big voice she do be having, but it's that happy-sounding."

It was after ten o'clock when Norah, having said good-night to her guests and shown Mrs. West to her room, went softly along the corridor. A light showed under Miss de Lisle's doorway, and she tapped gently.

The door opened, revealing the cook-lady's comfortable little sitting-room, with a fire burning merrily in the grate. The cook-lady herself was an extraordinarily altered being, in a pale-blue kimono with heavy white embroidery.

"I hoped you would come, " she said. "Are you tired? Poor child, what an evening! I wonder would you have a cup of cocoa with me here? I have it ready. "

She waved a large hand towards a fat brown jug standing on a trivet by the grate. There was a tray on a little table, bearing cups and saucers and a spongecake. Norah gave way promptly.

"I'd love it, " she said. "How good of you. I was much too excited to eat dinner. But the *souffle* was just perfect, Miss de Lisle. I never saw anything like it. Mrs. West raved about it after dinner. "

"I am glad, " said the cook-lady, with the rapt expression of a high-priestess. "Allenby told me how you arranged for a hot spoon. It was beautiful of you: beautiful! "

"Did he tell you how hot it was? " Norah inquired. They grew merry over the story, and the spongecake dwindled simultaneously with the cocoa in the jug.

"I must go, " Norah said at last. "It's been so nice: thank you ever so, Miss de Lisle. "

"It's I who should thank you for staying, " said the big woman, rising. "Will you come again, some time? "

"Rather! if I may. Good-night. " She shut the door softly, and scurried along to her room—unconscious that another doorway was a couple of inches ajar, and that through the space Mrs. Atkins regarded her balefully.

Her father's door was half-open, and the room was lit. Norah knocked.

"Come in, " said Mr. Linton. "You, you bad child! I thought you were in bed long ago. "

"I'm going now, " Norah said. "How did things go off, Daddy? "

"Quite well, " he said. "And my daughter made a good hostess. I think they all enjoyed themselves, Norah. "

"I think so, " said she. "They seemed happy enough. What about Captain Hardress, Dad? "

"He seemed comfortable, " Mr. Linton answered. "I found him on a couch, with a rug over him, reading. Allenby said he ate a fair dinner. He's a nice fellow, Norah; I like him. "

"Was he badly wounded, Dad? "

"He didn't say much about himself. I gathered that he had been a long while in hospital. But I'm sorry for him, Norah; he seems very down on his luck. "

"Jim said so, " remarked Norah. "Well, we must try to buck him up. I suppose Allenby will look after him, Dad, if he needs anything? "

"I told him to, " said Mr. Linton, with a grin. "He looked at me coldly, and said, 'I 'ope, sir, I know my duty to a wounded officer. ' I believe I found myself apologizing. There are times when Allenby quite fails to hide his opinion of a mere civilian: I see myself sinking lower and lower in his eyes as we fill this place up with khaki: Good-night, Norah. "

CHAPTER IX

HOMEWOOD GETS BUSY

"Good morning, Captain Hardress. "

Hardress turned. He was standing in the porch, looking out over the park towards the yellowing woods.

"Good morning, Miss Linton. I hope you'll forgive me for being so lazy as to stay in bed for breakfast. You'll have to blame your butler: he simply didn't call me. The first thing I knew was an enormous tray with enough breakfast for six men—and Allenby grinning behind it. "

"You stay in bed to breakfast here, or get up, just as you feel inclined, " Norah said. "There aren't any rules except two. "

"Isn't that a bit Irish? "

"Not exactly, because Jim says even those two may be broken. But I don't agree to that—at least, not for Rule 2. "

"Do tell me them, " he begged.

"Rule 1 is, 'Bed at ten o'clock. ' That's the one that may be broken when necessary. Rule 2 is, 'Please do just what you feel like doing. ' That's the one I won't have broken—unless any one wants to do things that aren't good for them. Then I shall remember that they are patients, and become severe. "

"But I'm not a patient. "

"No—but you're tired. You've got to get quite fit. What would you like to do? Would you care to come for a ride? "

Hardress flushed darkly.

"Afraid I can't ride. "

"Oh—I'm sorry, " said Norah, looking at him in astonishment. This lean, active-looking fellow with the nervous hands certainly looked as though he should be able to ride. Indeed, there were no men in Norah's world who could not. But, perhaps——

"What about a walk, then? " she inquired. "Do you feel up to it? "

Again Hardress flushed.

"I thought your brother would have explained, " he said heavily. "I can't do anything much, Miss Linton. You see, I've only one leg. "

Norah's grey eyes were wide with distress.

"I didn't know, " she faltered. "The telephone was out of order—Jim couldn't explain. I'm so terribly sorry—you must have thought me stupid. "

"Not a bit—after all, it's rather a compliment to the shop-made article. I was afraid it was evident enough. "

"Indeed it isn't, " Norah assured him. "I knew you limped a little—but it wasn't very noticeable. "

"It's supposed to be a special one, " Hardress said. "I'm hardly used to it yet, though, and it feels awkward enough. They've been experimenting with it for some time, and now I'm a sort of trial case for that brand of leg. The maker swears I'll be able to dance with it: he's a hopeful soul. I'm not. "

"You ought to try to be, " Norah said. "And it really must be a very good one. " She felt a kind of horror at talking of it in this cold-blooded fashion.

"I think most of the hopefulness was knocked out of me, " Hardress answered. "You see, I wanted to save the old leg, and they tried to: and then it was a case of one operation after another, until at last they took it off—near the hip. "

Norah went white.

"Near the hip! " Her voice shook. "Oh, it couldn't be—you're so big and strong! "

Hardress laughed grimly.

"I used to think it couldn't be, myself, " he said. "Well, I suppose one will get accustomed to it in time. I'm sorry I distressed you, Miss Linton—only I thought I had better make a clean breast of it. "

"I'm glad you did. " Norah had found control of her voice and her wits: she remembered that this maimed lad with the set face was there to be helped, and that it was part of her job to do it. Her very soul was wrung with pity, but she forced a smile.

"Now you have just got to let us help, " she said. "We can't try to make forget it, I know, but we can help to make the best of it. You can practise using it in all sorts of ways, and seeing just what you can do with it. And, Captain Hardress, I know they do wonders now with artificial legs: Dad knew of a man who played tennis with his— as bad a case as yours. "

"That certainly seems too good to be true, " said Hardress.

"I don't know about that, " said Norah eagerly. "Your leg must be very good—none of us guessed the truth about it. When you get used to it, you'll be able to manage all sorts of things. Golf, for instance—there's a jolly little nine-hole course in the park, and I know you could play. "

"I had thought golf might be a possibility, " he said. "Not that I ever cared much for it. My two games were polo and Rugby football. "

"I don't know about Rugby, " said Norah thoughtfully. "But of course you'll play polo again. Some one was writing in one of the papers lately, saying that so many men had lost a leg in the war that the makers would have to invent special riding-legs, for hunting and polo. I know very well that if Jim came home without a leg he'd still go mustering cattle, or know the reason why! And there was the case of an Irishman, a while ago, who had no legs at all—and he used to hunt. "

"By Jove! " said Hardress. "Well, you cheer a fellow up, Miss Linton."

"You see, I have Jim and Wally, " said Norah. "Do you know Wally, by the way? "

"Is that Meadows? —oh yes, I met him with your brother. "

"Well, he's just like my brother—he nearly lives with us. And from the time that they joined up we had to think of the chance of their losing a limb. Jim never says anything about it, but I know Wally dreads it. Dad and I found out all we could about artificial limbs, and what can be done with them, so that we could help the boys if they had bad luck. They are all right, so far, but of course there is always the chance. "

Hardress nodded.

"We planned that if bad luck came we would try to get them to do as much as possible. Of course an arm is worse: to lose a leg is bad enough, goodness knows—but it's better than an arm. "

"That's one of the problems I've been studying, " Hardress said grimly.

"Oh, but it is. And with you—why, in a few years no one will ever guess that you have anything wrong. It's luck in one way, because a leg doesn't make you conspicuous, and an arm does. "

"That's true, " he said energetically. "I have hoped desperately that I'd be able to hide it; I just couldn't stick the idea of people looking at me. "

"Well, they won't, " said Norah. "And the more you can carry on as usual, the less bad it will seem. Now, let's plan what you can tackle first. Can you walk much? "

"Not much. I get tired after about fifty yards. "

"Well, we'll do fifty yards whenever you feel like it, and then we'll sit down and talk until you can go on again. " She hesitated. "You— it doesn't trouble you to sit down? "

"Oh, no! " said Hardress, laughing for the first time. "It's an awfully docile leg! "

"Then, can you drive? There's the motor, and a roomy tub-cart, and the carriage. "

"Yes—I can drive. "

"Oh, I say! " cried Norah inelegantly, struck by a brilliant idea. "Can you drive a motor? "

"No, I can't! I'm sorry. "

"I'm not. Con will teach you—it will give you quite a new interest. Would you like to learn? "

"By Jove, I would, " he said eagerly. "You're sure your father won't mind my risking his car? "

"Dad would laugh at such a foolish question, " said Norah. "We'll go and see Con now—shall we? it's not far to the stables. You might have a lesson at once. "

"Rather! " he said boyishly. "I say, Miss Linton, you are a brick! "

"Now about golf, " Norah said, as they moved slowly away, Hardress leaning heavily on his stick. "Will you try to play a little with me? We could begin at the practice-holes beyond the terrace. "

"Yes, I'd like to, " he said.

"And billiards? We'll wait for a wet day, because I want you to live in the open air as much as possible. I can't play decently, but Captain Garrett is staying here, and Jim and Wally come over pretty often. "

"You might let me teach *you* to play, " he suggested. "Would you care to? "

"Oh, I'd love it, " said Norah, beaming. The beam, had he known it, was one of delight at the new ring in her patient's voice. Life had come back to it: he held his head erect, and his eyes were no longer hopeless.

"And riding? " she hesitated.

"I don't know, " he said. "I don't believe I could even get on. "

"There's a steady old pony, " Norah said. "Why not practise on him? He stands like a rock. I won't stay and look at you, but Con could— you see he's lost a leg himself, so you wouldn't mind him. I'm sure you'll find you can manage—and when you get confidence we'll go out together. "

"Well, you would put hope into—into a dead codfish! " he said. "Great Scott, if I thought I could get on a horse again! "

Norah laughed.

"We're all horse-mad, " she said. "If I were—like you, I know that to ride would be the thing that would help me most. So you have just got to. " They had arrived at the stables, where Con had the car out and was lovingly polishing its bonnet.

"Con, can you teach Captain Hardress to drive? "

"Is it the car? " asked Con. "And why not, miss? "

"Can I manage it, do you think? " asked Hardress. "I've only one leg."

"'Tis as many as I have meself, " returned Con cheerfully. "And I'm not that bad a driver, am I, Miss Norah? "

"You're not, " Norah answered. "Now I'll leave you to Con, Captain Hardress: I suppose you'll learn all about the car before you begin to drive her. Con can run you round to the house afterwards, if you're tired. The horses are in the stables, too, if you'd care to look at them."

"Jones have the brown pair out, miss, " said Con. "But the others are all here. "

"Well, you can show them to Captain Hardress, Con. I want him to begin riding Brecon. "

She smiled at Hardress, and ran off, looking back just before the shrubberies hid the stable-yard. Hardress was peering into the bonnet of the car, with Con evidently explaining its inner mysteries; just as she looked, he straightened up, and threw off his coat with a quick gesture.

"*He's* all right, " said Norah happily. She hurried on.

The Tired People were off her hands for the morning. Colonel and Mrs. West had gone for a drive; Captain Garrett was playing golf with Major Hunt, who was developing rapidly in playing a one-armed game, and was extremely interested in his own progress. It was the day for posting to Australia, and there was a long letter to Brownie to be finished, and one to Jean Yorke, her chum in Melbourne. Already it was late; in the study, her father had been deep in his letters for over an hour.

But as she came up to the porch she saw him in the hall.

"Oh—Norah, " he said with relief. "I've been looking for you. Here's a letter from Harry Trevor, of all people! "

"Harry! " said Norah delightedly. "Oh, I'm so glad! Where is he, Dad? "

"He's in London—this letter has been wandering round after us. We ought to have had it days ago. Harry has a commission now—got it on the field, in Gallipoli, more power to him: and he's been wounded and sent to England. But he says he's all right. "

"Oh, won't Jim and Wally be glad! " Harry Trevor was an old school-fellow whom Fate had taken to Western Australia; it was years since they had met.

"He has two other fellows with him, he says; and he doesn't know any one in London, nor do they. His one idea seems to be to see us. What are we to do, Norah? Can we have them here? "

"Why we *must* have them, " Norah said. She made a swift mental calculation. "Yes—we can manage it. "

"You're sure, " asked her father, evidently relieved. "I was afraid it might be too much for the house; and I would be very sorry to put them off. "

"Put off Australians, even if one of them wasn't Harry! " ejaculated Norah. "We couldn't do it! How will you get them, Dad? "

"I'll telephone to their hotel at once, " said her father. "Shall I tell them to come to-day? "

"Oh, yes. You can arrange the train, Dad. Now I'll go and see Mrs. Atkins. "

"'Tis yourself has great courage entirely, " said her father, looking at her respectfully. "I'd rather tackle a wild buffalo! "

"I'm not sure that I wouldn't, " returned Norah. "However, she's all the buffalo I've got, so I may as well get it over. " She turned as she reached the door. "Tell old Harry how glad we are, Dad. And don't you think you ought to let Jim know? "

"Yes—I'll ring him up too. " And off went Norah, singing. Three Australians—in "dear little Surrey! " It was almost too good to be true.

But Mrs. Atkins did not think so. She was sorting linen, with a sour face, when Norah entered her sanctum and made known her news. The housekeeper remained silent for a moment.

"Well, I don't see how we're to manage, miss, " she said at length. "The house is pretty full as it is. "

"There is the big room with two single beds, " Norah said. "We can put a third bed in. They won't mind being together. "

Mrs. Atkins sniffed.

"It isn't usual to crowd people like that, miss. "

"It won't matter in this case, " said Norah.

"Did you say Australians, miss? " asked the housekeeper. "Officers?"

"One is an officer. "

"And the others, miss? "

"I don't know—privates, very possibly, " said Norah. "It doesn't matter. "

"Not matter! Well, upon my word! " ejaculated Mrs. Atkins. "Well, all I can say, miss, is that it's very funny. And how do you think the maids are going to do all that extra work? "

Norah began to experience a curious feeling of tingling.

"I am quite sure the maids can manage it, " she said, commanding her voice with an effort. "For one thing, I can easily help more than I do now. "

"We're not accustomed in this country to young ladies doing that sort of thing, " said Mrs. Atkins. Her evil temper mastered her. "And your pet cook, the fine lady who's too grand to sit with me——"

Norah found her voice suddenly calm.

"You mustn't speak to me like that, Mrs. Atkins, " she said, marvelling at her own courage. "You will have to go away if you can't behave properly. "

Mrs. Atkins choked.

"Go away! " she said thickly. "Yes, I'll go away. I'm not going to stay in a house like this, that's no more and no less than a boarding-house! You and your friend the cook can——"

"Be quiet, woman! " said a voice of thunder. Norah, who had shrunk back before the angry housekeeper, felt a throb of relief as Allenby strode into the room. At the moment there was nothing of the butler about him—he was Sergeant Allenby, and Mrs. Atkins was simply a refractory private.

"I won't be quiet! " screamed the housekeeper. "I——"

"You will do as you're told, " said Allenby, dropping a heavy hand on her shoulder. "That's enough, now: not another word. Now go to your room. Out of 'ere, or I'll send for the police. "

Something in the hard, quiet voice filled Mrs. Atkins with terror. She cast a bitter look at Norah, and then slunk out of the room. Allenby closed the door behind her.

"I'm very sorry, miss, " he said—butler once more. "I hope she didn't frighten you. "

"Oh, no—only she was rather horrible, " said Norah. "Whatever is the matter with her, Allenby? I hadn't said anything to make her so idiotic. "

"I've been suspecting what was the matter these last three days, " said Allenby darkly. "Look 'ere, miss. " He opened a cupboard, disclosing rows of empty bottles. "I found these 'ere this morning when she was in the kitchen: I'd been missing bottles from the cellar. She must have another key to the cellar-door, 'owever she managed it. "

There came a tap at the door, and Mr. Linton came in—to have the situation briefly explained to him.

"I wouldn't have had it happen for something, " he said angrily. "My poor little girl, I didn't think we were letting you in for this sort of thing. "

"Why, you couldn't help it, " Norah said. "And she didn't hurt me— she was only unpleasant. But I think we had better keep her out of Miss de Lisle's way, or she might be hard to handle. "

"That's so, miss, " said Allenby. "I'll go and see. 'Ard to 'andle! I should think so! "

"See that she packs her box, Allenby, " said Mr. Linton. "I'll write her cheque at once, and Con can take her to the station as soon as she is ready. She's not too bad to travel, I suppose? "

"She's not bad at all, sir. Only enough to make her nasty. "

"Well, she can go and be nasty somewhere else, " said Mr. Linton. "Very well, Allenby. " He turned to Norah, looking unhappy. "Whatever will you do, my girl? —and this houseful of people! I'd better telephone Harry and put his party off. "

"Indeed you won't, " said Norah, very cheerfully. "I'll manage, Dad. Don't you worry. I'm going to talk to Miss de Lisle. "

The cook-lady was not in the kitchen. Katty, washing vegetables diligently, referred Norah to her sitting-room, and there she was found, knitting a long khaki muffler. She heard the story in silence.

"So I must do just the best I can, Miss de Lisle, " Norah ended. "And I'm wondering if you think I must really advertise for another housekeeper. It didn't seem to me that Mrs. Atkins did much except give orders, and surely I can do that, after a little practice. " Norah flushed, and looked anxious. "Of course I don't want to make a mess of the whole thing. I know the house must be well run. "

"Well, " said Miss de Lisle, knitting with feverish energy, "I couldn't have said it if you hadn't asked me, but as you have, I would like to propose something. Perhaps it may sound as if I thought too much of myself, but with a cook like me you don't need a housekeeper. I have a conscience: and I know how things ought to be run. So my proposal is this, and you and your father must just do as you like about it. Why not make me cook-housekeeper? "

"Oh, but could you? " Norah cried delightedly. "Wouldn't it be too much work? "

"I don't think so—of course I'm expecting that you're going to help in supervising things. I can teach you anything. You see, Katty is a treasure. I back down in all I ever thought about Irish maids, " said

123

the cook-lady, parenthetically. "And she makes me laugh all day, and I wouldn't be without her for anything. Give me a smart boy in the kitchen for the rough work; then Katty can do more of the plain cooking, which she'll love, and I shall have more time out of the kitchen. Now what do you say? "

"Me? " said Norah. "I'd like to hug you! "

"I wish you would, " said Miss de Lisle, knitting more frantically than ever. "You see, this is the first place I've been in where I've really been treated like a human being. You didn't patronize me, and you didn't snub me—any of you. But you laughed with me; and it was a mighty long time since laughing had come into my job. Dear me! " finished Miss de Lisle—"you've no idea how at home with you all I've felt since Allenby fell over me in the passage! "

"We loved you from that minute, " said Norah, laughing. "Then you think we can really manage? You'll have to let me consult with you over everything—ordering, and all that: because I do want to learn my job. And you won't mind how many people we bring in? "

"Fill the house to explosion-point, if you like, " said Miss de Lisle. "If you don't have a housekeeper you'll have two extra rooms to put your Tired People in. What's the good of a scheme like this if you don't run it thoroughly? "

She found herself suddenly hugged, to the no small disadvantage of the knitting.

"Oh, I'm so happy! " Norah cried. "Now I'm going to enjoy the Home for Tired People: and up till now Mrs. Atkins has lain on my soul like a ton of bricks. Bless you, Miss de Lisle! I'm going to tell Dad. " Her racing footsteps flew down the corridor.

But Miss de Lisle sat still, with a half smile on her rugged face. Once she put her hand up to the place where Norah's lips had brushed her cheek.

"Dear me! " she murmured. "Well, it's fifteen years since any one did *that*. " Still smiling, she picked up the knitting.

CHAPTER X

AUSTRALIA IN SURREY

The three Australians came that afternoon; and, like many Australians in the wilds of London with a vague idea of distances, having given themselves good time to catch their train, managed to catch the one before it; and so arrived at Homewood unheralded and unsung. Norah and Captain Hardress, who had been knocking golf-balls about, were crossing the terrace on their way to tea when the three slouched hats caught Norah's eye through the trees of the avenue. She gasped, dropped her clubs, and fled to meet them. Hardress stared: then, perceiving the newcomers, smiled a little and went on slowly.

"I'd like to see her doing a hundred yards! " he said.

The three soldiers jumped as the flying figure came upon them, round a bend in the drive. Then one of them sprang forward.

"Harry! " said Norah.

"My word, I am glad to see you! " said Harry Trevor, pumping her hand. "I say, Norah, you haven't changed a bit. You're just the same as when you were twelve—only that you've grown several feet. "

"Did you expect to find me bald and fat? " Norah laughed. "Oh, Harry, we are glad to see you! "

"Well, you might have aged a little, " said he. "Goodness knows *I* have! Norah, where's old Jim? "

"He's at Aldershot—but you can be certain that he'll be here as soon as he possibly can—and Wally too. "

"That's good business. " He suddenly remembered his friends, who were affecting great interest in the botanical features of a beech-tree. "Come here, you chaps; Norah, this is Jack Blake—and Dick Harrison. They're awfully glad to see you, too! "

"Well, you might have let us say it for ourselves, digger, " said the two, shaking hands. "We were just going to. "

"It's lovely to have you all, " said Norah. She looked over the tree — all tall fellows, lean and bronzed, with quiet faces and deep-set eyes, Blake bore a sergeant's stripes; Dick Harrison's sleeve modestly proclaimed him a lance-corporal.

"We've been wandering in that funny old London like lost sheep, " Blake said. "My word, that's a lonesome place, if you don't happen to know any one in it. And people look at you as if you were something out of a Zoo. "

"They're not used to you yet, " said Norah. "It's the hat, as much as anything. "

"I don't know about that, " Harry said. "No, I think they'd know we came out of a different mob, even if we weren't branded. "

"Perhaps they would — and you certainly do, " Norah answered. "But come on to the house. Dad is just as anxious to see you as any one. "

Indeed, as they came in sight of the house, David Linton was seen coming with long strides to meet them.

"Hardress told me you had suddenly turned into a Marathon runner at the sight of three big hats! " he said. "How are you, Harry? It's an age since we saw you. "

"Yes, isn't it? " Harry shook hands warmly, and introduced his friends. "You haven't changed either, Mr. Linton. "

"I ought to be aging — only Norah won't hear of it, " said Mr. Linton, laughing. "She bullies me more hopelessly than ever, Harry. "

"She always did, " Trevor agreed. "Oh, I want to talk about Billabong for an hour! How's Brownie, Nor? and Murty O'Toole? and Black Billy? How do you manage to live away from them? "

"It isn't easy, " Norah answered. "They're all very fit, only they want us back. We can't allow ourselves to think of the day that we'll get home, or we all grow light-headed. "

"It will be no end of a day for all of us, " said Harrison. "Think of marching down Collins Street again, with the crowd cheering us— keeping an eye out for the people one knew! It was fairly beastly marching up it for the last time. "

"It's not Collins Street I want, but a bit of the Gippsland track, " said Jack Blake. "You know, Dick, we took cattle there last year. Over the Haunted Hills—aren't they jolly in the spring! —and down through the scrub to Morwell and Traralgon. I'd give something to see that bit of country again. "

"Ah, it's all good country, " David Linton said. Then they were at the house, and a buzz of conversation floated out to them from the hall, where tea was in progress.

"Your father simply made me promise to go on without you, " said Mrs. West, as Norah made her apologies. "I said it was dreadful, but he wouldn't listen to me. And there are your friends! Dear me, how large they are, and so brown! Do introduce them to me: I'm planning to hear all about Australia. And a sergeant and lance-corporal! Isn't it romantic to see them among us, and quite at their ease. *Don't* tell them I'm a Colonel's wife, my dear; I would hate them to feel embarrassed! "

"I don't think you need worry, " said Norah, smiling to herself. She brought up the three newcomers and introduced them. They subsided upon a sofa, and listened solemnly while Mrs. West opened all her conversational batteries upon them. Norah heard the opening—"I've read such a *lot* about your charming country! " and felt a throb of pity for the three wanderers from afar.

Hardress came towards her with a cup of tea, his limb a little more evident.

"You're tired, " she said, taking it from him. "Sure you haven't done too much? "

"Not a bit, " he said. "I'm a little tired, but it's the best day I have had for many a month. I don't know when I enjoyed anything as much as my motor-lesson this morning. "

"Con says you'll be able to drive in Piccadilly in no time, " said Norah.

"He's hopeful, " Hardress said, laughing. "Particularly as we never started the car at all—he made me learn everything I could about it first. And did he tell you I rode Brecon? "

"No! How did you get on? " asked Norah delightedly.

"Well, I literally got on very badly—at first. The shop leg didn't seem to understand what was wanted of it at all, and any steed but Brecon would have strongly resented me. But he stood in a pensive attitude while I tried all sorts of experiments. In fact, I think he went to sleep!"

"I told you you could rely on Brecon, " Norah smiled. "What happened then? "

"Oh—I got used to myself, and found out the knack of getting on. It's not hard, with a steady horse, once you find out how. But I think Brecon will do me very well for awhile. "

"Oh, we'll soon get you on to Brunette, " Norah said. "You'd enjoy her. "

"Is that the black pony? "

"Yes—and she's a lovely hack. I'm going to hunt her in the winter: she jumps like a deer. "

"She looked a beauty, in the stable, " Hardress said. "She ought to make a good polo-pony. " He sighed. "I wonder if I'll really ever play polo again. "

"Of course you will, " Norah told him. "This morning you didn't think you would ever get on a horse again. "

"No, I certainly didn't. You have put an extraordinary amount of hope into me: I feel a different being. " He stopped, and a smile crept into his eyes. "Listen—aren't your friends having a time! "

"Life must be so exciting on your great cattle ranches, " Mrs. West was saying. "And the dear little woolly lambs on the farms—such pets! "

"We understood you people over here prefer them frozen, " Blake said gently. "So we send 'em that way. "

Norah choked over her tea. She became aware that Colonel West was speaking to her, and tried to command her wits—hearing, as she turned, Mrs. West's shrill pipe—"And what *is* a wheat-belt? Is it something you wear? " Norah would have given much to hear Blake's reply.

"Delightful place you have here! " barked the Colonel. "Your father and I have been spending an agricultural afternoon; planning all the things he means to do on that farm—Hawkins', isn't it? But I suppose you don't take much interest in that sort of thing? Dances and frocks more in your line—and chocolates, eh, what? "

"Then you've changed her in England, " said Harry Trevor suddenly. "Is it dances now, Norah? No more quick things over the grass after a cross-grained bullock? Don't say you've forgotten how to use a stockwhip! "

"It's hung up at Billabong, " Norah said laughing. "But you wait until I get back to it, that's all! "

"Dear me! " said Mrs. West. "And you do these wonderful things too! I always longed to do them as a girl—to ride over long leagues of plain on a fiery mustang, among your lovely eucalyptus trees. And do you really go out with the cowboys, and use a lasso? "

"She does, " said Harry, happily.

"Your wild animals, too, " said Mrs. West. "It's kangaroos you ride down with spears, is it not? And wallabies. We live in dear, quiet little England, but we read all about your wonderful life, and are oh! so interested. "

"What a life! " said Dick Harrison, under his breath.

"Quite. You know, I had a great friend who went out as A. D.C. to one of your Governors. He had to return after a month, because his father died and he came into the baronetcy, but some day he means to write a book on Australia. That is why I have always, as it were, kept in touch with your great country. I seem to know it so well, though I have never seen it. "

"You do, indeed, " said Blake gravely. "I wish we knew half as much about yours. "

"Ah, but you must let us show it to you. Is it not yours, too? Outposts of Empire: that is what I call you: outposts of Empire. Is it not that that brought you to fight under our flag? "

"Oh, rather, " said Blake vaguely. "But a lot of us just wanted a look in at the fun! "

"Well—you got a good deal for a start, " said Garrett.

"Yes—Abdul gave us all we wanted on his little peninsula. But he's not a bad fighting-man, old Abdul; we don't mind how often we take tea with him. He's a better man to fight than Fritz. "

"He could pretty easily be that, " Garrett said. "It's one of the worst grudges we owe Fritz—that he's taken all the decency out of war. It used to be a man's game, but the Boche made it one according to his own ideas—and everybody knows what they are. "

"Yes, " said Hardress. "I suppose the Boche will do a good deal of crawling to get back among decent people after the war; but he'll never live down his poison-gas and flame-throwers. "

"And wouldn't it have been a gorgeous old war if he'd only fought clean! " said Garrett longingly. They drew together and talked as fighting men will—veterans in the ways of war, though the eldest was not much over one-and-twenty.

The sudden hoot of a motor came from the drive, far-off; and then another, and another.

"Some one's joy-riding, " said Harry Trevor.

The hooting increased, and with it the hum of a racing car. The gravel outside the porch crunched as it drew up; and then came cheery voices, and two long figures in great coats dashed in: Jim and Wally, eager-eyed.

"Dad! Norah! Where's old Harry? "

But Harry was grasping a hand of each, and submitting to mighty pats on the back from their other hands.

"By Jove, it's great to see you! Where did you come from, you old reprobate? Finished Johnny Turk? "

Gradually the boys became aware that there were other people in the hall, and made apologies—interrupted by another burst of joy at discovering Garrett.

"You must think us bears, " said Jim, with his disarming smile, to Mrs. West. "But we hadn't seen Trevor for years, and he's a very old chum. It would have been exciting to meet him in Australia; but in England—well! "

"However did you manage to come? " Norah asked, beaming.

"Oh, we got leave. We've been good boys—at least, Wally was until we got your message this morning. Since then he has been wandering about like a lost fowl, murmuring, 'Harry! *My* Harry! '"

"Is it me? " returned Wally. "Don't believe him, Nor—it was all I could do to keep him from slapping the C. O. on the back and borrowing his car to come over. "

"I don't doubt it, " Norah laughed. "Whose car did you borrow, by the way? "

"Oh, we hired one. It was extravagant, but we agreed that it wasn't every day we kill a pig! "

"Thank you, " said Harry. "Years haven't altered your power of putting a thing nicely! " He smote Wally affectionately. "I say, you were a kid when I saw you last: a kid in knickerbockers. And look at you now! "

"Well, you were much the same, " Wally retorted. "And now you're a hardened old warrior—I've only played at it so far. "

"But you were gassed, weren't you? "

"Yes—but we hadn't had much war before they gassed us. That was the annoying part. "

"Well, didn't you have a little private war in Ireland? What about that German submarine? "

"Oh, that was sheer luck, " said Wally joyfully. "*Such* a lark—only for one thing. But we don't consider we've earned our keep yet. "

"Oh, well, you've got lots of time, " Harry said. "I wonder if they'll send any of us to France—it would be rather fun if we got somewhere in your part of the line. "

"Yes, wouldn't it? " Then Jack Blake, who had been at school with the boys, came up with Dick Harrison, and England ceased to exist for the five Australians. They talked of their own country—old days at school; hard-fought battles on the Melbourne Cricket Ground; boat-racing on the Yarra; Billabong and other stations; bush-fires and cattle-yarding; long days on the road with cattle, and nights spent watching them under the stars. All the grim business of life that had been theirs since those care-free days seemed but to make their own land dearer by comparison. Not that they said so, in words. But they lingered over their talk with an unspoken delight in being at home again—even in memory.

Norah slipped away, regretfully enough, after a time: her responsibilities as housekeeper weighed upon her, and she sought Miss de Lisle in the kitchen.

"What, your brother and Mr. Wally? How delightful! " ejaculated the cook-lady. "That's what I call really jolly. Their rooms are always ready, I suppose? "

"Oh, yes, " Norah said. "I've told Bride to put sheets on the beds. "

"Then that's all right. Dinner? My dear, you need never worry about a couple extra for dinner in a household of this size. Just tell the maids to lay the table accordingly, and let me know—that is all you need do. "

"Mrs. Atkins had destroyed my nerve! " said Norah, laughing. "I came down to tell you with the same scared feeling that I had when I used to go to her room. My very knees were shaking! "

"Then you're a very bad child, if you *are* my employer! " returned Miss de Lisle. "However, I'll forgive you: but some time I want you to make a list for me of the things those big boys of yours like most: I might just as well cook them as not, when they come. And of course, when they go out to France, we shall have to send them splendid hampers. "

"That will be a tremendous comfort, " Norah said. "You're a brick, Miss de Lisle. We used to send them hampers before, of course, but it seemed so unsatisfactory just to order them at the Stores: it will be ever so much nicer to cook them things. You *will* let me cook, won't you? "

"Indeed I will, " said Miss de Lisle. "We'll shut ourselves up here for a day, now and then, and have awful bouts of cookery. How did you like the potato cakes at tea, by the way? "

"They were perfect, " Norah said. "I never tasted better, even in Ireland. " At which Katty, who had just entered with a saucepan, blushed hotly, and cast an ecstatic glance at Miss de Lisle.

"I don't suppose you did, " remarked that lady. "You see, Katty made them. "

"Wasn't she good, now, to let me, Miss Norah? " Katty asked. "There's them at home that towld me I'd get no chance at all of learning under a grand cook here. 'Tis little the likes of them 'ud give you to do in the kitchen: if you asked them for a job, barring it was to wash the floor, they'd pitch you to the Sivin Divils. 'Isn't the scullery good enough for you? ' they'd say. 'Cock you up with the cooking! '

But Miss de Lisle isn't one of them—and the cakes to go up to the drawing-room itself! "

"Well, every one liked them, Katty, " Norah said.

"Yerra, hadn't I Bridie watching behind the big screen with the crack in it? " said the handmaid. "She come back to me, and she says, 'They're all ate, ' says she: ''tis the way ye had not enough made, ' she says. I didn't know if 'twas on me head or me heels I was! " She bent a look of adoration upon Miss de Lisle, who laughed.

"Oh, I'll make a cook of you yet, Katty, " she said. "Meanwhile you'd better put some coal on the fire, or the oven won't be hot enough for my pastry. Is it early breakfast for your brother and Mr. Wally, Miss Linton? "

"I'm afraid so, " Norah said. "Jim said they must leave at eight o'clock. "

"Then that means breakfast at seven-thirty. Will you have yours with them? "

"Oh yes, please—if it's not too much trouble. "

"Nothing's a trouble—certainly not an early breakfast, " said Miss de Lisle. "Now don't worry about anything. "

Norah went back to the hall—to find it deserted. A buzz of voices came from the billiard-room; she peeped in to find all the soldiers talking with her father listening happily in a big chair. No one saw her: she withdrew, and went in search of Mrs. West, but failed to find her. Bride, encountered in her evening tour with cans of hot water, reported that 'twas lying down she was, and not wishful for talk: her resht was more to her.

"Then I may as well go and dress, " Norah said.

She had just finished when a quick step came along the corridor, and stopped at her door. Jim's fingers beat the tattoo that was always their signal.

Captain Jim

"Come in, Jimmy, " Norah cried.

He came in, looming huge in the dainty little room.

"Good business—you're dressed, " he said. "Can I come and yarn? "

"Rather, " said Norah, beaming. "Come and sit down in my armchair. This electric heater isn't as jolly to yarn by as a good old log fire, but still, it's something. " She pulled her chair forward.

"Can't you wait for me to do that—bad kid! " said Jim. He sat down, and Norah subsided on the rug near him.

"Now tell me all about everything, " he said. "How are things going?"

"Quite well—especially Mrs. Atkins, " said Norah. "In fact she's gone! "

Jim sat up.

"Gone! But how? "

Norah told him the story, and he listened with joyful ejaculations.

"Well, she was always the black spot in the house, " he remarked. "It gave one the creeps to look at her sour face, and I'm certain she was more bother to you than she was worth. "

"Oh, I feel twenty years younger since she went! " Norah said. "And it's going to be great fun to housekeep with Miss de Lisle. I shall learn ever so much. "

"So will she, I imagine, " said Jim, laughing. "Put her up to all the Australian ways, and see if we can't make a good emigrant of her when we go back. "

"I might, " Norah said. "But she would be a shock to Brownie if she suggested putting her soul into a pudding! "

"Rather! " said Jim, twinkling. "I say, tell me about Hardress. Do you like him? "

"Oh, yes, ever so much. " She told him of her morning's work—indeed, by the time the gong boomed out its summons from the hall, there was very little in the daily life of Homewood that Jim had not managed to hear.

"We're always wondering how you are getting on, " he said. "It's jolly over there—the work is quite interesting, and there's a very nice lot of fellows: but I'd like to look in at you two and see how this show was running. " He hesitated. "It won't be long before we go out, Nor, old chap. "

"Won't it, Jimmy? " She put up a hand and caught his. "Do you know how long? "

"A week or two—not more. But you're not to worry. You've just got to think of the day when we'll get our first leave—and then you'll have to leave all your Tired People and come and paint London red. " He gave a queer laugh. "Oh, I don't know, though. It seems to be considered the right thing to do. But I expect we'll just amble along here and ask you for a job in the house! "

"Why, you'll be Tired People yourselves, " said Norah. "We'll have to look after you and give you nourishment at short intervals. "

"We'll take that, if it's Miss de Lisle's cooking. Now don't think about this business too much. I thought I'd better tell you, but nothing is definite yet. Perhaps I'd better not tell Dad. "

"No, don't; he's so happy. "

"I wish I didn't have to make either of you less happy, " Jim said in a troubled voice. "But it can't be helped. "

"No, I know it can't, Jimmy. Don't you worry. "

"Dear old chap, " said Jim, and stood up. "I had better go and make myself presentable before the second gong goes. " He paused. "You're all ready aren't you? Then you might go down. Wally will be wandering round everywhere, looking for you. "

CHAPTER XI

CHEERO!

It was ten days later that the summons to France came—ten days during which the boys had managed to make several meteoric dashes over to Homewood for the night, and had accomplished one blissful week-end, during which, with the aid of their fellow-countrymen, they had brought the household to the verge of exhaustion from laughter. Nothing could damp their spirits: they rode and danced, sang and joked, and, apparently, having no cares in the world themselves, were determined that no one else should have any. The Hunt family were drawn into the fun: the kitchen was frequently invaded, and Miss de Lisle declared that even her sitting-room was not sacred—and was privately very delighted that it was not. Allenby began to develop a regrettable lack of control over his once stolid features; Sarah herself was observed to stuff her apron into her mouth and rush from the dining-room on more than one occasion. And under cover of his most energetic fooling Jim Linton watched his father and sister, and fooled the more happily whenever he made them laugh.

They arrived together unexpectedly on this last evening, preferring to bring their news rather than give it by telephone; and found, instead of the usual cheery tea-party in the hall, only silence and emptiness. Allenby, appearing, broke into a broad smile of pleasure as he greeted them.

"Every one's out, Mr. Jim. "

"So it seems, " Jim answered. "Where are they? "

"Not very far, sir, " Allenby said. "Mrs. 'Unt has them all to tea with her to-day. "

"Oh, we'll go over, Wal, " Jim said. "Come and make yourself pretty: you've a splash of mud on your downy cheek. " At the foot of the stairs he turned. "We're off to-morrow, Allenby. "

Allenby's face fell.

"To France, sir? "

Jim nodded.

"The master and Miss Norah will be very sorry, sir. If I may say so, the 'ole 'ousehold will be sorry. "

"Thanks, Allenby. We'll miss you all, " Jim said pleasantly. He sprang upstairs after Wally.

Mrs. Hunt's sitting-room was already dangerously crowded—there seemed no room at all for the two tall lads for whom Eva opened the door ten minutes later. A chorus of welcome greeted them, nevertheless.

"This is delightful, " said Mrs. Hunt. "I'm sure I don't know how you're going to fit in, but you must manage it somehow. If necessary we'll all stand up and re-pack ourselves, but I warn you it is risky: the walls may not stand it! "

"Oh, don't trouble, Mrs. Hunt, " Jim said. "We're quite all right. " Both boys' eyes had sought Norah as they entered: and Norah, meeting the glance, felt a sudden pang at her heart, and knew.

"My chair is ever so much too big for me, " she said. "You can each have an arm. "

"Good idea! " said Wally, perching on the broad arm of the easy-chair that swallowed her up. "Come along, Jim, or we'll be lop-sided! "

"We put Norah in the biggest chair in the room, and everybody is treating her with profound respect, " Mrs. Hunt said. "This is the first day for quite a while that she hasn't been hostess, so we made her chief guest, and she is having a rest-cure. "

"If you treat Norah with respect it won't have at all a restful effect on her, " said Wally. "I've tried. " To which Norah inquired, "When? " in a voice of such amazement that every one laughed.

"Misunderstood as usual, " said Wally pathetically. "It really doesn't pay to be like me and have a meek spirit: people only think you are a worm, and trample on you. Come here, Geoff, and take care of me: " and Geoffrey, who adored him, came. "Have you been riding old Brecon lately? "

"'M! " said Geoffrey, nodding. "I can canter now! "

"Good man! Any tosses? "

"Well, just one, " Geoffrey admitted. "He cantered before I had gotted ready, and I fell off. But it didn't hurt. "

"That's right. You practise always falling on a soft spot, and you need never worry. "

"But I'd rather practise sticking on, " said Geoffrey. "It's nicer. "

"You might practise both, " said Wally. "You'll have plenty of both, you know. " He laughed at the puzzled face. "Never mind, old chap. How are the others, and why aren't they here? "

"They're too little, " Geoffrey said loftily. "Small childrens don't come in to tea, at least not when there's parties. I came, 'cause Mother says I'm getting 'normous. "

"So you are. Are the others quite well? "

"Oh yes, " Geoffrey answered, clearly regarding the question as foolish. "They're all right. Alison's got a puppy, and Michael's been eating plate-powder. His mouf was all pink. "

"What's that about my Michael, " demanded Mrs. Hunt. "Oh yes— we found him making a hearty meal of plate-powder this morning. Douglas says it should make him very bright. I'm thankful to say it doesn't seem to be going to kill him. "

"Michael never will realize that there is a war on, " said Major Hunt, aggrieved. "I found him gnawing the strap of one of my gaiters the other day. "

"You shouldn't underfeed the poor kid, " said Wally. "It's clear that he's finding his nourishment when and how he can. Isn't there a Society for dealing with people like you? "

"There is, " said Jim solemnly. "It's called the Police Force. "

"You're two horrible boys! " said their hostess, laughing. "And my lovely fat Michael! —he's getting so corpulent he can hardly waddle. He and the puppy are really very like each other; both of them find it easier to roll than to run. " She cast an inquiring eye round the room: "Some more tea, Norah? "

"No, thank you, Mrs. Hunt. " Norah's voice sounded strange in her own ears. She wanted to get away from the room, and the light-hearted chatter . .. to make sure, though she was sure already. The guns of France seemed to sound very near her.

The party broke up after a while. Jim and Wally lingered behind the others.

"Will you and the Major come over this evening, Mrs. Hunt? We're off to-morrow. "

"Oh—I'm sorry. " Mrs. Hunt's face fell. "Poor Norah! "

"Norah will keep smiling, " said Jim. "But I'm jolly glad you're so near her, Mrs. Hunt. You'll keep an eye on them, won't you? I'd be awfully obliged if you would. "

"You may be very sure I will, " she said. "And there will be a tremendous welcome whenever you get leave. "

"We won't lose any time in coming for it, " Jim said. "Blighty means more than ever it did, now that we've got a real home. Then you'll come to-night? "

"Of course we will. " She watched them stride off into the shrubbery, and choked back a sigh.

Norah came back to them through the trees.

"It's marching orders, isn't it? "

"Yes, it's marching orders, old kiddie, " Jim answered. They looked at each other steadily: and then Norah's eyes met Wally's.

"When? " she asked.

"To-morrow morning. "

"Well——" said Norah; and drew a long breath. "And I haven't your last week's socks darned! That comes of having too many responsibilities. Any buttons to be sewn on for either of you? "

"No, thanks, " they told her, greatly relieved. She tucked a hand into an arm of each boy, and they went towards the house. David Linton came out hurriedly to meet them.

"Allenby says——" he began. He did not need to go further.

"We were trotting in to tell you, " said Jim.

"We'll be just in time to give the Boche a cheery Christmas, " said Wally. "Norah, are you going to send us a Christmas hamper? With a pudding? "

"Rather! " Norah answered. "And I'll put a lucky pig, and a button, and a threepenny-bit in it, so you'd better eat it with care, or you may damage your teeth. Miss de Lisle and I are going to plan great parcels for you; she's going to teach me to cook all sorts of things. "

"After which you'll try them on the dogs—meaning us, " Jim said, laughing. "Well, if we don't go into hospital after them, we'll let you know. "

They came into the house, where already the news of the boys' going had spread, and the "Once-Tired's, " as Wally called their guests, were waiting to wish them luck. Then everybody faded away unobtrusively, and left them to themselves. They went into the morning-room, and Norah darned socks vigorously while the boys kept up a running fire of cheery talk. Whatever was to come they would meet it with their heads up—all four.

They made dinner a revel—every one dressed in their best, and "playing-up" to their utmost, while Miss de Lisle—the only person in the house who had wept—had sent up a dinner which really left her very little extra chance of celebrating Peace, when that most blessed day should come. Over dessert, Colonel West rose unexpectedly, and made a little speech, proposing the health of the boys, who sat, for the first time, with utterly miserable faces, restraining an inclination to get under the table.

"I am sure, " said the Colonel, "that we all wish the—ah—greatest of luck to our host's sons—ah, that is, to his son and to—ah—his—ah"

"Encumbrance, " said Wally firmly.

"Quite, " said the Colonel, without listening. "We know they will—ah—make things hot for the Boche—ah—whenever they get a chance. I—we—hope they will get plenty of chances: and—ah—that we will see them—ah—back, with decorations and promotion. We will miss them—ah—very much. Speaking—ah—personally, I came here fit for nothing, and have—ah—laughed so much that I—ah—could almost believe myself a subaltern! "

The Tired People applauded energetically, and Mrs. West said "Quite—quite! " But there was something like tears in her eyes as she said it.

The Hunts arrived after dinner, and they all woke the house with ringing choruses—echoed by Allenby in his pantry, as he polished the silver; and Garrett sang a song which was not encored because something in his silver tenor made a lump come into Norah's throat; and there was no room for that, to-night, of all nights. Jack Blake sang them a stockrider's song, with a chorus in which all the Australians joined; and Dick Harrison recited "The Geebung Polo Club, " without any elocutionary tricks, and brought down the house. Jim had slipped out to speak to Allenby: and presently, going out, they found the hall cleared, and the floor waxed for dancing. They danced to gramophone music, manipulated by Mr. Linton: and Norah and Mrs. Hunt had to divide each dance into three, except those with Jim and Wally, which they refused to partition, regardless of disconsolate protests from the other warriors. It was eleven o'clock when Allenby announced stolidly, "Supper is served, sir! "

Captain Jim

"Supper? " said Mr. Linton. "How's this, Norah? "

"*I* don't know, " said his daughter. "Ask Miss de Lisle! "

They filed in, to find a table laden and glittering; in the centre a huge cake, bearing the greeting, "Good Luck! " with a silken Union Jack waving proudly. Norah whispered to her father, and then ran away. She returned, presently, dragging the half-unwilling cook-lady.

"It's against *all* my rules! " protested the captive.

"Rules be hanged! " said Jim cheerfully. "Just you sit there, Miss de Lisle. " And the cook-lady found herself beside Colonel West, who paid her great attention, regarding her, against the evidence of his eyes, as a Tired Person whom he had not previously chanced to meet.

"My poor, neglected babies! " said Mrs. Hunt tragically, as twelve strokes chimed from the grandfather clock in the hall. Wally and Norah, crowned with blue and scarlet paper caps, the treasure of crackers, were performing a weird dance which they called, with no very good reason, a tango. It might have been anything, but it satisfied the performers. The music stopped suddenly, and Mr. Linton wound up the gramophone for the last time, slipping on a new record. The notes of "Auld Lang Syne, " stole out.

They gathered round, holding hands while they sang it; singing with all their lungs and all their hearts: Norah between Jim and Wally, feeling her fingers crushed in each boyish grip.

> *"Then here's a hand, my trusty friend,*
> *And gie's a hand o' thine. "*

Over the music her heart listened to the booming of the guns across the Channel. But she set her lips and sang on.

*****

It was morning, and they were on the station. The train came slowly round the corner.

"I'll look after him, Nor. " Wally's voice shook. "Don't worry too much, old girl. "

"And yourself, too, " she said.

"Oh, I'll keep an eye on *him*, " said Jim. "And Dad's your job. "

"And we'll plan all sorts of things for your next leave, " said David Linton. "God bless you, boys. "

They gripped hands. Then Jim put his arms round Norah's shoulder.

"You'll keep smiling, kiddie? Whatever comes? "

"Yes, I promise, Jimmy. "

The guard was shouting.

"All aboard. "

"Cheero, Norah! " Wally cried from the window. "We'll be back in no time! "

"Cheero! " She made the word come somehow. The train roared off round the curve.

CHAPTER XII

OF LABOUR AND PROMOTION

The months went by quickly enough, as David Linton and his daughter settled down to their work at the Home for Tired People. As the place became more widely known they had rarely an empty room. The boys' regiment sent them many a wearied officer, too fagged in mind and body to enjoy his leave: the hospitals kept up a constant supply of convalescent and maimed patients; and there was a steady stream of Australians of all ranks, who came, homesick for their own land, and found a little corner of it planted in the heart of Surrey. Gradually, as the Lintons realized the full extent of the homesickness of the lads from overseas, Homewood became more and more Australian in details. Pictures from every State appeared on the walls: aboriginal weapons and curiosities, woven grass mats from the natives of Queensland, Australian books and magazines and papers—all were scattered about the house. They filled vases with blue-gum leaves and golden wattle-blossom from the South of France: Norah even discovered a flowering boronia in a Kew nurseryman's greenhouse and carried it off in triumph, to scent the house with the unforgettable delight of its perfume. She never afterwards saw a boronia without recalling the bewilderment of her fellow-travellers in the railway carriage at her exquisitely-scented burden.

"You should have seen their wondering noses, Dad! " said Norah, chuckling.

No one, of course, stayed very long at Homewood, unless he were hopelessly unfit. From ten days to three weeks was the average stay: then, like ships that pass in the night, the "Once-Tireds, " drifted away. But very few forgot them. Little notes came from the Fronts, in green Active Service envelopes: postcards from Mediterranean ports; letters from East and West Africa; grateful letters from wives in garrison stations and training camps throughout the British Isles. They accumulated an extraordinary collection of photographs in uniform; and Norah had an autograph book with scrawled signatures, peculiar drawings and an occasional scrap of very bad verse.

Major Hunt, his hand fully recovered, returned to the Front in February, and his wife prepared to seek another home. But the Lintons flatly refused to let her go.

"We couldn't do it, " said David Linton. "Doesn't the place agree with the babies? "

"Oh, you know it does, " said Mrs. Hunt. "But we have already kept the cottage far too long—there are other people. "

"Not for that cottage, " Norah said.

"It really isn't fair, " protested their guest. "Douglas never dreamed of our staying: if he had not been sent out in such a hurry at the last he would have moved us himself. "

David Linton looked at her for a moment.

"Go and play with the babies, Norah, " he said. "I want to talk to this obstinate person. "

"Now look, Mrs. Hunt, " he said, as Norah went off, rather relieved—Norah hated arguments. "You know we run this place for an ideal—a dead man's ideal. *He* wanted more than anything in the world to help the war; we're merely carrying on for him. We can only do it by helping individuals. "

"But you have done that for us. Look at Douglas—strong and fit, with one hand as good as the other. Think of what he was when he came here! "

"He may not always be fit. And if you stay here you ease his worries by benefiting his children—and saving for their future. Then, if he has the bad luck to be wounded again, his house is all ready for him."

"I know, " she said. "And I would stay, but that there are others who need it more. "

"Well, we haven't heard of them. Look at it another way. I am getting an old man; it worries me a good deal to think that Norah has no woman to mother her. I used to think, " he said with a sigh, "that it was worse for them to lose their own mother when they were wee things; now, I am not sure that Norah's loss is not just beginning. It's no small thing for her to have an influence like yours; and Norah loves you. "

Mrs. Hunt flushed.

"Indeed, I love her, " she said.

"Then stay and mother her. There are ever so many things you can teach her that I can't: that Miss de Lisle can't, good soul as she is. They're not things I can put into words—but you'll understand. I know she's clean and wholesome right through, but you can help to mould her for womanhood. Of course, she left school far too early, but there seemed no help for it. And if—if bad news comes to us from the Front—for any of us—we can all help each other. "

Mrs. Hunt thought deeply.

"If you really think I can be of use I will stay, " she said. "I'm not going to speak of gratitude—I tried to say all that long ago. But indeed I will do what I can. "

"That's all right: I'm very glad, " said David Linton.

"And if you really want her taught more, " Mrs. Hunt said—"well, I was a governess with fairly high certificates before I was married. She could come to me for literature and French; I was brought up in Paris. Her music, too: she really should practise, with her talent. "

"I'd like it above all things, " exclaimed Mr. Linton. "Norah's neglected education has been worrying me badly. "

"We'll plan it out, " Mrs. Hunt said. "Now I feel much happier. "

Norah did not need much persuasion; after the first moment of dismay at the idea of renewed lessons she saw the advantages of the plan—helped by the fact that she was always a little afraid of failing to come up to Jim's standard. A fear which would considerably have amazed Jim, had he but guessed it! It was easy enough to fit hours of study into her day. She rose early to practise, before the Tired People were awake; and most mornings saw her reading with Mrs. Hunt or chattering French, while Eva sang shrilly in the kitchen, and the babies slept in their white bunks; and Geoffrey followed Mr. Linton's heels, either on Brecon or afoot. The big Australian squatter and the little English boy had become great friends: there was something in the tiny lad that recalled the Jim of long ago, with his well-knit figure and steady eyes.

One man alone, out of all Tired People, had never left Homewood.

For a time after his arrival Philip Hardress had gained steadily in strength and energy; then a chill had thrown him back, and for months he sagged downwards; never very ill, but always losing vitality. The old depression seemed to come back to him tenfold. He could see nothing good in life: a cripple, a useless cripple. His parents were dead; save for a brother in Salonica, he was alone in the world. He was always courteous, always gentle; but a wall of misery seemed to cut him off from the household.

Then the magnificent physique of the boy asserted itself, and gradually he grew stronger, and the hacking cough left him. Again it became possible to tempt him to try to ride. He spent hours in the keen wintry air, jogging round the fields and lanes with Mr. Linton and Geoffrey, returning with something of the light in his eyes that had encouraged Norah in his first morning, long ago.

"I believe all he wants is to get interested in something, " Norah said, watching him, one day, as he sat on the stone wall of the terrace, looking across the park. "He was at Oxford before he joined the Army, wasn't he, Dad? "

Mr. Linton assented. "His people arranged when he was little that he should be a barrister. But he hated the idea. His own wish was to go out to Canada. "

Norah pondered.

"Couldn't you give him a job on the farm, Dad? "

"I don't know, " said her father. "I never thought of it. I suppose I might find him something to do; Hawkins and I will be busy enough presently. "

"He's beginning to worry at being here so long, " Norah said. "Of course, we couldn't possibly let him go: he isn't fit for his own society. I think if you could find him some work he would be more content. "

So David Linton, after thinking the matter over, took Hardress into his plans for the farm which was to be the main source of supply for Homewood. He found him a quick and intelligent helper. The work was after the boy's own heart: he surrounded himself with agricultural books and treaties on fertilizers, made a study of soils, and took samples of earth from different parts of the farm—to the profound disgust of Hawkins. War had not done away with all expert agricultural science in England: Hardress sent his little packets of soil away, and received them back with advice as to treatment which, later on, resulted in the yield of the land being doubled—which Hawkins attributed solely to his own skill as a cultivator. But the cure was worked in Philip Hardress. The ring of hope came back into his voice: the "shop-leg" dragged ever so little, as he walked across the park daily to where the ploughs were turning the grass of the farm fields into stretches of brown, dotted with white gulls that followed the horses' slow plodding up and down. The other guests took up a good deal of Mr. Linton's time: he was not sorry to have an overseer, since Hawkins, while honest and painstaking, was not afflicted with any undue allowance of brains. Together, in the study at night, they planned out the farm into little crops. Already much of the land was ready for the planting, and a model poultry-run built near the house was stocked with birds; while a flock of sheep grazed in the park, and to the tiny herd of cows had been added half a dozen pure-bred Jerseys. David Linton had taken Hardress with him on the trip to buy the stock, and both had enjoyed it thoroughly.

Meanwhile the boys at the Front sent long and cheery letters almost daily. Astonishment had come to them almost as soon as they rejoined, in finding themselves promoted; they gazed at their second stars in bewilderment which was scarcely lessened by the fact that their friends in the regiment were not at all surprised.

"Why, didn't you have a war on your own account in Ireland? " queried Anstruther. "You got a Boche submarine sunk and caught half the crew, didn't you? "

"Well, but that was only a lark! " said Wally.

"You were wounded, anyhow, young Meadows. Of course *we* know jolly well you don't deserve anything, but you can't expect the War Office to have our intimate sources of information. " He patted Wally on the back painfully. "Just be jolly thankful you get more screw, and don't grumble. No one'll ever teach sense to the War Office! "

There was no lack of occupation in their part of the line. They saw a good deal of fighting, and achieved some reputation as leaders of small raids: Jim, in particular, having a power of seeing and hearing at night that had been developed in long years in the Bush—but which seemed to the Englishmen almost uncanny. There was reason to believe that the enemy felt even more strongly about it—there was seldom rest for the weary Boche in the trenches opposite Jim Linton's section. Some of his raids were authorized: others were not. It is probable that the latter variety was more discouraging to the enemy.

Behind the fighting line they were in fairly comfortable billets. The officers were hardworked: the daily programme of drill and parades was heavy, and in addition there was the task of keeping the men interested and fit: no easy matter in the bitter cold of a North France winter. Jim proved a tower of strength to his company commander, as he had been to his school. He organized football teams, and taught them the Australian game: he appealed to his father for aid, and in prompt response out came cases of boxing-gloves, hockey and lacrosse sets, and footballs enough to keep every man going. Norah sent a special gift—a big case of indoor games for wet weather, with a splendid bagatelle board that made the battalion deeply envied by less fortunate neighbours: until a German shell disobligingly burst just above it, and reduced it to fragments. However, Norah's disgust at the news was so deep that the Tired People in residence at Homewood at the moment conspired together, and supplied the battalion with a new board in her name; and this time it managed to escape destruction.

The battalion had some stiff fighting towards the end of the winter, and earned a pat on the back from high quarters for its work in capturing some enemy trenches. But they lost heavily, especially in officers. Jim's company commander was killed at his side: the boy went out at night into No-Man's Land and brought his body in single-handed, in grim defiance of the Boche machine-guns. Jim had liked Anstruther: it was not to be thought of that his body should be dishonoured by the touch of a Hun. Next day he had a far harder task, for Anstruther had asked him to write to his mother if he failed to come back. Jim bit his pen for two hours over that letter, and in his own mind stigmatized it as "a rotten effort, " after it was finished. But the woman to whom it carried whatever of comfort was left in the world for her saw no fault in it. It was worn and frayed with reading when she locked it away with her dead son's letters.

Jim found himself a company commander after that day's fighting—doing captain's work without captain's rank. Wally was his subaltern, an arrangement rather doubted at first by the Colonel, until he saw that the chums played the game strictly, and maintained in working hours a discipline as firm as was their friendship. The men adored them: they knew their officers shirked neither work nor play, and that they knew their own limitations—neither Jim nor Wally ever deluded themselves with the idea that they knew as much as their hard-bitten non-commissioned officers. But they learned their men by heart, knowing each one's nickname and something of his private affairs; losing no opportunity of talking to them and gaining their confidence, and sizing them up, as they talked, just as in old days, as captains of the team, they had learned to size up boys at football. "If I've got to go over the top I want to know what Joe Wilkins and Tiny Judd are doing behind me, " said Jim.

They had hoped for leave before the spring offensive, but it was impossible: the battalion was too shorthanded, and the enemy was endeavouring to be the four-times-armed man who "gets his fist in fust. " In that early fighting it became necessary to deal with a nest of machine-guns that had got the range of their trenches to a nicety. Shells had failed to find them, and the list of casualties to their discredit mounted daily higher. Jim got the chance. He shook hands with Wally—a vision of miserable disappointment—in the small hours of a starlit night, and led a picked body of his men out of the front trench: making a long *detour* and finally working nearer and nearer to the spot he had studied through his periscope for hours during the day. Then he planted his men in a shell-hole, and wriggled forward alone.

The men lay waiting, inwardly chafing at being left. Presently their officer came crawling back to them.

"We've got 'em cold, " he whispered. "Come along—and don't fire a shot. "

It was long after daylight before the German guards in the main trenches suspected anything wrong with that particular nest of machine-guns, and marvelled at its silence. For there was no one left to tell them anything—of the fierce, silent onslaught from the rear; of men who dropped as it were from the clouds and fought with clubbed rifles, led by a boy who seemed in the starlight as tall as a young pine-tree. The gun-crews were sleeping, and most of them never woke again: the guards, drowsy in the quiet stillness, heard nothing until that swift, wordless avalanche was upon them.

In the British trench there was impatience and anxiety. The men waiting to go forward, if necessary, to support the raiders, crouched at the fire-step, muttering. Wally, sick with suspense, peered forward beside the Colonel, who had come in person to see the result of the raid.

"I believe they've missed their way altogether, " muttered the Colonel angrily. "There should hove been shots long ago. It isn't like Linton. Dawn will be here soon, and the whole lot will be scuppered. " He wheeled at a sudden commotion beyond him in the trench. "Silence there! What's that? "

"That" was Jim Linton and his warriors, very muddy, but otherwise undamaged. They dropped into the trench quietly, those who came first turning to receive heavy objects from those yet on top. Last of all Jim hopped down.

"Hullo, Wal! " he whispered. "Got 'em. "

"Got 'em! " said the Colonel sternly. "What? Where have you been, sir? "

"I beg your pardon, sir—I didn't know you were there, " Jim said, rather horrified. It is not given to every subaltern to call his commanding officer "Wal, " when that is not his name. "I have the guns, sir. "

"You have—*what*? "

"The Boche—I mean, the enemy, machine-guns. We brought them back, sir. "

"You brought them back! " The Colonel leaned against the wall of the trench and began to laugh helplessly. "And your men? "

"All here, sir. We brought the ammunition, too, " said Jim mildly. "It seemed a pity to waste it! "

Which things, being told in high places, brought Jim a mention in despatches, and, shortly afterwards, confirmation of his acting rank. It would be difficult to find fitting words to tell of the effect of this matter upon a certain grizzled gentleman and a very young lady who, when the information reached them were studying patent manures in a morning-room in a house in Surrey.

"He's—why, " gasped Norah incredulously—"he's actually Captain Linton! "

"I suppose he is, " said her father. "Doesn't it sound ridiculous! "

"I don't think it's ridiculous at all, " said Norah warmly. "He deserved it. I think it sounds simply beautiful! "

"Do you know, " said her father, somewhat embarrassed—"I really believe I agree with you! " He laughed. "Captain Linton! "

"Captain Linton! " reiterated Norah. "Our old Jimmy! " She swept the table clear. "Oh, Daddy, bother the fertilizers for to-night—I'm going to write to Billabong! "

"But it isn't mail-day to-morrow, " protested her father mildly.

"No, " said Norah. "But I'll explode if I don't tell Brownie! "

"And will the Captain be coming 'ome soon, Miss Norah? " inquired Allenby, a little later. The household had waxed ecstatic over the news.

"The Captain? " Norah echoed. "Oh, how nice of you, Allenby! It does sound jolly! "

"Miss de Lisle wishes to know, miss. The news 'as induced 'er to invent a special cake. "

"We'll have to send it to the poor Captain, I'm afraid, " said Norah, dimpling. "Dear me, I haven't told Mrs. Hunt! I must fly! " She dropped her pen, and fled to the cottage—to find her father there before her.

"I might have known you couldn't wait to tell, " said Norah, laughing. "And he pretends he isn't proud, Mrs. Hunt! "

"I've given up even pretending, " said her father, laughing. "I found myself shaking hands with Allenby in the most affectionate manner. You see, Mrs. Hunt, this sort of thing hasn't happened in the family before. "

"Oh, but those boys couldn't help doing well, " Mrs. Hunt said, looking almost as pleased as the two beaming faces before her. "They're so keen. I don't know if I should, but shall I read you what Douglas says about them? " They gathered eagerly together over the curt words of praise Major Hunt had written. "Quite ordinary boys, and not a bit brainy, " he finished. "But I wish I had a regiment full of them! "

Out in Australia, two months later, a huge old woman and a lean Irishman talked over the letter Norah had at length managed to finish.

"And it's a Captin he is! " said Murty O'Toole, head stockman.

"A Captain! " Brownie echoed. "Don't it seem only yesterday he was tearing about in his first little trousis, and the little mistress watching him! "

"And riding his first pony. She put him over her head, and I med sure he was kilt. 'Howld her, will ye, Murty, ' says he, stamping his little fut, and blood trickling down his face. 'Give me a leg up again, ' he says, 'till we see who's boss! ' And I put him up, and off he went down the paddock, digging his little heels into her. And he's a Captin! Little Masther Jim! "

"I don't know why you're surprised, " said Brownie loftily. "The only wonder to *me* is he wasn't one six months ago! "

CHAPTER XIII

THE END OF A PERFECT DAY

"Are you ready, Norah? "

"Coming, Phil—half a minute! "

Hardress, in riding kit, looked into the kitchen, where Norah was carrying on a feverish consultation with Miss de Lisle.

"You'll be late, " he said warningly. "Your father and Geoffrey have gone on. "

"Will I truly? " said Norah distractedly. "Yes, Miss de Lisle, I'll write to the Stores about it to-night. Now, what about the fish? "

"Leave the fish to me, " said Miss de Lisle, laughing. "If I can't manage to worry out a fish course without you, I don't deserve to have half my diplomas. Run away: the house won't go to pieces in a single hunting day. "

"Bless you! " said Norah thankfully, dragging on her gloves and casting a wild glance about the kitchen for her hunting crop. "Oh, there it is. Good-bye. You won't forget that Major Arkwright is only allowed white meat? "

"Oh, run away—I won't forget anything. "

"Well, he only came last night, so I thought you mightn't know, " said the apologetic mistress of the house. "All right, Phil—I'm truly coming. Good-bye, Miss de Lisle! " The words floated back as she raced off to the front door, where the horses were fretting impatiently, held by the groom.

They jogged down the avenue—Hardress on one of the brown cobs, Norah on Brunette, the black pony—her favourite mount. It was a perfect hunting morning: mild and still, with almost a hint of spring warmth in the air. The leafless trees bore faint signs of swelling leaf-buds. Here and there, in the grass beside the drive crocus bells peeped out at them—purple, white and gold.

"We'll have daffodils soon, I do believe, " Norah said. "Well, I love Australia, but there isn't anything in the world lovelier than your English spring! "

Ahead of them, as they turned into the road, they could see Mr. Linton, looking extraordinarily huge on Killaloe, beside Geoffrey's little figure on Brecon.

"This is a great day for Geoff, " Hardress said.

"Yes—he has been just longing to go to a meet. Of course he has driven a good many times, but Mrs. Hunt has been a bit nervous about his riding. But he's perfectly safe—and it isn't as if Brecon ever got excited. "

"No. Come along, Norah, there's a splendid stretch of grass here: let's canter! "

They had agreed upon a Christian-name footing some time before, when it seemed that Hardress was likely to be a permanent member of the household. She looked at him now, as they cantered along through the dew-wet grass at the side of the road. No one would have guessed at anything wrong with him: he was bronzed and clear-eyed, and sat as easily in the saddle as though he had never been injured.

"Sometimes, " said Norah suddenly, "I find myself wondering which of your legs is the shop one! " She flushed. "I suppose I oughtn't to make personal remarks, but your leg does seem family property! "

"So it is, " said Hardress, grinning. "Anyhow, you couldn't make a nicer personal remark than that one. So I forgive you. But it's all thanks to you people. "

"We couldn't have done anything if you hadn't been determined to get on, " Norah answered. "As soon as you made up your mind to that—well, you got on. "

"I don't know how you stood me so long, " he muttered. Then they caught up to the riders ahead, and were received by Geoffrey with a joyful shout.

"You were nearly late, Norah, " said Mr. Linton.

"I dragged her from the kitchen, sir, " Hardress said. "She and Miss de Lisle were poring over food—if we get no dinner to-night it will be our fault. "

"If *you* had the responsibility of feeding fourteen hungry people you wouldn't make a joke of it, " said Norah. "It's very solemn, especially when the fishmonger fails you hopelessly. "

"There's always tinned salmon, " suggested her father.

"Tinned salmon, indeed! " Norah's voice was scornful. "We haven't come yet to giving the Tired People dinner out of a tin. However, it's all right: Miss de Lisle will work some sort of a miracle. I'm not going to think of housekeeping for a whole day! "

The meet was four miles away, near a marshy hollow thickly covered with osiers and willows. A wood fringed the marsh, and covered a hill which rose from a little stream beyond it. Here and there was a glimpse of the yellow flame of gorse. There were rolling fields all round, many of them ploughed: it had not yet been made compulsory for every landowner to till a portion of his holding, but English farmers were beginning to awake to the fact that while the German submarine flourished it would be both prudent and profitable to grow as much food as possible, and the plough had been busy. The gate into the field overlooking the marsh stood open; a few riders were converging towards it from different points. The old days of crowded meets and big fields of riders were gone. Only a few plucky people struggled to keep the hounds going, and to find work for the hunters that had escaped the first requisition of horses for France.

The hounds came into view as Mr. Linton's party arrived. The "Master" came first, on a big, workmanlike grey; a tall woman, with a weatherbeaten face surmounted by a bowler hat. The hounds trotted meekly after her, one or another pausing now and then to drink at a wayside puddle before being rebuked for bad manners by a watchful whip. Mrs. Ainslie liked the Lintons; she greeted them pleasantly.

"Nice morning, " she said. "Congratulations: I hear the boy is a Captain. "

"We can't quite realize it, " Norah said, laughing. "You see, we hardly knew he had grown up! "

"Well, he grew to a good size, " said Mrs. Ainslie, with a smile. "Hullo, Geoff. Are you going to follow to-day? "

"They won't let me, " said Geoffrey dolefully. "I know Brecon and I could, but Mother says we're too small. "

"Too bad! " said Mrs. Ainslie. "Never mind; you'll be big pretty soon. "

A tall old man in knickerbockers greeted her: Squire Brand, who owned a famous property a few miles away, and who had the reputation of never missing a meet, although he did not ride. He knew every inch of the country; it was said that he could boast, at the end of a season, that he had, on the whole, seen more of the runs than any one else except the Master. He was a tireless runner, with an extraordinarily long stride, which carried him over fields and ditches and gave him the advantage of many a short cut impossible to most people. He knew every hound by name; some said he knew every fox in the country; and he certainly had an amazing knowledge of the direction a fox was likely to take. Horses, on the other hand, bored him hopelessly; he consented to drive them, in the days when motors were not, but merely as a means of getting from place to place. A splendid car, with a chauffeur much smarter than his master, had just dropped him: a grant figure in weatherbeaten Harris tweeds, grasping a heavy stick.

"We should get a good run to-day, " he said.

"Yes—with luck, " Mrs. Ainslie answered.

"Any news from the Colonel? "

"Nothing in particular—plenty of hard fighting. But he never writes much of that. He's much more interested in a run he had with a queer scratch pack near their billets. I can't quite gather how it was organized, but it comprised two beagles and a greyhound and a fox-terrier and a pug. He said they had a very sporting time! "

Squire Brand chuckled.

"I don't doubt it, " he said. "Did he say what they hunted? "

"Anything they could get, apparently. They began with a hare, and then got on to a rabbit, in some mysterious fashion. They finished up with a brisk run in the outskirts of a village, and got a kill—it turned out this time to be a cat! " Mrs. Ainslie's rather grim features relaxed into a smile. "If any one had told Val two years ago that he would be enthusiastic over a day like that! "

A few other riders had come up: two or three officers from a neighbouring town; a couple of old men, and a sprinkling of girls. Philip Hardress was the only young man in plain clothes, and strangers who did not suspect anything amiss with his leg looked at him curiously.

"Look at that dear old thing! " he whispered to Norah, indicating a prim maiden lady who had arrived on foot. "I know she's aching for a chance to ask me why I'm not in khaki! " He grinned delightedly. "She's rather like the old lady who met me in the train the other day, and after looking at me sadly for a few minutes said, 'My dear young man, do you not know that your King and Country want you? '"

"Phil! What did you say? "

"I said, 'Well, they've got one of my legs, and they don't seem to have any use for the remnant! ' I don't think she believed me, so I invited her to prod it! " He chuckled at his grim joke. Three months ago he had shrunk from any mention of his injury as from the lash of a whip.

Mrs. Ainslie never wasted time. Two minutes' grace for any laggards—which gave time for the arrival of a stout lady on a weight-carrying cob—and then she moved on, and in a moment the hounds were among the osiers, hidden except that now and then a waving stern caught the eye. Occasionally there was a brief whimper, and once a young hound gave tongue too soon, and was, presumably, rebuked by his mother, and relapsed into hunting in shamed silence.

The osiers proved blank: they drew out, and went up the hill into the covert, while the field moved along to be as close as possible, and the followers on foot dodged about feverishly, hoping for luck that would make a fox break their way. Too often the weary lot of the foot contingent is to see nothing whatever after the hounds once enter covert, since the fox is apt to leave it as unobtrusively as possible at the far side, and to take as short a line as he can across country to another refuse. To follow the hounds on foot needs a stout heart and patience surpassing that of Job.

But those on horses know little of the blighting experiences of the foot-plodders: and when Norah went a-hunting everything ceased to exist for her except the white-and-black-and-tan hounds and the green fields, and Brunette under her, as eager as she for the first long-drawn-out note from the pack. They moved restlessly back and forth along the hillside, the black pony dancing with impatience at the faintest whimper from an unseen hound. Near them Killaloe set an example of steadiness—but with watchful eyes and pricked ears.

Squire Brand came up to them.

"I'd advise you to get up near the far end of the covert, " he said. "It's almost a certainty that he'll break away there and make a bee-line across to Harley Wood. I hope he will, for there's less plough there than in the other direction. " He hurried off, and Norah permitted Brunette to caper after him. A young officer on a big bay followed their example.

"Come along, " he said to a companion. "It's a safe thing to follow old Brand's lead if you want to get away well. "

Where the covert ended the hill sloped gently to undulating fields, divided by fairly stiff hedges with deep ditches, and occasionally by post-and-rail fences, more like the jumps that Norah knew in Australia. The going was good and sound, and there was no wire—that terror of the hunter. Norah had always hated wire, either plain or barbed. She held that it found its true level in being used against Germans.

Somewhere in a tangle of bracken an old hound spoke sharply. A little thrill ran through her. She saw her father put his pipe in his pocket and pull his hat more firmly down on his forehead, while she held back Brunette, who was dancing wildly. Then came another note, and another, and a long-drawn burst of music from the hounds; and suddenly Norah saw a stealthy russet form, with brush sweeping the ground, that stole from the covert and slid down the slope, and after him, a leaping wave of brown and white and black as hounds came bounding from the wood and flung themselves upon the scent, with Mrs. Ainslie close behind. Some one shouted "Gone awa-a-y! " in a voice that went ringing in echoes round the hillside.

Brunette bucked airily over the low fence near the covert, and Killaloe took it almost in his stride. Then they were racing side by side down the long slope, with the green turf like wet velvet underfoot; and the next hedge seemed rushing to meet them. Over, landing lightly in the next field; before them only the "Master" and whip, and the racing hounds, with burning eyes for the little red speck ahead, trailing his brush.

"By Jove, Norah! " said David Linton, "we're in for a run! "

Norah nodded. Speech was beyond her; only all her being was singing with the utter joy of the ride. Beneath her Brunette was spurning the turf with dainty hooves; stretching out in her gallop, yet gathering herself cleverly at her fences, with alert, pricked ears— judging her distance, and landing with never a peck or stumble. The light weight on the pony's back was nothing to her; the delicate touch on her mouth was all she needed to steady her at the jumps.

Near Harley Wood the fox decided regretfully that safety lay elsewhere: the enemy, running silently and surely, were too hot on his track. He crept through a hedge, and slipped like a shadow down a ditch; and hounds, jumping out, were at fault for a moment. The slight check gave the rest of the field time to get up.

"That's a great pony! " Norah heard the young officer say. She patted Brunette's arching neck.

Then a quick cast of the hounds picked up the scent, and again they were off, but no longer with the fences to themselves; so that it was necessary to be watchful for the cheerful enthusiast who jumps on top of you, and the prudent sportsman who wobbles all over the field in his gallop, seeking for a gap. Killaloe drew away again: there was no hunter in the country side to touch him. After him went Brunette, with no notion of permitting her stable companion to lose her in a run like this.

A tall hedge faced them, with an awkward take-off from the bank of a ditch. Killaloe crashed through; Brunette came like a bird in his tracks, Norah's arm across her face to ward off the loose branches. She got through with a tear in her coat, landing on stiff plough through which Mrs. Ainslie's grey was struggling painfully. Brunette's light burden was all in her favour here—Norah was first to the gate on the far side, opening it just in time for the "Master, " and thrilling with joy at that magnate's brief "Thank you! " as she passed through and galloped away. The plough had given the hounds a long lead. But ahead were only green fields, dotted by clumps of trees: racing ground, firm and springy. The air sang in their ears. The fences seemed as nothing; the good horses took them in racing style, landing with no shock, and galloping on, needing no touch of whip or spur.

The old dog-fox was tiring, as well he might, and yet, ahead, he knew, lay sanctuary, in an old quarry where the piled rocks hid a hole where he had lain before, with angry hounds snuffing helplessly around him. He braced his weary limbs for a last effort. The cruel eyes and lolling tongues were very close behind him; but his muscles were steel, and he knew how to save every short cut that gave him so much as a yard. He saw the quarry, just ahead, and snarled his triumph in his untamed heart.

Brunette's gallop was faltering a little, and Norah's heart sank. She had never had such a run: it was hard if she could not see it out, when they had led the field the whole way—and while yet Killaloe was going like a galloping-machine in front. Then she heard a shout from her father and saw him point ahead. "Water! " came to her. She saw the gleam of water, fringed by reeds: saw Killaloe rise like a deer at it, taking off well on the near side, and landing with many feet to spare.

"Oh—we can do that, " Norah thought. "Brunette likes water. "

She touched the pony with her heel for the first time, and spoke to her. Brunette responded instantly, gathering herself for the jump. Again Norah heard a shout, and was conscious of the feeling of vague irritation that we all know when some one is trying to tell us something we cannot possibly hear. She took the pony at the jump about twenty yards from the place where Killaloe had flown it. Nearer and nearer. The water gleamed before her, very close: she felt the pony steady herself for the leap. Then the bank gave way under her heels: there was a moment's struggle and a stupendous splash.

Norah's first thought was that the water was extremely cold; then, that the weight on her left leg was quite uncomfortable. Brunette half-crouched, half-lay, in the stream, too bewildered to move; then she sank a little more to one side and Norah had to grip her mane to keep herself from going under the surface. It seemed an unpleasantly long time before she saw her father's face.

"Norah—are you hurt? "

"No, I'm not hurt, " she said. "But I can't get my leg out—and Brunette seems to think she wants to stay here. I suppose she finds the mud nice and soft. " She tried to smile at his anxious face, but found it not altogether easy.

"We'll get you out, " said David Linton. He tugged at the pony's bridle; and Mrs. Ainslie, arriving presently, came to his assistance, while some of the other riders, coming up behind, encouraged Brunette with shouts and hunting-crops. Thus urged, Brunette decided that some further effort was necessary, and made one, with a mighty flounder, while Norah rolled off into the water. Half a dozen hands helped her at the bank.

"You're sure you're not hurt? " her father asked anxiously. "I was horribly afraid she'd roll on your leg when she moved. "

"I'm quite all right—only disgustingly wet, " said Norah. "Oh, and I missed the finish—did you ever know such bad luck? "

"Well, you only missed the last fifty yards, " said Mrs. Ainslie, pointing to the quarry, from which the whips were dislodging the aggrieved hounds. "We finished there; and that old fox is good for another day yet. I'd give you the brush, if he hadn't decided to keep it himself. "

"Oh! " said Norah, blushing, while her teeth chattered. "Wasn't it a beautiful run! "

"It was—but something has got to be done with you, " said Mrs. Ainslie firmly. "There's a farmhouse over there, Mr. Linton: I know the people, and they'll do anything they can for you. Hurry her over and get her wet things off—Mrs. Hardy will lend her some clothes. " And Norah made a draggled and inglorious exit.

Mrs. Hardy received her with horrified exclamations and offers of all that she had in the house: so that presently Norah found herself drinking cup after cup of very hot tea and eating buttered toast with her father—attired in a plaid blouse of green and red in large checks, and a black velvet skirt that had seen better days; with carpet slippers lending a neat finish to a somewhat striking appearance. Without, farm hands rubbed down Killaloe and Brunette in the stable. Mrs. Hardy fluttered in and out, bringing more and yet more toast, until her guests protested vehemently that exhausted nature forbade them to eat another crumb.

"And wot is toast? " grumbled Mrs. Hardy, "and you ridin' all day in the cold! " She had been grievously disappointed at her visitors' refusing bacon and eggs. "The young lady'll catch 'er death, sure's fate! Just another cup, miss. Lor, who's that comin' in at the gate! "

"That" proved to be Squire Brand, who had appeared at the scene of Norah's disaster just after her retreat—being accused by Mrs. Ainslie of employing an aeroplane.

"I came to see if I could be of any use, " he said. His eye fell on Norah in Mrs. Hardy's clothes, and he said, "Dear me! " suddenly, and for a moment lost the thread of his remarks. "You can't let her ride home, Linton—my car is here, and if your daughter will let me drive her home I'm sure Mr. Hardy will house her pony until to-morrow—you can send a groom over for it. I've a spare coat in the car. Yes, thank you, Mrs. Hardy, I should like a cup of tea very much. "

Captain Jim

Now that the excitement of the day was over, Norah was beginning to feel tired enough to be glad to escape the long ride home on a jaded horse. So, with Mrs. Hardy's raiment hidden beneath a gorgeous fur coat, she was presently in the Squire's car, slipping through the dusk of the lonely country lanes. The Squire liked Jim, and asked questions about him: and to talk of Jim was always the nearest way to Norah's heart. She had exhausted his present, and was as far back in his past as his triumphs in inter-State cricket, when they turned in at the Homewood avenue.

"I'm afraid I've talked an awful lot, " she said, blushing. "You see, Jim and I are tremendous chums. I often think how lucky I was to have a brother like him, as I had only one! "

"Possibly Jim thinks the same about his sister, " said the old man. He looked at her kindly; there was something very child-like in the small face, half-lost in the great fur collar of his coat.

"At all events, Jim has a good champion, " he said.

"Oh, Jim doesn't need a champion, " Norah answered. "Every one likes him, I think. And of course we think there's no one like him. "

The motor stopped, and the Squire helped her out. It was too late to come in, he said; he bade her good night, and went back to the car.

Norah looked in the glass in the hall, and decided that her appearance was too striking to be kept to herself. A very battered felt riding-hat surmounted Mrs. Hardy's finery; it bore numerous mud-splashes, some of which had extended to her face. No one was in the hall; it was late, and presumably the Tired People were dressing for dinner. She headed for the kitchen, meeting, on the way, Allenby, who uttered a choking sound and dived into his pantry. Norah chuckled, and passed on.

Miss de Lisle sat near the range, knitting her ever-present muffler. She looked up, and caught her breath at the apparition that danced in—Norah, more like a well-dressed scarecrow than anything else, with her grey eyes bright among the mud-splashes. She held up Mrs. Hardy's velvet skirt in each hand, and danced solemnly up the long kitchen, pointing each foot daintily, in the gaudy carpet slippers.

"Oh my goodness! " ejaculated Miss de Lisle—and broke into helpless laughter.

Norah sat down by the fender and told the story of her day—with a cheerful interlude when Katty came in hurriedly, failed to see her until close upon her, and then collapsed. Miss de Lisle listened, twinkling.

"Well, you must go and dress, " she said at length. "It would be only kind to every one if you came down to dinner like that, but I suppose it wouldn't do. "

"It wouldn't be dignified, " said Norah, looking, at the moment, as though dignity were the last thing she cared about. "Well, I suppose I must go. " She gathered up her skirts and danced out again, pausing at the door to execute a high kick. Then she curtsied demurely to the laughing cook-lady, and fled to her room by a back staircase.

She came down a while later, tubbed and refreshed, in a dainty blue frock, with a black ribbon in her shining curls. The laughter had not yet died out of her eyes; she was humming one of Jim's school songs as she crossed the hall. Allenby was just turning from the door.

"A telegram, Miss Norah. "

"Thanks, Allenby. " She took it, still smiling. "I hope it isn't to say any one is coming to-night, " she said, as she carried it to the light. "Wouldn't it be lovely if it was to tell us they had leave! " There was no need to specify whom "they" meant. "But I'm afraid that's too much to hope, just yet. " She tore open the envelope.

There was a long silence as she stood there with the paper in her hand: a silence that grew gradually more terrible, while her face turned white. Over and over she read the scrawled words, as if in the vain hope that the thing they told might yet prove only a hideous dream from which, presently, she might wake. Then, as if very far away, she heard the butler's shaking voice.

"Miss Norah! Is it bad news? "

"You can send the boy away, " she heard herself say, as though it were some other person speaking. "There isn't any answer. He has been killed. "

"Not Mr. Jim? " Allenby's voice was a wail.

"Yes. "

She turned from him and walked into the morning-room, shutting the door. In the grate a fire was burning; the leaping light fell on Jim's photograph, standing on a table near. She stared at it, still holding the telegram. Surely it was a dream—she had so often had it before. Surely she would soon wake, and laugh at herself.

The door was flung open, and her father came in, ruddy and splashed. She remembered afterwards the shape of a mud-splash on his sleeve. It seemed to be curiously important.

"Norah! —what is wrong? "

She put out her hands to him then, shaking. Jim had said it was her job to look after him, but she could not help him now. And no words would come.

"Is it Jim? " At the agony of his voice she gave a little choking cry, catching at him blindly. The telegram fluttered to the floor, and David Linton picked it up and read it. He laid the paper on the table and turned to her, holding out his hands silently, and she came to him and put her face on his breast, trembling. His arm tightened round her. So they stood, while the time dragged on.

He put her into a chair at last, and they looked at each other: they had said no word since that first moment.

"Well, " said David Linton slowly, "we knew it might come. And we know that he died like a man, and that he never shirked. Thank God we had him, Norah. And thank God my son died a soldier, not a slacker. "

CHAPTER XIV

CARRYING ON

After that first terrible evening, during which no one had looked upon their agony, David Linton and his child took up their life again and tried to splice the broken ends as best they might. Their guests, who came down to breakfast nervously, preparing to go away at once, found them in the dining-room, haggard and worn, but pleasantly courteous; they talked of the morning's news, of the frost that seemed commencing, of the bulbs that were sending delicate spear-heads up through the grass or the bare flower-beds. There were arrangements for the day to be made for those who cared to ride or drive: the trains to be planned for a gunner subaltern whose leave was expiring next day. Everything was quite as usual, outwardly.

"Pretty ghastly meal, what? " remarked the young gunner to a chum, as they went out on the terrace. "Rather like dancing at a funeral. "

Philip Hardress came into the morning-room, where Mr. Linton and Norah were talking.

"I don't need to tell you how horribly sorry I am, " he faltered.

"No—thanks, Phil. "

"You—you haven't any details? "

"No. "

"Wally will write as soon as he can, " Norah added.

"Yes, of course. The others want me to say, sir, of course they will go away. They all understand. I can go too, just to the hotel. I can supervise Hawkins from there. "

"I hope none of you will think of doing any such thing, " David Linton said. "Our work here is just the same. Jim would never have wished us not to carry on. "

"But— —" Hardress began.

"There isn't any 'but. ' Norah and I are not going to sit mourning, with our hands in front of us. We mean to work a bit harder, that's all. You see" —the ghost of a smile flickered across the face that had aged ten years in a night—"more than ever now, whatever we do for a soldier is done for Jim. "

Hardress made a curious little gesture of protest.

"And I'm left—half of me! "

"You have got to help us, Phil, " Norah said. "We need you badly. "

"I can't do much, " he said. "But as long as you want me, I'm here. Then I'm to tell the others, sir— —"

"Tell them we hope they will help us to carry on as usual, " said David Linton. "I'll come across with you presently, Phil, to look at the new cultivator: I hear it arrived last night. "

He looked at Norah as the door closed.

"You're sure it isn't too much for you, my girl? I will send them away if you would rather we were by ourselves for a while. "

"I promised Jim that whatever happened we'd keep smiling, " Norah said. "He wouldn't want us to make a fuss. Jim always did so hate fusses, didn't he, Dad? "

She was quite calm. Even when Mrs. Hunt came hurrying over, and put her kind arms about her, Norah had no tears.

"I suppose we haven't realized it, " she said. "Perhaps we're trying not to. I don't want to think of Jim as dead—he was so splendidly alive, ever since he was a tiny chap. "

"Try to think of him as near you, " Mrs. Hunt whispered.

"Oh, he is. I know Jim never would go far from us, if he could help it. I know he's watching, somewhere, and he will be glad if we keep

170

our heads up and go straight on. He would trust us to do that. " Her face changed. "Oh, Mrs. Hunt, —but it's hard on Dad! "

"He has you still. "

"I'm only a girl, " said Norah. "No girl could make up for a son: and such a son as Jim. But I'll try. "

There came racing little feet in the hall, and Geoffrey burst in.

"It isn't true! " he shouted. "Say it isn't true, Norah! Allenby says the Germans have killed Jim—I know they couldn't. " He tugged at her woollen coat. "Say it's a lie, Norah—Jim couldn't be dead! "

"Geoff—Geoff, dear! " Mrs. Hunt tried to draw him away.

"Don't! " Norah said. She put her arms round the little boy—and suddenly her head went down on his shoulder. The tears came at last. Mrs. Hunt went softly from the room.

There were plenty of tears in the household: The servants had all loved the big cheery lad, with the pleasant word for each one. They went about their work red-eyed, and Allenby chafed openly at the age that kept him at home, doing a woman's work, while boys went out to give their lives, laughing, for Empire.

"It ain't fair, " he said to Miss de Lisle, who sobbed into the muffler she was knitting. "It ain't fair. Kids, they are—no more. They ain't meant to die. Oh, if I could only get at that there Kayser! "

Then, after a week of waiting, came Wally's letter.

*****

"Norah, Dear, —

"I don't know how to write to you. I can't bear to think about you and your father. It seems it must be only a bad dream—and all the time I know it isn't, even though I keep thinking I hear his whistle—the one he used for me.

Captain Jim

"I had better tell you about it.

"We had orders to attack early one morning. Jim was awfully keen; he had everything ready, and he had been talking to the men until they were all as bucked up as they could be. You know, he was often pretty grave about his work, but I don't think I ever saw him look so happy as he did that morning. He looked just like a kid. He told me he felt as if he were going out on a good horse at Billabong. We were looking over our revolvers, and he said, 'That's the only thing that feels wrong; it ought to be a stock whip! '

"We hadn't much artillery support. Our guns were short of shells, as usual. But we took the first trench, and the next. Jim was just everywhere. He was always first; the men would have followed him down a precipice. He was laughing all the time.

"We didn't get much time before they counter-attacked. They came on in waves—as if there were millions of them, and we had a pretty stiff fight in the trench. It was fairly well smashed about. I was pretty busy about fifty yards away, but I saw Jim up on a broken traverse, using his revolver just as calmly as if he were practising in camp, and cheering on the men. He gave me a 'Coo-ee! '

"And then—oh, I don't know how to tell you. Just as I was looking at him a shell burst near him: and when the smoke blew over there was nothing—traverse and trench and all, it was just wiped out. I couldn't get near him—the Boches were pouring over in fresh masses, and we got the signal to retire—and I was the only one left to get the men back.

"He couldn't have felt anything; that's the only thing.

"I wish it had been me. I'm nobody's dog, and he was just everything to you two—and the best friend a fellow ever had. It would have been so much more reasonable if it had been me. I just feel that I hate myself for being alive. I would have saved him for you if I could, Norah, "Wally. "

*****

There were letters, too, from Jim's Colonel, and from Major Hunt, and Garrett, and every other brother-officer whom Jim had sent to

172

Homewood; and others that Norah and her father valued almost more highly—from men who had served under him. Letters that made him glow with pride—almost forgetting grief as they read them. It seemed so impossible to think that Jim would never come again.

"I can't feel as though he were dead, " Norah said, looking up at her father. "I know I've got to get used to knowing he has gone away from us for always. But I like to think of him as having only changed work. Jim never could be idle in Heaven; he always used to say it seemed such a queer idea to sit all day in a white robe and play a harp. Jim's Heaven would have to be a very busy one, and I know he's gone there, Dad. "

David Linton got up and went to the bookcase. He came back with *Westward Ho!* in his hand.

"I was reading Kingsley's idea of it last night, " he said. "I think it helps, Norah. Listen. 'The best reward for having wrought well already, is to have more to do; and he that has been faithful over a few things, must find his account in being made ruler over many things. That is the true and heroical rest, which only is worthy of gentlemen and sons of God. ' Jim was only a boy, but he went straight and did his best all his life. I think he has just been promoted to some bigger job. "

So they held their heads high, as befitted people with just cause for being proud, and set themselves to find the rest that comes from hard work. There was plenty to do, for the house was always full of Tired People. Not that the Lintons ever tried to entertain their guests. Tired People came to a big, quiet house, where everything ran smoothly, and all that was possible was done for comfort. Beyond that, they did exactly as they chose. There were horses and the motor for those who cared to ride and drive; the links for golfers; walks with beautiful scenery for energetic folk, and dainty rooms with big easy-chairs, or restful lounges under the trees on the lawn, for those who asked from Fate nothing better than to be lazy. No one was expected to make conversation or to behave as an ordinary guest. Everywhere there was a pleasant feeling of homeliness and welcome; shy men became suddenly at their ease; nerve-racked men, strained with long months of the noise and horror of war, relaxed in the peace of Homewood, and went back to duty with a light step and a clear eye. Only there was missing the wild merriment of the first few weeks, when Jim and Wally dashed in and out perpetually and kept the house in a simmer of uncertainty and laughter. That could never come again.

But beyond the immediate needs of the Tired People there was much to plan and carry out. Conscription in England was an established fact; already there were few fit men to be seen out of uniform. David Linton looked forward to a time when shortage of labour, coupled with the deadly work of the German submarines, should mean a shortage of food; and he and Norah set themselves to provide against that time of scarcity. Miss de Lisle and Philip Hardress entered into every plan, lending the help of brains as well as hands. The farm was put under intensive culture, and the first provision made for the future was that of fertilizers, which, since most of them came from abroad, were certain to be scarce. Mr. Linton and Hardress breathed more freely when they had stored a two years' supply. The flock of sheep was increased; the fowl-run doubled in size, and put in charge of a disabled soldier, a one-armed Australian, whom Hardress found in London, ill and miserable, and added to the list of Homewood's patients—and cures. Young heifers were bought, and "boarded-out" at neighbouring farms; a populous community of grunting pigs occupied a little field. And in the house Norah and Miss de Lisle worked through the spring and summer, until the dry and spacious cellars and storerooms showed row upon row of shelves covered with everything that could be preserved or salted or pickled, from eggs to runner beans.

Sometimes the Tired People lent a hand, becoming interested in their hosts' schemes. Norah formed a fast friendship with a cheerful subaltern in the Irish Guards, who was with them for a wet fortnight, much of which he spent in the kitchen stoning fruit, making jam, and acting as bottler-in-chief to the finished product. There were many who asked nothing better than to work on the farm, digging, planting or harvesting: indeed, in the summer, one crop would have been ruined altogether by a fierce storm, but for the Tired People, who, from an elderly Colonel to an Australian signaller, flung themselves upon it, and helped to finish getting it under cover— carrying the last sheaves home just as the rain came down in torrents, and returning to Homewood in a soaked but triumphant procession. Indeed, nearly all the unending stream of guests came under the spell of the place; so that Norah used to receive anxious inquiries from various corners of the earth afterwards—from Egypt or Salonica would come demands as to the success of a catch-crop which the writer had helped to sow, or of a brood of Buff Orpingtons which he had watched hatching out in the incubator: even from German East Africa came a letter asking after a special litter of pigs! Perhaps it was that every one knew that the Lintons were shouldering a burden bravely, and tried to help.

They kept Jim very close to them. A stranger, hearing the name so often on their lips, might have thought that he was still with them. Together, they talked of him always; not sadly, but remembering the long, happy years that now meant a memory too dear ever to let go. Jim had once asked Norah for a promise. "If I go West, " he said, "don't wear any horrible black frocks. " So she went about in her ordinary dresses, especially the blue frocks he had loved — with just a narrow black band on her arm. There were fresh flowers under his picture every day, but she did not put them sadly. She would smile at the frank happy face as she arranged leaves and blossoms with a loving hand.

Later on, David Linton fitted up a carpenter's bench and a workshop; the days were too full for much thinking, but he found the evenings long. He enlisted Hardress in his old work of splint-making, and then found that half his guests used to stray out to the lit workshop after dinner and beg for jobs, so that before long the nearest Hospital Supply Depot could count on a steady output of work from Homewood. Mrs. Hunt and Norah used to come as polishers; Miss de Lisle suddenly discovered that her soul for cooking included a corner for carpentry, and became extraordinarily skilful in the use of chisel and plane. When the autumn days brought a chill into the air, Mr. Linton put a stove into the workshop; and it became a kind of club, where the whole household might often be found; they extended their activities to the manufacture of crutches, bed-rests, bed-tables, and half a dozen other aids to comfort for broken men. No work had helped David Linton so much.

In the early summer Wally came back on leave: a changed Wally, with grim lines where there had once been only merry ones in his lean, brown face. He did not want to come to Homewood; only when begged to come did he master the pitiful shrinking he felt from meeting them.

"I didn't know how to face you, " he said. Norah had gone to meet him, and they were walking back from the station.

"Don't, Wally; you hurt, " she said.

"It's true, though; I didn't. I feel as if you must hate me for coming back—alone. "

"Hate you! —and you were Jim's chum! "

"I always came as Jim's chum, " Wally said heavily. "From the very first, when I was a lonely little nipper at school, I sort of belonged to Jim. And now—well, I just can't realize it, Norah. I can't keep on thinking about him as dead. I know he is, and one minute I'm feeling half-insane about it, and the next I forget, and think I hear him whistling or calling me. " He clenched his hands. "It's the minute after that that is the worst of all, " he said.

For a time they did not speak. They walked on slowly, along the pleasant country lane with its blossoming hedges.

"I know, " Norah said. "There's not much to choose between you and Dad and me, when it comes to missing Jim. But as for you—well you did come as Jim's chum first—and always; but you came just as much because you were yourself. You know you belonged to Billabong, as we all did. You can't cut yourself off from us now, Wally. "

"I? " he echoed. "Well, if I do, I have mighty little left. But I felt that you couldn't want to see me. I know what it must be like to see me come back without him. "

"I'm not going to say it doesn't hurt, " said Norah. "Only it hurts you as much as it does us. And the thing that would be ever so much worse is for you not to come. Why, you're the only comfort we have left. Don't you see, you're like a bit of Jim coming back to us? "

"Oh, Norah—Norah! " he said. "If I could only have saved him! "

"Don't we know you'd have died quite happily if you could! " Norah said. "Just as happily as he would have died for you. "

"He did, you know, " Wally said. All the youth and joy had gone out of his voice, leaving it flat and toneless. "Two or three times that morning he kept me out of a specially hot spot, and took it himself.

176

He was always doing it: we nearly punched each other's heads about it the day before—I told him he was using his rank unfairly. He just grinned and said subalterns couldn't understand necessary strategy in the field! "

"He would! " said Norah, laughing.

Wally stared at her.

"I didn't think I'd ever see you laugh again! "

"Not laugh! " Norah echoed. "Why, it wouldn't be fair to Jim if we didn't. We keep him as near us as we can—talk about him, and about all the old, happy times. We did have such awfully good times together, didn't we? We're never going to get far away from him. "

The boy gave a great sigh.

"I've been getting a long way from everything, " he said. "Since— since it happened I couldn't let myself think: it was just as if I were going mad. The only thing I've wanted to do was to fight, and I've had that. "

"He looks as if his mind were more tired than his body, " David Linton said that evening. "One can see that he has just been torturing himself with all sorts of useless thoughts. You'll have to take him in hand, Norah. Put the other work aside for a while and go out with him—ride as much as you can. It won't do you any harm, either. "

"We never thought old Wally would be one of the Tired People, " Norah said musingly.

"No, indeed. And I think there has been no one more utterly tired. It won't do, Norah: the boy will be ill if we don't look after him. "

"We've just got to make him feel how much we want him, " Norah said.

"Yes. And we have to teach him to think happily about Jim—not to fight it all the time. Fighting won't make it any better, " said David Linton, with a sigh.

But there was no riding for Wally, for a while. The next day found him too ill to get up, and the doctor, sent for hastily, talked of shock and over-strain, and ordered bed until his temperature should be pleased to go down: which was not for many a weary day. Possibly it was the best thing that could have happened to Wally. He grew, if not reconciled, at least accustomed to his loss; grew, too, to thinking himself a coward when he saw the daily struggle waged by the two people he loved best. And Norah was wise enough to call in other nurses: chief of them the Hunt babies, Alison and Michael, who rolled on his bed and played with him, while Geoffrey sat as close to him as possible, and could hardly be lured from the room. It was not for weeks after his return that they heard Wally laugh; and then it was at some ridiculous speech of Michael's that he suddenly broke into the ghost of his old mirth.

Norah's heart gave a leap.

"Oh, he's better! " she thought. "You blessed little Michael! "

And so, healing came to the boy's bruised soul. Not that the old, light-hearted Wally came back: but he learned to talk of Jim, and no longer to hug his sorrow in silence. Something became his of the peace that had fallen upon Norah and her father. It was all they could hope for, to begin with.

They said good-bye to him before they considered him well enough to go back to the trenches. But the call for men was insistent, and the boy himself was eager to go.

"Come back to us soon, " Norah said, wistfully.

"Oh, I'm safe to come back, " Wally said. "I'm nobody's dog, you know. "

"That's not fair! " she flashed. "Say you're sorry for saying it! "

He flushed.

"I'm sorry if I hurt you, Nor. I suppose I was a brute to say that. " Something of his old quaint fun came into his eyes for a moment. "Anyhow it's something to be somebody's dog—especially if one happens to belong to Billabong-in-Surrey! "

CHAPTER XV

PRISONERS AND CAPTIVES

The church was half in ruins. Great portions of the roof had been torn away by shell-fire, and there were gaping holes in the walls through which could be caught glimpses of sentries going backwards and forwards. Sometimes a grey battalion swung by; sometimes a German officer peered in curiously, with a sneer on his lips. The drone of aircraft came from above, through the holes where the rafters showed black against the sky. Ever the guns boomed savagely from beyond.

There were no longer any seats in the church. They had all been broken up for camp-fires—even the oaken pulpit had gone. The great empty space had been roughly cleared of fallen masonry, which had been flung in heaps against the wall; on the stone floor filthy straw was thinly spread. On the straw lay row upon row of wounded men—very quiet for the most part; they had found that it did not pay to make noise enough to annoy the guards who smoked and played cards in a corner.

The long day—how long only the men on the straw knew—was drawing to a close. The sun sank behind the western window, which the guns had spared; and the stained glass turned to a glory of scarlet and gold and blue. The shafts of colour lay across the broken altar, whence everything had been stripped; they bathed the shattered walls in a beauty that was like a cloak over the nakedness of their ruin. Slowly they crept over the floor, as the sun sank lower, touching the straw with rosy fingers, falling gently on broken bodies and pain-drawn faces; and weary eyes looked gratefully up to the window where a figure of Christ with a child in His arms stood glorious in the light, and blessed them with the infinite pity of His smile.

A little Cockney lad with a dirty bandage round his head, who had tossed in pain all day on the chancel steps, turned to the window to greet the daily miracle of the sunset.

"Worf waiting for, all the day, that is! " he muttered. The restlessness left him, and his eyes closed, presently, in sleep.

Slowly the glory died away, and as it passed a little figure in a rusty black cassock came in, making his way among the men on the straw. It was the French priest, who had refused to leave his broken church: a little, fat man, not in the least like a hero, but with as knightly a soul as was ever found in armour and with lance in rest. He passed from man to man, speaking in quaint English, occasionally dropping gladly into French when he found some one able to answer him in his own language. He had nothing to give them but water; but that he carried tirelessly many times a day. His little store of bandages and ointment had gone long ago, but he bathed wounds, helped cramped men to change their position, and did the best he could to make the evil straw into the semblance of a comfortable bed. To the helpless men on the floor of the church his coming meant something akin to Paradise.

He paused near a little Irishman with a broken leg, a man of the Dublin Fusiliers, whose pain had not been able to destroy his good temper.

"How are you to-night, *mon garcon?* "

"Yerra, not too bad, Father, " said the Irishman. "If I could have just a taste of water, now? " He drank deeply as the priest lifted his head, and sank back with a word of thanks.

"This feather pillow of mine is apt to slip if I don't watch it, " he said, wriggling the back of his head against the cold stone of the floor, from which the straw had worked away. "I dunno could you gather it up a bit, Father. " He grinned. "I'd ask you to put me boots under me for a pillow, but if them thieving guards found them loose, they'd shweep them from me. "

"Ss-h, my son! " the priest whispered warningly. He shook up a handful of straw and made it as firm as he could under the man's head. "It is not prudent to speak so loud. Remember you cannot see who may be behind you. "

"Indeed and I cannot, " returned Denny Callaghan. "I'll remember, Father. That's great! " He settled his head thankfully on the straw pillow. "I'll sleep aisier to-night for that. "

"And *Monsieur le Capitaine*—has he moved yet? " The priest glanced at a motionless form near them.

"Well, indeed he did, Father, this afternoon. He gev a turn, an' he said something like 'Tired People. ' I thought there was great sense in that, if he was talkin' to us, so I was cheered up about him—but not a word have I got out of him since. But it's something that he spoke at all. "

The *cure* bent over the quiet figure. Two dark eyes opened, as if with difficulty, and met his.

"Norah, " said Jim Linton. "Are you there, Norah? "

"I am a friend, my son, " said the *cure*. "Are you in pain? "

The dark eyes looked at him uncomprehendingly. Then he murmured, "Water! "

"It is here. " The little priest held the heavy head, and Jim managed to drink a little. Something like a shadow of a smile came into his eyes as the priest wiped his lips. Then they closed again.

"If they would send us a doctor! " muttered the *cure*, in his own language, longingly. "*Ma joi*, what a lad! " He looked down in admiration at the splendid helpless body.

"He won't die, Father, will he? "

"I do not know, my son. I can find no wound, except the one on his head—nothing seems broken. Perhaps he will be better to-morrow. " He gave the little Irishman his blessing and moved away. There were many eager eyes awaiting him.

Jim was restless during the night; Denny Callaghan, himself unable to sleep, watched him muttering and trying to turn, but unable to move.

"I doubt but his back's broken, " said the little man ruefully. "Yerra, what a pity! " He tried to soothe the boy with kind words; and towards the dawn Jim slept heavily.

He woke when the sun was shining upon him through a rift in the wall. The church was full of smothered sounds—stifled groans from helpless men, stiffened by lying still, and trying to move. Jim managed to raise himself a little, at which Denny Callaghan gave an exclamation of relief.

"Hurroo! Are you better, sir? "

"Where am I? " Jim asked thickly.

"'Tis in a church you are, sir, though it's not much like it, " said the little man. "The Germans call it a hospital. 'Tis all I wish they may have the like themselves, and they wounded. Are you better, sir? "

"I . .. think I'm all right, " Jim said. He was trying to regain his scattered faculties. "So they've got me! " He tried to look at Callaghan. "What's your regiment? "

"The Dubs, sir. 'Tis hard luck; I kem back wounded from Suvla Bay and they sent me out to the battalion here; and I'd not been with them a week before I got landed again. Now 'tis a German prison ahead—and by all one hears they're not rest-camps. "

"No, " said Jim. He tried to move, but failed, sinking back with a stifled groan. "I wish I knew if I was damaged much. Are there any doctors here? "

"There was two, a while back. They fixed us up somehow, and we haven't seen a hair of them since. The guards throw rations—of a sort—at us twice a day. 'Tis badly off we'd be, if it weren't for the priest. "

"Is he French? "

"He is—and a saint, if there ever was one. There he comes now. " Callaghan crossed himself reverently.

A hush had come over the church. The *cure,* in his vestments, had entered, going slowly to the altar.

Captain Jim

Jim struggled up on his elbow. There was perfect silence in the church; men who had been talking ceased suddenly, men who moaned in their pain bit back their cries. So they lay while the little priest celebrated Mass, as he had done every morning since the Germans swept over his village: at first alone, and, since the first few days to a silent congregation of helpless men. They were of all creeds and some of no creed at all: but they prayed after him as men learn to pray when they are at grips with things too big for them. He blessed them, at the end, with uplifted hand; and dim eyes followed him as he went slowly from the church.

He was back among them, presently, in the rusty black cassock. The guards had brought in the men's breakfast—great cans of soup and loaves of hard, dark bread. They put them down near the door, tramping out with complete disregard of the helpless prisoners. The priest would see to them, aided by the few prisoners who could move about, wounded though they were. In any case the guard had no order to feed prisoners; they were not nurse-maids, they said.

"Ah, my son! You are awake! "

Jim smiled up at the *cure.*

"Have I been asleep long, sir? "

"Three days. They brought you in last Friday night. Do you not remember? "

"No, " said Jim. "I don't remember coming here. " He drank some soup eagerly, but shook his head at the horrible bread. The food cleared his head, and when the little *cure* had gone away, promising to return as soon as possible, he lay quietly piecing matters together in his mind. Callaghan helped him: the Dublins had been in the line next his own regiment when they had gone "over the top" on that last morning.

"Oh, I remember all that well enough, " Jim said. "We took two lines of trench, and then they came at us like a wall; the ground was grey with them. And I was up on a smashed traverse, trying to keep the men together, when it went up too. "

"A shell was it? "

Captain Jim

Jim shook his head.

"A shell did burst near us, but it wasn't that. No, the trench was mined, and the mine went off a shade too late. They delayed, somehow; it should have gone off if we took the trench, before they counter-attacked. As it was, it must have killed as many of their men as ours. They told me about it afterwards. "

"Afterwards? " said Callaghan, curiously. He looked at Jim, a little doubtful as to whether he really knew what he was talking about. "Did ye not come straight here then, sir? "

"I did not; I was buried, " said Jim grimly. "The old mine went up right under me, and I went up too. I came down with what seemed like tons of earth on top of me; I was covered right in, I tell you, only I managed to get some of the earth away in front of my nose and mouth. I was lying on my side, near the edge of a big heap of dirt, with my hands near my face. If I'd been six inches further back there wouldn't have been the ghost of a chance for me. I got some of the earth and mud away, and found I could breathe, just as I was choking. But I was buried for all that. All our chaps were fighting on top of me! "

"D'ye tell me! " gasped Callaghan incredulously.

"I could feel the boots, " Jim said. "I'm bruised with them yet. What time did we go over that morning? —nine o'clock, wasn't it? "

"It was, sir. "

"Well, it was twelve or one o'clock when they dug me out. They re-took the trench, and started to dig themselves in, and they found me; I've a spade-cut on my hand. My Aunt, that was a long three hours!"

"Did they treat you decent, sir? "

"They weren't too bad, " Jim said. "I couldn't move; I suppose it was the weight on me, and the bruising—at least, I hope so. They felt me all over—there was a rather decent lieutenant there, who gave me some brandy. He told me he didn't think there was anything broken. But I couldn't stir, and it hurt like fury when they touched me. "

Captain Jim

"And how long were you there, sir? "

"They had to keep me until night—there was no way of sending back prisoners. So I lay on a mud-heap, and the officer-boy talked to me—he had been to school in England. "

"That's where they larned him any decency he had, " said Callaghan.

"It might be. But he wasn't a bad sort. He looked after me well enough. Then, after nightfall, they sent a stretcher party over with me. The German boy shook hands with me when we were starting, and said he was afraid he wouldn't see me again, as we were pretty sure to be shelled by the British. "

"And were you, sir? "

"Rather. The first thing I knew was a bit of shrapnel through the sleeve of my coat; I looked for the hole this morning, to see if I was remembering rightly, and sure enough, here it is. " He held up his arm, and showed a jagged tear in his tunic. "But that's where I stop remembering anything. I suppose I must have caught something else then. Why is my head tied up? It was all right when they began to carry me over. "

"Ye have a lump the size of an egg low down on the back of your head, sir, " said Callaghan. "And a nasty little cut near your temple. "

"H'm! " said Jim. "I wondered why it ached! Well I must have got those from our side on the way across. I hope they got a Boche or two as well. "

"I dunno, " Callaghan said. "The fellas that dumped you down said something in their own haythin tongue. I didn't understand it, but it sounded as if they were glad to be rid of you. "

"Well, I wouldn't blame them, " Jim said. "I'm not exactly a featherweight, and it can't be much fun to be killed carrying the enemy about, whether you're a Boche or not. "

185

He lay for a while silently, thinking. Did they know at home yet? he wondered anxiously. And then he suddenly realized that his fall must have looked like certain death: that if they had heard anything it would be that he had been killed. He turned cold at the thought. *What* had they heard—his father, Norah? And Wally—what did he think? Was Wally himself alive? He might even be a prisoner. He turned at that thought to Callaghan, his sudden move bringing a stifled cry to his lips.

"Did they—are there any other officers of my regiment here? "

"There are not, " said Callaghan. "I got the priest to look at your badges, sir, the way he could find out if there was anny more of ye. But there is not. Them that's here is mostly Dublins and Munsters, with a sprinkling of Canadians. There's not an officer or man of the Blankshires here at all, barring yourself. "

"Will the Germans let us communicate with our people? "

"Communicate, is it? " said the Irishman. "Yerra, they'll not let anyone send so much as a scratch on a post-card. " He dropped his voice. "Whisht now, sir: the priest's taking all our addresses, and he'll do his best to send word to every one at home. "

"But can he depend on getting through? "

"Faith, he cannot. But 'tis the only chance we've got. The poor man's nothing but a prisoner himself; he's watched if he goes tin yards from the church. So I dunno, at all, will he ever manage it, with the suspicions they have of him. "

Jim sighed impatiently. He could do nothing, then, nothing to keep the blow from falling on the two dear ones at home. He thought of trying to bribe the German guards, and felt for his pocket-book, but it was gone; some careful Boche had managed to relieve him of it while he had been unconscious. And he was helpless, a log—while over in England Norah and his father were, perhaps, already mourning him as dead. His thoughts travelled to Billabong, where Brownie and Murty O'Toole and the others kept the home ready for them all, working with the love that makes nothing a toil, and planning always for the great day that should bring them all back. He pictured the news arriving—saw Brownie's dismayed old face, and heard her cry of incredulous pain. And there was nothing he could do. It seemed unbelievable that such things could be, in a sane world. But then, the world was no longer sane; it had gone mad nearly two years before, and he was only one of the myriad atoms caught into the swirl of its madness.

The *cure* came again, presently, and saw his troubled face. "You are in pain, my son? "

"No—I'm all right if I keep quiet, " Jim answered. "But it's my people. Callaghan says you will try to let them know, Father. "

"I am learning you all, " said the priest, "names, regiments, and numbers is it not? I dare not put them on paper: I have been searched three times already, even to my shoes. But I hope that my chance will come before long. Then I will send them to your War Office. " He beamed down on Jim so hopefully that it seemed rather likely that he would find a private telegraph office of his own, suddenly. "Now I will learn your name and regiment. " He repeated them several times, nodding his head.

"Yes, that is an easy one, " he said. "Some of them are very terrible, to a Frenchman; our friend here"—he looked quaintly at Callaghan—"has a name which it twists the tongue to say. And now, my son, I would like to examine you, since you are conscious. I am the only doctor—a poor one, I fear. But perhaps we will find out together that there is nothing to be uneasy about. "

That, indeed, was what they did find out, after a rather agonizing half-hour. Jim was quite unable to move his legs, being so bruised that there was scarcely a square inch of him that was not green and blue and purple. One hip bore the complete impress of a foot, livid and angry.

"Yes, that chap jumped on me from a good height, " Jim said when the *cure* exclaimed at it. "I thought he had smashed my leg. "

"He went near it, " said the *cure*. "Indeed, my son, you are beaten to a jelly. But that will recover itself. You can breathe without pain? That is well. Now we will look at the head. " He unwrapped the bandages and felt the lump tenderly. "Ah, that is better; a little concussion, I think, *mon brave*; it is that which kept you so quiet when you stayed with us at first. And the cut heals well; that comes of being young and strong, with clean, healthy blood. " He bathed the head, and replaced the bandages, sighing that he had no clean ones. "But with you it matters little; you will not need them in a few days. Then perhaps we will wash these and they will be ready for the next poor boy. " He smiled at Jim. "Move those legs as much as you can, my son, and rub them. " He trotted away.

"And that same is good advice, " said Callaghan. "It will hurt to move, sir, and you beaten to a pulp first and then stiffening for the three days you're after lying here; 'tis all I wish I could rub you, with a good bottle of Elliman's to do it with. But if them Huns move you 'twill hurt a mighty lot more than if you move yourself. Themselves is the boys for that; they think they've got a feather in their caps if they get an extra yelp out of annywan. So do the best you can, sir. "

"I will, " said Jim—and did his best, for long hours every day. It was weary work, with each movement torture, and for a time very little encouragement came in the shape of improvement: then, slowly, with rubbing and exercise, the stiffened muscles began to relax. Callaghan cheered him on, forgetting his own aching leg in his sympathy for the boy in his silent torment. In the intervals of "physical jerks, " Jim talked to his little neighbour, whose delight knew no bounds when he heard that Jim knew and cared for his country. He himself was a Cork man, with a wife and two sons; Jim gathered that their equal was not to be found in any town in Ireland. Callaghan occasionally lamented the "foolishness" that had kept him in the Army, when he had a right to be home looking after Hughie and Larry. "'Tis not much the Army gives you, and you giving it the best years of your life, " he said. "I'd be better out of it, and home with me boys. "

"Then you wouldn't let them go to the war, if they were old enough? " Jim asked.

"If they were old enough 'twould not be asking my liberty they'd be, " rejoined Mr. Callaghan proudly. "Is it *my* sons that 'ud shtand out of a fight like this? " He glared at Jim, loftily unconscious of any inconsistency in his remarks.

"Well, there's plenty of your fellow-countrymen that won't go and fight, Cally! " said the man beyond him—a big Yorkshireman.

"There's that in all countries, " said Callaghan calmly. "They didn't all go in your part of the country, did they, till they were made? Faith, I'm towld there's a few there yet in odd corners—and likely to be till after the war. " The men round roared joyfully, at the expense of the Yorkshireman.

"And 'tis not in Ireland we have that quare baste the con-sci-en-tious objector, " went on Callaghan, rolling the syllables lovingly on his tongue. "That's an animal a man wouldn't like to meet, now! Whatever our objectors are in Ireland, they're surely never con-sci-en-tious! "

Jim gave a crack of laughter that brought the roving grey eye squarely upon him.

"Even in Australia, that's the Captain's country, " said the soft Irish voice, "I've heard tell there's a boy or two there out of khaki—maybe they're holding back for conscription too. But wherever the boys are that don't go, none of them have a song and dance made about them, barring only the Irish. "

"What about your Sinn Feiners? " some one sang out. Callaghan's face fell.

"Yerra, they have the country destroyed, " he admitted. "And nine out of every ten don't know annything about politics or annything else at all, only they get talked over, and towld that they're patriots if they'll get howld of a gun and do a little drilling at night—an' where's the country boy that wouldn't give his ears for a gun! An' the English Gov'mint, that could stop it all with the stroke of a pen, hasn't the pluck to bring in conscription in Ireland. "

"You're right there, Cally, " said some one.

"I know well I'm right. But the thousands and tens of thousands of Irish boys that went to the war and fought till they died—they'll be forgotten, and the Sinn Fein scum'll be remembered. If the Gov'mint had the pluck of a mouse they'd be all right. I tell you, boys, 'twill be the Gov'mint's own fault if we see the haythin Turks parading the fair fields of Ireland, with their long tails held up by the Sinn Feiners! " Callaghan relapsed into gloomy contemplation of this awful possibility, and refused to be drawn further. Even when Jim, desiring to be tactful, mentioned a famous Irish V. C. who had, single-handed, slain eight Germans, he declined to show any enthusiasm.

"Ah, what V. C.! " he said sourly. "Sure, his owld father wouldn't make a fuss of him. 'Why didn't he do more? ' says he. 'I often laid out twenty men myself with a stick, and I coming from Macroom Fair. It is a bad trial of Mick that he could kill only eight, and he having a rifle and bayonet! ' he says. Cock him up with a V. C.! " After which Jim ceased to be consoling and began to exercise his worst leg—knowing well that the sight of his torments would speedily melt Denny's heart and make him forget the sorrows of Ireland.

The guards did not trouble them much; they kept a strict watch, which was not difficult, as all the prisoners were partially disabled; and then considered their duty discharged by bringing twice a day the invariable meal of soup and bread. No one liked to speculate on what had gone to the making of the soup; it was a pale, greasy liquid, with strange lumps in it, and tasted as dish-water may be supposed to taste. Jim learned to eat the sour bread by soaking it in the soup. He had no inclination to eat, but he forced himself to swallow the disgusting meals, so that he might keep up his strength, just as he worked his stiff limbs and rubbed them most of the day. For there was but one idea in Jim Linton's mind—escape.

Gradually he became able to sit up, and then to move a little, hobbling painfully on a stick which had been part of a broken pew, and endeavouring to take part in looking after the helpless prisoners, and in keeping the church clean, since the guards laughed at the idea of helping at either. Jim had seen something of the treatment given to wounded German soldiers in England, and he writhed to think of them, tended as though they were our own sick, while British prisoners lay and starved in filthy holes. But the little *cure* rebuked him.

"But what would you, my son? They are *canaille*—without breeding, without decency, without hearts. Are we to put ourselves on that level? "

"I suppose not—but it's a big difference, Father, " Jim muttered.

"The bigger the difference, the more honour on our side, " said the little priest. "And things pass. Long after you and I and all these poor lads are forgotten it will be remembered that we came out of this war with our heads up. But they— —! " Suddenly fierce scorn filled his quiet eyes. "They will be the outcasts of the world! "

Wherefore Jim worked on, and tried to take comfort by the *cure's* philosophy; although there were many times when he found it hard to digest. It was all very well to be cheerful about the verdict of the future, but difficult to forget the insistent present, with the heel of the Hun on his neck. It was sometimes easier to be philosophic by dreaming of days when the positions should be reversed.

He was able to walk a little when the order came to move. The guards became suddenly busy; officers whom the prisoners had not seen before came in and out, and one evening the helpless were put roughly into farm carts and taken to the station, while those able to move by themselves were marched after them—marched quickly, with bayonet points ready behind them to prod stragglers. It was nearly dark when they were thrust roughly into closed trucks, looking back for the last time on the little *cure*, who had marched beside them, with an arm for two sick men, and now stood on the platform, looking wistfully at them. He put up his hand solemnly.

"God keep you, my sons! "

A German soldier elbowed him roughly aside. The doors of the trucks were clashed together, leaving them in darkness; and presently, with straining and rattling and clanging, the train moved out of the station.

"Next stop, Germany! " said Denny Callaghan from the corner where he had been put down. "And not a ticket between the lot of us! "

CHAPTER XVI

THROUGH THE DARKNESS

"I think that's the last load, " Jim Linton said.

He had wriggled backwards out of a black hole in the side of a black cupboard; and now sat back on his heels, gasping. His only article of attire was a pair of short trousers. From his hair to his heels he was caked with dirt.

"Well, praise the pigs for that, " said a voice from the blackness of the cupboard.

Some one switched on a tiny electric light. Then it could be seen, dimly, that the cupboard was just large enough to hold four men, crouching so closely that they almost touched each other. All were dressed—or undressed—as Jim was; all were equally dirty. Their blackened faces were set and grim. And whether they spoke, or moved, or merely sat still, they were listening—listening.

All four were British officers. Marsh and Fullerton were subalterns belonging to a cavalry regiment. Desmond was a captain—a Dublin Fusilier; and Jim Linton completed the quartette; and they sat in a hole in the ground under the floor of an officers' barrack in a Westphalian prison-camp. The yawning opening in front of them represented five months' ceaseless work, night after night. It was the mouth of a tunnel.

"I dreamed to-day that we crawled in, " Marsh said, in a whisper— they had all learned to hear the faintest murmur of speech. "And we crawled, and crawled, and crawled: for years, it seemed. And then we saw daylight ahead, and we crawled out—in Piccadilly Circus! "

"That was 'some' tunnel, even in a dream, " Desmond said.

"I feel as if it were 'some' tunnel now, " remarked Jim—still breathing heavily.

"Yes—you've had a long spell, Linton. We were just beginning to think something was wrong. "

"I thought I might as well finish—and then another bit of roof fell in, and I had to fix it, " Jim answered. "Well, it won't be gardening that I'll go in for when I get back to Australia; I've dug enough here to last me my life! "

"Hear, hear! " said some one. "And what now? "

"Bed, I think, " Desmond said. "And to-morrow night—the last crawl down that beastly rabbit-run, if we've luck. Only this time we won't crawl back. "

He felt within a little hollow in the earth wall, and brought out some empty tins and some bottles of water; and slowly, painstakingly, they washed off the dirt that encrusted them. It was a long business, and at the end of it Desmond inspected them all, and was himself inspected, to make sure that no tell-tale streaks remained. Finally he nodded, satisfied, and then, with infinite caution, he slid back a panel and peered out into blackness—having first extinguished their little light. There was no sound. He slipped out of the door, and returned after a few moments.

"All clear, " he whispered, and vanished.

One by one they followed him, each man gliding noiselessly away. They had donned uniform coats and trousers before leaving, and closed the entrance to the tunnel with a round screen of rough, interlaced twigs which they plastered with earth. The tins were buried again, with the bottles. Ordinarily each man carried away an empty bottle, to be brought back next night filled with water; but there was no further need of this. To-morrow night, please God, there would be no returning; no washing, crouched in the darkness, to escape the eagle eye of the guards; no bitter toil in the darkness, listening with strained ears all the while.

Jim was the last to leave. He slid the panel into position, and placed against it the brooms and mops used in keeping the barrack clean. As he handled them one by one, a brush slipped and clattered ever so slightly. He caught at it desperately, and then stood motionless, beads of perspiration breaking out upon his forehead. But no sound came from without, and presently he breathed more freely.

He stood in a cupboard under the stairs. It was Desmond who first realized that there must be space beyond it, who had planned a way in, and thence to cut a tunnel to freedom. They had found, or stolen, or manufactured, tools, and had cut the sliding panel so cunningly that none of the Germans who used the broom-cupboard had suspected its existence. The space on the far side of the wall had given them room to begin their work. Gradually it had been filled with earth until there was barely space for them to move; then the earth as they dug it out had to be laboriously thrust under the floor of the building, which was luckily raised a little above ground. They had managed to secrete some wire, and, having tapped the electric supply which lit the barrack, had carried a switch-line into their "dug-out. " But the tunnel itself had, for the most part, been done in utter blackness. Three times the roof had fallen in badly, on the second occasion nearly burying Jim and Fullerton; it was considered, now, that Linton was a difficult man to bury, with an unconquerable habit of resurrecting himself. A score of times they had narrowly escaped detection. For five months they had lived in a daily and nightly agony of fear—not of discovery itself, or its certain savage punishment, but of losing their chance.

There were eight officers altogether in the "syndicate, " and four others knew of their plan—four who were keen to help, but too badly disabled from wounds to hope for anything but the end of the war. They worked in shifts of four—one quartette stealing underground each night, as soon as the guards relaxed their vigil, while the others remained in the dormitories, ready to signal to the working party, should any alarm occur, and, if possible, to create a disturbance to hold the attention of the Germans for a little. They had succeeded in saving the situation three times when a surprise roll-call was made during the night—thanks to another wire which carried an electric alarm signal underground from the dormitory. Baylis, who had been an electrical engineer in time of peace, had managed the wiring; it was believed among the syndicate that when Baylis needed any electric fitting very badly he simply went and thought about it so hard that it materialized, like the gentleman who evolved a camel out of his inner consciousness.

One of the romances of the Great War might be written about the way in which prisoners bent on escape were able to obtain materials for getting out, and necessary supplies when once they were away from the camp. Much of how it was done will never be known, for the organization was kept profoundly secret, and those who were helped by it were often pledged solemnly to reveal nothing. Money—plenty of money—was the only thing necessary; given the command of that, the prisoner who wished to break out would find, mysteriously, tools or disguises, or whatever else he needed within the camp, and, after he had escaped, the three essentials, without which he had very little chance—map, compass, and civilian clothes. Then, having paid enormous sums for what had probably cost the supply system a few shillings, he was at liberty to strike for freedom—with a section of German territory—a few miles or a few hundred—to cross; and finally the chance of circumventing the guards on the Dutch frontier. It was so desperate an undertaking that the wonder was, not that so many failed, but that so many succeeded.

Jim Linton had no money. His was one of the many cases among prisoners in which no letters over seemed to reach home—no communication to be opened up with England. For some time he had not been permitted to write, having unfortunately managed to incur the enmity of the camp commandant by failing to salute him with the precise degree of servility which that official considered necessary to his dignity. Then, when at length he was allowed to send an occasional letter, he waited in vain for any reply, either from his home or his regiment. Possibly the commandant knew why; he used to look at Jim with an evil triumph in his eye which made the boy long to take him by his fat throat and ask him whether indeed his letters ever got farther than the office waste-paper basket.

Other officers in the camp would have written about him to their friends, so that the information could be passed on to Jim's father; but in all probability their letters also would have been suppressed, and Jim refused to allow them to take the risk. Letters were too precious, and went astray too easily; it was not fair to add to the chances of their failing to reach those who longed for them at home. And then, there was always the hope that his own might really have got through, even though delayed; that some day might come answers, telling that at last his father and Norah and Wally were no longer mourning him as dead. He clung to the hope though one mail day after another left him bitterly disappointed. In a German prison-camp there was little to do except hope.

Jim would have fared badly enough on the miserable food of the camp, but for the other officers. They received parcels regularly, the contents of which were dumped into a common store; and Jim and another "orphan" were made honorary members of the mess, with such genuine heartiness that after the first protests they ceased to worry their hosts with objections, and merely tried to eat as little as possible.

Jim thought about them gratefully on this last night as he slipped out of the cupboard and made his way upstairs, moving noiselessly as a cat on the bare boards. What good chaps they were! How they had made him welcome! —even though his coming meant that they went hungrier. They were such a gay, laughing little band; there was not one of them who did not play the game, keeping a cheery front to the world and meeting privation and wretchedness with a joke and a shrug. If that was British spirit, then Jim decided that to be British was a pretty big thing.

It was thanks to Desmond and Fullerton that he had been able to join the "syndicate. " They had plenty of money, and had insisted on lending him his share of the expenses, representing, when he had hesitated, that they needed his strength for the work of tunnelling— after which Jim had laboured far more mightily than they had ever wished, or even suspected. He was fit and strong again now; lean and pinched, as were they all, but in hard training. Hope had keyed him up to a high pitch. The last night in this rat-hole; to-morrow—!

A light flashed downstairs and a door flung open just as he reached the landing. Jim sprang to his dormitory, flinging off his coat as he ran with leaping, stealthy strides. Feet were tramping up the stairs behind him. He dived into his blankets and drew them up under his chin, just as he had dived hurriedly into bed a score of times at school when an intrusive master had come upon a midnight "spread"; but with his heart pounding with fear as it had never pounded at school. What did they suspect? Had they found out anything?

The guard tramped noisily into the room, under a big Feldwebel, or sergeant-major. He flashed his lantern down the long room, and uttered a sharp word of command that brought the sleepers to their feet, blinking and but half awake. Then he called the roll, pausing when he came to Jim.

"You sleep in a curious dress. Where is your shirt? "

"Drying, " said Jim curtly. "I washed it—I've only one. "

"Enough for an English swine-hound, " said the German contemptuously. He passed on to the next man, and Jim sighed with relief.

Presently the guard clanked out, and the prisoners returned to their straw mattresses.

"That was near enough, " whispered Baylis, who was next to Jim.

"A good deal too near, " Jim answered. "However, it ought to be fairly certain that they won't spring another surprise-party on us to-morrow. And a miss is as good as a mile. " He turned over, and in a moment was sleeping like a baby.

The next day dragged cruelly.

To the eight conspirators it seemed as long as the weary stretch of months since they had come to the camp. For a long while they had avoided each other as far as possible in public, knowing that even two men who talked much together were liable to be suspected of plotting; on this last day they became afraid even to look at each other, and wandered about, each endeavouring to put as great a distance as possible between himself and the other seven. It became rather like a curious game of hide-and-seek, and by evening they were thoroughly "jumpy, " with their nerves all on edge.

They had no preparations to make. Scarcely any of their few possessions could be taken with them; they would find outside—if ever they got there—food and clothing. They had managed to make rough knives that were fairly serviceable weapons; beyond these, and a few small personal belongings they took nothing except the clothes they wore—and they wore as little as possible, and those the oldest and shabbiest things to be found. So there was nothing to do, all that last day, but watch the slow hours pass, and endeavour to avoid falling foul of any of the guards—no easy matter, since every German delighted in any chance of making trouble for a prisoner. Nothing but to think and plan, as they had planned and thought a thousand times before; to wonder desperately was all safe still—had the door been found in the cupboard under the stairs? was the tunnel safe, or had it chosen to-day of all days to fall in again? was the exit—in a bed of runner beans—already known and watched? The Huns were so cunning in their watchfulness; it was quite likely that they knew all about their desperate enterprise, and were only waiting to pounce upon them in the instant that success should seem within their grasp. That was how they loved to catch prisoners.

The age-long afternoon dragged to a close. They ate their supper, without appetite—which was a pity, since the meagre store of food in the mess had been recklessly ransacked, to give them a good send-off. Then another hour—muttering good-byes now and then, as they prowled about; and finally, to bed, to lie there for hours of darkness and silence. Gradually the noise of the camp died down. From the guard-room came, for a while, loud voices and harsh laughter; then quiet fell there too, and presently the night watch tramped through the barrack on its last visit of inspection, flashing lanterns into the faces of the prisoners. To-night the inspection seemed unusually thorough. It set their strained nerves quivering anew.

Then came an hour of utter stillness and darkness; the eight prisoners lying with clenched hands and set teeth, listening with terrible intentness. Finally, when Jim was beginning to feel that he must move, or go mad, a final signal came from the doorway. He heard Baylis say "Thank God! " under his breath, as they slipped out of bed in the darkness and felt their way downstairs. They were the last to come. The others were all crouched in the cupboard, waiting for them, as they reached its door; and just as they did so, the outer doorway swung open, with a blaze of light, and the big Feldwebel strode in.

"Shut the door! " Jim whispered. He launched himself at the German as he spoke, with a spring like a panther's. His fist caught him between the eyes and he went down headlong, the lantern rolling into a corner. Jim knew nothing of what followed. He was on top of the Feldwebel, pounding his head on the floor; prepared, in his agony of despair, to do as much damage as possible before his brief dash for freedom ended. Then he felt a hand on his shoulder, and heard Desmond's sharp whisper.

"Steady—he's unconscious. Let me look at him, Linton. "

Jim, still astride his capture, sat back, and Desmond flashed the Feldwebel's own lantern into that hero's face.

"H'm, yes, " he said. "Hit his head against something. He's stunned, anyhow. What are we going to do with him? "

"Is he the only one? " Jim asked.

"It seems like it. But there may be another at any moment. We've got to go on; if he wakes up he'll probably be able to identify you. " He felt in his pocket, and produced a coil of strong cord. "Come along, Linton—get off and help me to tie him up. "

They tied up the unconscious Feldwebel securely, and lifted him into the cupboard among the brooms, gagging him in case he felt inclined for any outcry on coming to his senses. The others had gone ahead, and were already in the tunnel; with them, one of the four disabled officers, whose job it was to close up the hole at the entrance and dismantle the electric light, in the faint hope that the Germans might fail to discover their means of escape, and so leave it free for another party to try for freedom. He stood by the yawning hole, holding one end of a string by which they were to signal from the surface, if all went well. The wistfulness of his face haunted Jim long afterwards.

"Good-bye, old man, " he said cheerily, gripping Jim's hand. "Good luck. "

"I wish you were coming, Harrison, " Jim said, unhappily.

"No such luck. Cheero, though: the war won't last for ever. I'll see you in Blighty. " They shook hands again, and Jim dived into the tunnel.

He knew every inch of it, and wriggled quickly along until the top of his head encountered the boots of the man in front of him, after which he went more slowly. There seemed a long delay at the end— long enough to make him break into a sweat of fear lest something should have gone wrong. Such thoughts come easily enough when you are lying full length in black darkness, in a hole just large enough to hold a man; in air so stifling that the laboured breath can scarcely come; with the dank earth just under mouth and nose, and overhead a roof that may fall in at any moment. The dragging minutes went by. Then, just as despair seized him, the boots ahead moved. He wriggled after them, finding himself praying desperately as he went. A rush of sweet air came to him, and then a hand, stretching down, caught his shoulder, and helped him out.

It was faintly moonlight. They stood in a thick plantation of runner beans, trained on rough trellis-work, in a garden beyond the barbed-wire fence of the camp. The tunnel had turned sharply upwards at the end; they had brought with them some boards and other materials for filling it up, and now they set to work furiously, after giving the signal with the string to Harrison; the three sharp tugs that meant "All Clear! " The boards held the earth they shovelled in with their hands; they stamped it flat, and then scattered loose earth on top, with leaves and rubbish, working with desperate energy — fearing each moment to hear the alarm raised within the barrack. Finally all but Desmond gained the beaten earth of the path, while he followed, trying to remove all trace of footprints on the soft earth. He joined them in a moment.

"If they don't worry much about those beans for a few days they may not notice anything, " he said. "Come along. "

So often had they studied the way from behind the barbed-wire that they did not need even the dim moonlight. They hurried through the garden with stealthy strides, bending low behind a row of currant-bushes, and so over a low hedge and out into a field beyond. There they ran; desperately at first, and gradually slackening to a steady trot that carried them across country for a mile, and then out upon a highroad where there was no sign of life. At a cross-roads two miles further on they halted.

"We break up here, " Desmond said. "You can find your *cache* all right, you think, Baylis? "

"Oh, yes, " Baylis nodded. It had been thought too dangerous for so many to try to escape together, so two hiding-places of clothes and food had been arranged. Later they would break up again into couples.

"Then we'd better hurry. Good night, you fellows, and good luck. We'll have the biggest dinner in Blighty together—when we all get there! "

"Good luck! "

Baylis led his party down a road to the east, and Jim, Fullerton and Marsh struck south after Desmond, who paused now and then to consult a rough map, by a pocket-lamp. On and on, by a network of lanes, skirting farmhouses where dogs might bark; flinging themselves flat in a ditch once, when a regiment of Uhlans swept by, unconscious of the gasping fugitives a few yards away. Jim sat up and looked after their retreating ranks.

"By Jove, I wish we could borrow a few of their horses! "

"Might buck you off, my son, " said Desmond. "Come on. "

A little wood showed before them presently, and Desmond sighed with relief.

"That's our place, I think. " He looked at the map again. "We've got to make for the south-west corner and find a big, hollow tree. "

They brushed through the close-growing firs, starting in fear as an owl flew out above them, hooting dismally. It was not easy to find anything, for the moonlight was scarcely able to filter through the branches. Jim took the lead, and presently they scattered to look for the tree. Something big loomed up before Jim presently.

"It should be about here, " he muttered, feeling with his hand for the hollow. Then, as he encountered a roughly-tied bundle, he whistled softly, and in a moment brought them all to his side.

There were four rough suits of clothes in the package; a big bag of bread, meat, and chocolate; and, most precious of all, a flat box containing maps, compasses, and some German money. They changed hurriedly, thrusting their uniforms deep into the hollow of the tree and covering them with leaves; and then divided the food. There was a faint hint of dawn in the sky when at length their preparations were complete.

"Well, you know your general direction, boys, " Desmond said to Marsh and Fullerton. "Get as far as you can before light, and then hide for the day. Hide well, remember; they'll be looking for us pretty thoroughly to-day. Good luck! " They shook hands and hurried away in different directions.

Desmond and Jim came out into open fields beyond the wood, and settled down to steady running over field after field. Sometimes they stumbled over ploughed land; sometimes made their way between rows of mangolds or turnips, where their feet sank deeply into the yielding soil; then, with a scramble through a ditch or hedge, came upon grass land where sheep or cows gazed stolidly at the shadowy, racing figures. The east brightened with long streaks of pink; slowly the darkness died, and the yellow circle of the sun came up over the horizon, and found them still running—casting anxious glances to right and left in search of a hiding-place.

"Hang these open fields! —will they never end! " Desmond gasped. "We should be under cover now. "

Behind a little orchard a farm-house came into view; they were almost upon a cow-house. It was daylight; a window in the house rattled up, and a man shouted to a barking dog. The fugitives ducked by a sudden impulse, and darted into the cow-shed.

It was a long, low building, divided into stables. There was no hiding-place visible, and despair held them for a moment. Then Jim caught sight of a rough ladder leading to an opening in the ceiling, and flung his hand towards it; he had no speech left. They went up it hand over hand, and found themselves in a dim loft, with pea-straw heaped at one end. Desmond was almost done.

"Lie down—quick! " Jim pushed him into the straw and covered him over with great bundles of it. Then he crawled in himself, pulling the rough pea-stalks over him until he had left himself only a peep-hole commanding the trap-door. As he did so, voices came into the stable.

They held their breath, feeling for their knives. Then Desmond smothered a laugh.

"What did they say? " Jim whispered.

"It would be 'Bail up, Daisy! ' in English, " Desmond whispered back. "They're beginning to milk the cows. "

"I wish they'd milk Daisy up here, " Jim grinned. "Man, but I'm thirsty! "

It was thirsty work, lying buried in the dusty pea-straw, in the close, airless loft. Hours went by, during which they dared not move, for when the milking was done, and the cows turned out, people kept coming and going in the shed. They picked up a little information about the war from their talk—Jim's German was scanty, but Desmond spoke it like a native; and in the afternoon a farmer from some distance away, who had apparently come to buy pigs, let fall the remark that a number of prisoners had escaped from the English camp. No one seemed much interested; the war was an incident, not really mattering so much, in their estimation, as the sale of the pigs. Then every one went away, and Jim and his companion fell asleep.

It was nearly dark when they awoke. The sleep had done them good, but they were overpoweringly thirsty—so thirsty that the thought of food without drink was nauseating. The evening milking was going on; they could hear the rattle of the streams of milk into the pails, in the intervals of harsh voices. Then the cows were turned out and heavy feet stamped away.

"They should all be out of the way pretty soon, " Desmond whispered. "Then we can make a move. We must get to water somehow, or——" He broke off, listening. "Lie still! " he added quickly. "Some one is coming up for straw. "

"How do you know? "

"'Tis a young lady, and she volunteering to see to bedding for the pigs! " Desmond answered.

The ladder creaked, and, peering out, they saw a shock yellow head rise into the trap-door. The girl who came up was about twenty—stoutly built, with a broad, good-humoured face. She wore rough clothes, and but for her two thick plaits of yellow hair, might easily have passed for a man.

The heavy steps came slowly across the floor, while the men lay trying to breath so softly that no unusual movement should stir the loose pea-straw. Then, to their amazement, she spoke.

"Where are you? " she said in English.

Astonishment as well as fear held them silent. She waited a moment, and spoke again.

"I saw you come in. You need not be afraid. "

Still they made no sign. She gave a short laugh.

"Well, if you will not answer, I must at least get my straw for my pigs. "

She stooped, and her great arms sent the loose stalks flying in every direction. Desmond and Jim sat up and looked at her in silence.

"You don't seem to want to be killed, " Desmond said. "But assuredly you will be, if you raise an alarm. "

The girl laughed.

"I could have done that all day, if I had wished, " she said. "Ever since I saw you run in when I put up my window this morning. "

"Well—what do you want? Money? "

"No. " She shook her head. "I do not want anything. I was brought up in England, and I think this is a silly war. There is a bucket of milk for you downstairs; it will come up if one of you will pull the string you will find tied to the top of the ladder. " She laughed. "If I go to get it you will think I am going to call for help. "

Jim was beyond prudence at the moment. He took three strides to the ladder, found the cord, and pulled up a small bucket, three parts full of new milk. The girl sat down on an empty oil-drum and watched them drink.

"So! You are thirsty, indeed, " she said. "Now I have food. "

She unearthed from a huge pocket a package of bread and sausage.

"Now you can eat. It is quite safe, and you could not leave yet; my uncle is still wandering about. He is like most men; they wander about and are very busy, but they never do any work. I run the farm, and get no wages, either. But in England I got wages. In Clapham. That is the place of all others which I prefer. "

"Do you, indeed? " Desmond said, staring at this amazing female. "But why did you leave Clapham? "

"My father came back to fight. He knew all about the war; he left England two months before it began. I did not wish to leave. I desired to remain, earning good wages. But my father would not permit me. "

"And where is he now? "

She shrugged her shoulders.

"I do not know. Fighting: killed, perhaps. But my uncle graciously offered me a home, and here am I. I do the work of three men, and I am—how did we say it in Clapham? —bored stiff for England. I wish this silly old war would end, so that I could return. "

"We're trying to return without waiting for it to end, " said Jim solemnly. "Only I'd like to know how you knew what we were. "

"But what else could you be? It is so funny how you put on these clothes, like the ostrich, and think no one will guess who you are. If you wore his suit of feathers you would still look like British officers and nothing else. "

"You're encouraging, " said Desmond grimly. "I hope all your nation won't be as discerning. "

"Ach—they! " said the girl. "They see no farther than their noses. I, too, was like that before I went to Clapham. "

"It's a pleasant spot, " said Desmond. "I don't wonder you improved there. But all the same, you are German, aren't you? I don't quite see why you want to befriend us. " He took a satisfying mouthful of sausage. "But I'm glad you do. "

"In England I am—well, pretty German, " said his fair hostess. "The boys in Clapham, they call me Polly Sauer Kraut. And I talk of the

Fatherland, and sing 'Die Wacht am Rhein. ' Oh yes. But when I come back here and work for my so economical uncle on this beastly farm, then I remember Clapham and I do not feel German at all. I cannot help it. But if I said so, I would skinned be, very quickly. So I say 'Gott Strafe England! ' But that is only eyewash! "

"Well, we'll think kindly of one German woman, anyhow, " said Desmond. "The last of your charming sisters I met was a Red Cross nurse at a station where our train pulled up when I was going through, wounded. I asked her for a glass of water, and she brought it to me all right—only just as she gave it to me she spat in it. I've been a woman-hater ever since, until I met you. " He lifted the bucket, and looked at her over its rim. "Here's your very good health, Miss Polly Sauer Kraut, and may I meet you in Clapham! "

The girl beamed.

"Oh, I will be there, " she said confidently. "I have money in the Bank in London: I will have a little baker shop, and you will get such pastry as the English cannot make. "

Jim laughed.

"And then you will be pretty German again! "

"I do not know. " She shook her head. "No, I think I will just be Swiss. They will not know the difference in Clapham. And I do not think they will want Germans back. Of course, the Germans will go—but they will call themselves Swiss, Poles, any old thing. Just at first, until the English forget: the English always forget, you know. "

"If they forget all they've got to remember over this business—well then, they deserve to get the Germans back, " said Desmond, grimly. "Always excepting yourself, Miss Polly. You'd be an ornament to whichever nation you happened to favour at the moment. " He finished the last remnant of his sausage. "That was uncommonly good, thank you. Now, don't you think we could make a move? "

"I will see if my uncle is safely in. Then I will whistle. " She ran down the ladder, and presently they heard a low call, and going down, found her awaiting them in the cow-shed.

"He is at his supper, so all is quite safe, " she said. "Now you had better take the third road to the right, and keep straight on. It is not so direct as the main road, but that would lead you through several places where the police are very active—and there is a reward for you, you know! " She laughed, her white teeth flashing in the dim shed. "Good-bye; and when I come back to Clapham you will come and take tea at my little shop. "

"We'll come and make you the fashion, Miss Polly, " said Desmond. "Thank you a thousand times. " They swung off into the dusk.

CHAPTER XVII
LIGHTS OUT

"There was two of every single thing in the Ark, " said Geoffrey firmly. "The man in Church read it out of the Bible. "

"Two Teddy-bears? " asked Alison.

"No; Teddies are only toys. There was real bears, though. "

"Meat ones? " asked his sister hopefully.

"Yes. And all the other nanimals. "

"Who drived 'em in? "

"Ole Noah and Mrs. Noah. Mustn't they have had a time! If you tried to drive in our turkeys an sheep and cows together there'd be awful trouble—and Noah had lions and tigers and snakes too. "

"Perhaps he had good sheep-dogs, " Norah suggested. She was sewing with Mrs. Hunt under a tree on the lawn, while the children played with a Noah's Ark on a short-legged table near them.

"He'd need them, " Geoffrey said. "But would sheep-dogs be any good at driving snakes and porklepines, Norah? "

"Noah's might have been, " Norah answered prudently. "They must have been used to it, you see. And I believe a good sheep-dog would get used to anything. "

"Funny things ole Noah and his fam'ly wore, " said Geoffrey, looking at Japhet with disfavour. "Like dressing-gowns, only worse. Wouldn't have been much good for looking after nanimals in. Why, even the Land Army girls wear trousers now! "

"Well, fashions were different then, " said Mrs. Hunt. "Perhaps, too, they took off the dressing-gowns when they got inside the Ark, and had trousers underneath. "

"Where'd they keep all the food for the nanimals, anyhow? " Geoffrey demanded. "They'd want such a lot, and it would have to be all different sorts of food. Tigers wouldn't eat vegi-tubbles, like rabbits. "

"And efalunts would eat buns, " said Alison anxiously. "Did Mrs. Noah make vem buns? "

"She couldn't, silly, unless she had a gas-stove, " said Geoffrey. "They couldn't carry firewood as well. I say, Mother, don't you think the Ark must have had a supply-ship following round, like the Navy has? "

"It isn't mentioned, " said Mrs. Hunt.

"I say! " said Geoffrey, struck by a new idea that put aside the question of supply. "Just fancy if a submarine had torpedoed the Ark! Wouldn't it have been exciting! "

"Let's do it in the bath, " said Alison, delightedly.

"All right, " Geoffrey said. "May we, Mother? "

"Oh, yes, if you don't get too wet, " his mother said resignedly. "They can all swim, that's a comfort.

"We'll muster them, " said Geoffrey, bundling the animals into a heap. "Hand over that bird, Alison. I say, Mother, which came first, a fowl or an egg? "

Mrs. Hunt sighed.

"It isn't mentioned, " she said. "Which do you think? "

"Fowl, I 'specs, " answered her son.

"*I* fink it was ve egg, " said Alison.

"How would it be hatched if it was, silly? " demanded her brother. "They didn't have ink-ink-inklebaters then. "

Captain Jim

Alison puckered her brows, and remained undefeated.

"P'raps Adam sat on it, " she suggested.

"I cannot imagine Adam being broody, " said Mrs. Hunt.

"Well, anyhow, he hatched out Eve! " said Geoffrey. No one ventured to combat this statement, and the children formed themselves into a stretcher party, bearing the Ark and its contents upon a tray in the direction of the bathroom.

"Aren't they darlings? " Norah said, laughing. "Look at that Michael! "

Michael was toddling behind the stretcher-party as fast as his fat legs would permit, uttering short and sharp shrieks of anguish lest he should be forgotten. Geoffrey gave the order, "Halt! " and the Ark and its bearers came to a standstill.

"Come along, kid, " said the commanding officer. "You can be the band. " The procession was re-formed with Michael in the lead, tooting proudly on an imaginary bugle. They disappeared within the house.

"They are growing so big and strong, " said Mrs. Hunt thankfully. "Michael can't wear any of the things that fitted Geoff at his age; as for Alison, nothing seems to fit her for more than a month or two; then she gracefully bursts out of her garments! As for Geoff——! But he is getting really too independent: he went off by himself to the village yesterday, and I found him playing football behind one of the cottages with a lot of small boys. "

"Oh—did you? " Norah said, looking a little worried. "We heard just before I came over this morning that there is a case of fever in the village—some travelling tinker-people seem to have brought it. Dad said I must tell you we had better not let the children go down there for the present. "

"There were some gipsy-looking boys among the crowd that Geoff was playing with, " Mrs. Hunt said anxiously. "I do hope he hasn't run any risk. He is wearing the same clothes, too—I'll take them off him, and have them washed. " She gathered up her sewing hurriedly. "But I think Geoff is strong enough now to resist any germ. "

"Oh, of course he is, " Norah answered. "Still, it doesn't do any harm to take precautions. I'll come and help you, Mrs. Hunt. "

Geoffrey, congenially employed as a submarine commander about to torpedo the Ark, was distinctly annoyed at being reduced to a mere small boy, and an unclad one at that.

"I don't see why you want to undress me in the middle of the morning, " he said, wriggling out of his blue jersey. "And it isn't washing-day, either, and Alison and Michael'll go and sink the Ark without me if you don't hurry. "

"I won't let them, Geoff, " Norah reassured him. "I'm an airship commander cruising round over the submarine, and she doesn't dare to show so much as the tip of her periscope. Of course, when her captain comes back, he'll know what to do! "

"Rather! " said the Captain, wriggling this time in ecstasy. "I'll just put up my anti-aircraft gun and blow the old airship to smithereens."

Alison uttered a howl.

"*Won't* have Norah made into smivvereens! "

"Don't you worry darling, I'll dodge, " said Norah.

"Michael, what are you doing with Mrs. Noah? "

"Not want my dear 'ickle Mrs. Noah dwowned, " said Michael, concealing the lady yet more securely in his tiny pocket. "She good. Michael *loves* her. "

"Oh, rubbish, Michael! put her back in the Ark, " said Geoffrey wrathfully. "However can we have a proper submarining if you go and collar half the things? "

"Never collared nuffig, " said Michael, unmoved. "Only tooked my dear 'ickle Mrs. Noah. "

"Never mind Geoff—he's only a small boy, " Mrs. Hunt said.

"*Isn't* a small boy! " protested Michael furiously. "Daddy said I was 'normous. "

"So you are, best-beloved, " laughed Norah, catching him up. "Now the submarine commander has on clean clothes, and you'd better get ready to go on duty. " Geoffrey dashed back to the bath with a shout of defiance to the airship, and the destruction of the Ark proceeded gaily.

"There! " said Mrs. Hunt, putting Geoffrey's garments into a tub. "It's just as well to have them washed, but I really don't think there's any need to worry. "

"I don't think you need, indeed! " said Norah, laughing, as a medley of sound came from the bathroom.

It was an "off" day for Norah. With Miss de Lisle she had potted and preserved every variety of food that would lend itself to such treatment, and now the working season was almost over. For the first time the Home for Tired People had not many inmates, owing to the fact that leave had been stopped for several men at the Front who had arranged to spend their holiday at Homewood. They had with them an elderly colonel and his wife; Harry Trevor and another Australian; a silent Major who played golf every hour of daylight, and read golf literature during the other part of the day; and a couple of sappers, on final leave after recovering from wounds. To-day the Colonel and his wife had gone up to London; the others, with the exception of Major Mackay, who, as usual, might be seen afar upon the links, had gone with Mr. Linton to a sale where he hoped to secure some unusually desirable pigs; the sappers, happy in ignorance, promised themselves much enjoyment in driving them home. Left alone, therefore, Norah had gone for the day to Mrs. Hunt, ostensibly to improve her French and needlework, but in reality to play with the babies. Just how much the Hunt babies had helped her only Norah herself knew.

"I'm asked to a festivity the day after to-morrow, " Mrs. Hunt said that afternoon. They were having tea in the pleasant sitting-room of the cottage; sounds from the kitchen indicated that Eva was giving her celebrated performance of a grizzly bear for the benefit of the children. The performance always ended with a hunt, and with the slaying of the quarry by Geoffrey, after which the bear expired with lingering and unpleasant details. "Douglas's Colonel is in London on leave, and he and his wife have asked me to dine and go to a theatre afterwards. It would mean staying in London that night, of course. "

"So of course you'll go? "

"I should love to go, " Mrs. Hunt admitted. "It would be jolly in itself, and then I should hear something about Douglas; and all he ever tells me about himself might be put on a field postcard. If the babies are quite well, Norah, do you think you would mind taking charge? "

Norah laughed. She had occasionally come to sleep at the cottage during a brief absence on Mrs. Hunt's part, and liked nothing better.

"I should love to come, " she said. "But you'd better not put it that way, or Eva will be dreadfully injured. "

"I don't—to Eva, " smiled Mrs. Hunt. "She thinks you come over in case she should need any one to run an errand, and therefore permits herself to adore you. In fact, she told me yesterday, that for a young lady you had an uncommon amount of sense! "

"Jim would have said that was as good as a diploma, " Norah said, laughing.

"I rather think so, myself, " Mrs. Hunt answered. "What about Wally, Norah? Have you heard lately? "

"Yesterday, " Norah replied. "He decorated his letter with beautiful people using pen-wipers, so I suppose he is near Ypres. He says he's very fit. But the fighting seems very stiff. I'm not happy about Wally."

"Do you think he isn't well? "

"I don't think his mind is well, " said Norah. "He was better here, before he went back, but now that he is out again I believe he just can't bear being without Jim. He can't think of him happily, as we do; he only fights his trouble, and hates himself for being alive. He doesn't say so in words, but when you know Wally as well as Dad and I do, you can tell form his letters. He used to write such cheery, funny letters, and now he deliberately tries to be funny—and it's pretty terrible. "

She paused, and suddenly a little sob came. Mrs. Hunt stroked her hand, saying nothing.

"Do you know, " Norah said presently, "I think we have lost Wally more than Jim. Jim died, but the real Jim is ever close in our hearts, and we never let him go, and we can talk and laugh about him, just as if he was here. But the real Wally seems to have died altogether, and we've only the shell left. Something in him died when he saw Jim killed. Mrs. Hunt—do you think he'll ever be better? "

"I think he will, " Mrs. Hunt said. "He is too fine and plucky to be always like this. You have to remember that he is only a boy, and that he had the most terrible shock that could come to him. It must take time to recover. "

"I know, " Norah said. "I tried to think like that—but it hurts so, that one can't help him. We would do anything to make him feel better. "

"And you will, in time. Remember, you and your father are more to him than any one else in the world. Make him feel you want him; I think nothing else can help him so much. " Mrs. Hunt's eyes were full of tears. "He was such a merry lad—it breaks one's heart to think of him as he is. "

"He was always the cheerfullest person I ever saw, " said Norah. "He just laughed through everything. I remember once when he was bitten by a snake, and it was hours before we could get a doctor. We were nearly mad with anxiety, and he was in horrible pain with the tourniquet, but he joked through it all in the most ridiculous way. And he was always so eager. It's the last thing you could call him now. All the spring has gone out of him. "

"It will come back, " Mrs. Hunt said. "Only keep on trying—let him see how much he means to you. "

"Well, he's all we have left, " said Norah. There was silence for a moment; and then it was a relief when the children burst into the room.

They all went to the station two days later to see Mrs. Hunt off for her excursion. Michael was not to be depended upon to remain brave when a train actually bore his mother away, so they did not wait to see her go; there were errands to be done in the village, and Norah bundled them all into the governess-cart, giving Geoffrey the reins, to his huge delight. He turned his merry face to his mother.

"Good-bye, darling! Take care of yourself in London Town! "

"I will, " said his mother. "Mind you take care of all the family. You're in charge, you know, Geoff. "

"Rather! " he said. "I'm G. O.C., and they've got to do what I tell them, haven't they? And Mother—tell the Colonel to send Father home. "

"Then you won't be G. O.C., " said Norah.

"Don't want to be, if Father comes, " said Geoffrey, his eyes dancing. "You'll tell him, won't you, Mother? "

"Indeed I will, " she said. "Now, off you go. Don't put the cart into the ditch, Geoff! "

"Isn't you insulting, " said her son loftily. "But womens don't understand! " He elevated his nose—and then relented to fling her kisses as the pony trotted off. Mrs. Hunt stood at the station entrance to watch him for a moment—sitting very straight and stiff, holding his whip at the precise angle taught by Jones. It was such a heartsome sight that the incoming train took her by surprise, and she had barely time to get her ticket and rush for a carriage.

Norah and her charges found so much to do in the village that when they reached home it was time for Michael's morning sleep. Eva brooked no interference with her right of tucking him up for this period of peace, but graciously permitted Norah to inspect the process and kiss the rosy cheek peeping from the blankets. Then Alison and Geoffrey accompanied her to the house, and visited Miss de Lisle in her kitchen, finding her by a curious chance, just removing from the oven a batch of tiny cakes of bewildering attractions. Norah lost them afterwards, and going to look for them, was guided by sound to Allenby's pantry, where that most correct of butlers was found on his hands and knees, being fiercely ridden by both his visitors, when it was very pleasant to behold Allenby's frantic endeavours to get to his feet before Norah should discover him, and yet to avoid upsetting his riders. Then they called upon Mr. Linton in his study, but finding him for once inaccessible, being submerged beneath accounts and cheque-books, they fell back upon the billiard-room, where Harry Trevor and Bob McGrath, his chum, welcomed them with open arms, and romped with them until it was time for Norah to take them home to dinner.

"Awful jolly kids, " said Harry. "Why don't you keep them here for lunch, Norah? "

"Eva would be terribly hurt, " said Norah. "She always cooks everything they like best when Mrs. Hunt is away—quite regardless of their digestions. "

"Well, can't they come back afterwards? Let's all go for a walk somewhere. "

"Oh, do! " pleaded Geoffrey. "Could we go to the river, Norah? "

"Yes, of course, " said Norah. "Will it be too far for Alison, though? "

"Not it—she walked there with Father when he was home last time. Do let's. "

"Then we must hurry, " said Norah. "Come along, or Eva will think we have deserted her. "

They found Eva slightly truculent.

"I was wonderin' was you stayin' over there to dinner, " she said. "I know I ain't one of your fine lady cooks with a nime out of the

'Family 'Erald, ' but there ain't no 'arm in that there potato pie, for all that! "

"It looks beautiful, " said Norah, regarding the brown pie affectionately. "I'm so glad I'm here for lunch. What does Michael have, Eva? "

"Michael 'as fish—an' 'e 'as it out in the kitchen with me, " said Eva firmly. "An' 'is own little baby custid-puddin'. No one but me ever cooks anythink for that kid. Well, of course, you send 'im cakes an' things, " she added grudgingly.

"Oh, but they're not nourishment, " said Norah with tact.

"No, " said Eva brightening. "That's wot I says. An' nourishment is wot counts, ain't it? "

"Oh, rather! " Norah said. "And isn't he a credit to you! Well, come on, children—I want pie! " She drew Alison's high chair to the table, while Eva, departing to the kitchen, relieved her feelings with a burst of song.

They spent a merry afternoon at the river—a little stream which went gurgling over pebbly shallows, widening now and then into a broad pool, or hurrying over miniature rapids where brown trout lurked. Harry and Bob, like most Australian soldiers in England, were themselves only children when they had the chance of playing with babies; they romped in the grass with them, swung them on low-growing boughs, or skimmed stones across placid pools, until the sun grew low in the west, and they came back across the park. Norah wheeled Michael in a tiny car; Bob carried Alison, and presently Geoffrey admitted that his legs were tired, and was glad to ride home astride Harry's broad shoulders. Mr. Linton came out to meet them, and they all went back to the cottage, where Eva had tea ready and was slightly aggrieved because her scones had cooled.

"Now, you must all go home, " Norah told her men-folk, after tea. "It's late, and I have to bath three people. "

"Don't we see you again? " Harry asked.

"You may come over to-night if you like—Dad is coming, " Norah said. "Geoff, you haven't finished, have you? "

"I don't think I'm very hungry, " Geoffrey said. "May I go and shut up my guinea-pigs? "

"Yes, of course. Alison darling, I don't think you ought to have any more cakes. "

"I always has free-four-'leven when mother is at home, " said Alison firmly, annexing a chocolate cake and digging her little white teeth into it in the hope of averting any further argument. "Michael doesn't want more, he had Geoff's. "

"Geoff's? But didn't Geoff eat any? "

"Geoff's silly to-night, " said his sister. "Fancy not bein' hungry when there was choc'lit cakes! "

"I hope he didn't get too tired, " Norah said to herself anxiously. "I'll hurry up and get them all to bed. "

She bathed Michael and Alison, with Eva in attendance, and tucked them up. They were very sleepy—too sleepy to be troubled that Mother was not there to kiss them good night; indeed, as Norah bent over Michael, he thought she was his mother, and murmured, "Mum-mum, " in the dusk in a little contented voice. Norah put her cheek down to the rose-leaf one for a moment, and then hurried out.

"Geoff! Where are you, Geoff? "

"I'm here, " said Geoffrey, from the back doorstep. He rose and came towards her slowly. Something in his face made her vaguely uneasy.

"Ready for bed, old chap? " she asked. "Come on—are you tired? "

"My legs are tired, " Geoffrey said. "And my head's queer. It keeps turning round. " He put out a little appealing hand, and Norah took it in her own. It was burning hot.

"I—I wish Mother was home, " the boy said.

Norah sat down and took him on her knee. He put his head against her.

"You must just let old Norah look after you until Mother comes back, " she said gently. The memory of the fever in the village came to her, and she turned sick with fear. For a moment she thought desperately of what she must do both for Geoffrey and for the other children.

"I won't bath Master Geoff; he is tired, " she said to Eva. She carried the little fellow into his room and slipped off his clothes; he turned in the cool sheets thankfully.

"Lie still, old man; I'll be back in a moment, " Norah said. She went out and called to Eva, reflecting with relief that the girl's hard Cockney sense was not likely to fail her.

"Eva, " she said, "I'm afraid Master Geoff is ill. You know there is fever in the village, and I think he has it. I mustn't go near any one, because I've been looking after him. Run over to the house and tell Mr. Linton I would like him to come over—as quickly as possible. Don't frighten him. "

"Right-oh! " said Eva. "I won't be 'arf a tick. "

Her flying feet thudded across the grass as Norah went back to the room where Geoffrey was already sleeping heavily. She looked down at the little face, flushed and dry; in her heart an agony of dread for the Mother, away at her party in London. Then she went outside to wait for her father.

He came quickly, accompanied by Miss de Lisle and Harry Trevor.

"I telephoned for the doctor directly I got your message, " he said. "He'll be up in a few minutes. "

"Thank goodness! " said Norah. "Of course it may not be the fever. But it's something queer. "

"The little chap wasn't all right down at the river, " Harry said. "Only he kept going; he's such a plucky kid. But he sat jolly quiet on me coming home. "

"I knew he was quiet; I just thought he was a bit tired, " Norah said. "I say, Daddy, what about the other children? "

"What about you? " he asked. His voice was hard with anxiety.

"Me? " said Norah, staring. "Why, of course I must stay with him, Dad. He's in my charge. "

"Yes, I suppose you must, " said David Linton heavily. "We'll find out from the doctor what precautions can be taken. "

"Oh, I'll be all right, " Norah said. "But Alison and Michael mustn't stay here. "

"No, of course not. Well, they must only come to us. "

"But the Tired People? " Norah asked.

Miss de Lisle interposed.

"There are hardly any now—and two of the boys go away to-morrow, " she said. "The south wing could be kept entirely for the children, couldn't it, Mr. Linton? Katty could look after them there—they are fond of her. "

"That's excellent, " said Mr. Linton. "I really think the risk to the house wouldn't be much. Any of the Tired People who were worried would simply have to go away. But the children would not come near any of them; and, please goodness, they won't develop fever at all. "

"Then I'll go back and have a room prepared, " Miss de Lisle said; "and then I'll get you, Mr. Harry, to help me bundle them up and carry them over. We mustn't leave them in this place a minute longer than we can help. That lovely fat Michael! " murmured Miss de Lisle incoherently. She hurried away.

There was a hum of an approaching motor presently, and the doctor's car came up the drive. Dr. Hall, a middle-aged and over-worked man, looked over Geoffrey quickly, and nodded to himself, as he tucked his thermometer under the boy's arm. Geoffrey scarcely stirred in his heavy sleep.

"Fever of course, " said the doctor presently, out in the hall. "No, I can't say yet whether he'll be bad or not, Miss Norah. We'll do our best not to let him be bad. Mrs. Hunt away, is she? Well, I'll send you up a nurse. Luckily I've a good one free—and she will bring medicines and will know all I want done. " He nodded approval of their plans for Alison and Michael. Mr. Linton accompanied him to his car.

"Get your daughter away as soon as you can, " the doctor said. "It's a beastly species of fever; I'd like to hang those tinkers. The child in the village died this afternoon. "

"You don't say so! " Mr. Linton exclaimed.

"Yes; very bad case from the first. Fine boy, too—but they didn't call me in time. Well, this village had forgotten all about fever. " He jumped into the car. "I'll be up in the morning, " he said; and whirred off into the darkness.

Alison and Michael, enormously amused at what they took to be a new game, were presently bundled up in blankets and carried across to Homewood; and soon a cab trundled up with a brisk, capable-looking nurse, who at once took command in Geoffrey's room.

"I don't think you should stay, " she said to Norah. "The maid and I can do everything for him—and his mother will be home to-morrow. A good hot bath, with some disinfectant in it, here; then leave all your clothes here that you've worn near the patient, and run home in fresh things. No risk for you then. "

"I couldn't leave Geoff, " Norah said. "Of course I won't interfere with you; but his mother left him to me while she was away. And he might ask for me. "

"Well, it's only for your own sake I was advising you, " said the nurse. "What do you think, Mr. Linton? "

"I think she ought to stay, " said David Linton shortly—with fear tugging at his heart as he spoke. "Just make her take precautions, if there are any; but the child comes first—he was left in our care. "

He went away soon, holding Norah very tightly to him for a moment; and then the nurse sent Norah to bed.

"There's nothing for you to do, " she said. "I shall have a sleep near the patient. "

"But you'll call me if he wants me? "

"Yes—I promise. Now be off with you. "

At the moment Norah did not feel as though she could possibly sleep; but very soon her eyes grew heavy and she dozed off to dream, as she often dreamed, that she and Jim were riding over the Far Plain at Billabong, bringing in a mob of wild young bullocks. The cattle had never learned to drive, and broke back constantly towards the shelter of the timber behind them. There was one big red beast, in particular, that would not go quietly; she had half a dozen gallops after him in her dream with Bosun under her swinging and turning with every movement of the bullocks, and finally heading him, wheeling him, and galloping him back to the mob. Then another broke away, and Jim shouted to her, across the paddock.

"Norah! Norah! "

She woke with a start. A voice was calling her name, hoarsely; she groped for her dressing-gown and slippers, and ran to Geoffrey's room. The nurse, also in her dressing-gown, was bending over the bed.

"You're quick, " she said approvingly. "He only called you once. Take this, now, sonnie. "

"Norah! "

She bent down to him, taking the hot hand.

"I'm here, Geoff, old man. Take your medicine. "

"All right, " said Geoffrey. He gulped it down obediently and lay back. "Will Mother come? "

"Very soon now, " Norah said. "You know she had to be in London—just for one night. She'll be back to-morrow. "

"It's nearly to-morrow, now, " the nurse said. "Not far off morning. "

"That's nice! " the child said. "Stay with me, Norah. "

"Of course I will, old man. Just shut your eyes and go to sleep; I won't go away. "

She knelt by his bed, patting him gently, until his deep breaths told that sleep had come to him again. The nurse touched her shoulder and pointed to the door; she got up softly and went out, looking through her open window at the first streaks of dawn in the east. Her dream was still vivid in her mind; even over her anxiety for the child in her care came the thought of it, and the feeling that Jim was very near now.

"Jim! " she whispered, gazing at the brightening sky.

In Germany, at that moment, two hunted men were facing dawn— running wildly, in dread of the coming daylight. But of that Norah knew nothing. The Jim she saw was the big, clean-limbed boy with whom she had ridden so often at Billabong. It seemed to her that his laughing face looked at her from the rose and gold of the eastern sky.

Then Geoffrey turned, and called to her, and she went to him swiftly.

*****

It was four days later.

"Mother. " Geoffrey's voice was only a thread of sound now. "Will Father come? "

"I have sent for him, little son. He will come if he can. "

"That's nice. Where's Norah? "

223

"I'm here, sweetheart. " Norah took the wasted hand in hers, holding it gently. "Try to go to sleep. "

"Don't go away, " Geoffrey murmured. "I'm awful sleepy. " He half turned, nestling his head into his mother's arm. Across the bed the mother's haggard eyes met Norah's. But hope had almost died from them.

"If he lives through the night there's a chance, " the doctor said to David Linton. "But he's very weak, poor little chap. An awful pity; such a jolly kid, too. And all through two abominable families of tinkers! However, there are no fresh cases. "

"Can you do nothing more for Geoffrey? "

The doctor shook his head.

"I've done all that can be done. If his strength holds out there is a bare chance. "

"Would it be any good to get in another nurse? " Mr. Linton asked. "I'm afraid of the mother and Norah breaking down. "

"If they do, we shall have to get some one else, " the doctor answered. "But they wouldn't leave him; neither of them has had any sleep to speak of since the boy was taken ill. Norah is as bad as Mrs. Hunt; the nurse says that even if they are asleep they hear Geoffrey if he whispers. I'll come again after a while, Mr. Linton. "

He hurried away, and David Linton went softly into the little thatched cottage. Dusk was stealing into Geoffrey's room; the blind fluttered gently in the evening breeze. Mrs. Hunt was standing by the window looking down at the boy, who lay sleeping, one hand in that of Norah, who knelt by the bed. She smiled up at her father. Mrs. Hunt came softly across the room and drew him out into the passage.

"He may be better if he sleeps, " she said. "He has hardly had any real sleep since he was taken ill. "

"Poor little man! " David Linton's voice was very gentle. "He's putting up a good fight, Mrs. Hunt. "

"Oh, he's so good! " The mother's eyes filled with tears. "He does everything we tell him—you know he fought us a bit at first, and then we told him he was on parade and we were the officers, and he has done everything in soldier-fashion since. I think he even tried to take his medicine smartly—until he grew too weak. But he never sleeps more than a few moments unless he can feel one of us; it doesn't seem to matter whether it's Norah or me. "

Geoffrey stirred, and they heard Norah's low voice.

"Go to sleep, old chap; it's 'Lights Out, ' you know. You mustn't wake up until Reveille. "

"Has 'Last Post' gone? " Geoffrey asked feebly.

"Oh yes. All the camp is going to sleep. "

"Is Father? "

"Yes. Now you must go to sleep with him, the whole night long. "

"Stay close, " Geoffrey whispered. His weak little fingers drew her hand against his face. Then no sound came but fitful breathing.

The dark filled the little room. Presently the nurse crept in with a shaded lamp and touched Norah's shoulder.

"You could get up, " she whispered.

Norah shook her head, pointing to the thin fingers curled in her palm.

"I'm all right, " she murmured back.

They came and went in the room from time to time; the mother, holding her breath as she looked down at the quiet face; the nurse, with her keen, professional gaze; after a while the doctor stood for a long time behind her, not moving. Then he bent down to her.

"Sure you're all right? "

Norah nodded. Presently he crept out; and soon the nurse came and sat down near the window.

"Mrs. Hunt has gone to sleep, " she whispered as she passed.

Norah was vaguely thankful for that. But nothing was very clear to her except Geoffrey's face; neither the slow passing of the hours nor her own cramped position that gradually became pain. Geoffrey's face, and the light breathing that grew harder and harder to bear. Fear came and knelt beside her in the stillness, and the night crept on.

CHAPTER XVIII

THE WATCH ON THE RHINE

Evening was closing upon a waste of muddy flats. Far as the eye could see there was no rise in the land; it lay level to the skyline, with here and there a glint of still water, and, further off, flat banks between which a wide river flowed sluggishly. If you cared to follow the river, you came at length to stone blockhouses, near which sentries patrolled the banks—and would probably have turned you back rudely. From the blockhouses a high fence of barbed wire, thickly criss-crossed, stretched north and south until it became a mere thread of grey stretching over the country. There was something relentless, forbidding, in that savage fence. It was the German frontier. Beyond it lay Holland, flat and peaceful. But more securely than a mountain range between the two countries, that thin grey fence barred the way.

If you turned back from the sentries and followed the muddy path along the river bank, you were scarcely likely to meet any one. The guards in the blockhouses were under strict discipline, and were not encouraged to allow friends to visit them, either from the scattered farms or from the town of Emmerich, where lights were beginning to glimmer faintly in the twilight. It was not safe for them to disregard regulations, since at any moment a patrol motor-launch might come shooting down the river, or a surprise visit be paid by a detachment from the battalion of infantry quartered, for training purposes, at Emmerich. Penalties for lax discipline were severe; the guards were supposed to live on the alert both by day and by night, and the Emmerich commandant considered that the fewer distractions permitted to the sentries, the more likely they were to make their watch a thorough one. There had been too many escapes of prisoners of war across the frontier; unpleasant remarks had been made from Berlin, and the Commandant was on his mettle. Therefore the river-bank was purposely lonely, and any stray figure on it was likely to attract attention.

A mile from the northern bank a windmill loomed dark against the horizon; a round brick building, like a big pepper-castor, with four great arms looking like crossed combs. A rough track led to it from the main road. Within, the building was divided into several floors, lit by narrow windows. The heavy sails had plied lazily during the

227

day; now they had been secured, and two men were coming down the ladder that led from the top. On the ground floor they paused, looking discontentedly at some barrels that were ranged against the wall, loosely covered with sacking.

"Those accursed barrels are leaking again, " one said, in German. "Look! " He pointed to a dark stain spreading from below. "And Rudolf told me he had caulked them thoroughly. "

"Rudolf does nothing thoroughly—do you not know that? " answered his companion scornfully. "If one stands over him—well and good; if not, then all that Master Rudolf cares for is how soon he may get back to his beerhouse. Well, they must be seen to in the morning; it is too late to begin the job to-night. "

"I am in no hurry, " said the first man. "If you would help me I would attend to them now. All the stuff may not be wasted. "

"Himmel! I am not going to begin work again at this hour, " answered the other with a laugh. "I am not like Rudolf, but I see no enjoyment in working overtime; it will be dark, as it is, before we get to Emmerich. Come on, my friend. "

"You are a lazy fellow, Emil, " rejoined the first man. "However, the loss is not ours, after all, and we should be paid nothing extra for doing the work to-night. Have you the key? "

"I do not forget it two nights running, " returned Emil. "What luck it was that the master did not come to-day! —if he had found the mill open I should certainly have paid dearly. "

"Luck for you, indeed, " said his companion. They went out, shutting and locking the heavy oaken door behind them. Then they took the track that led to the main road.

The sound of their footsteps had scarcely died away when the sacking over one of the barrels became convulsed by an internal disturbance and fell to the floor; and Jim Linton's head popped up in the opening, like a Jack-in-the box.

"Come on, Desmond—they've gone at last! " he whispered.

Desmond's head came up cautiously from another barrel.

"Take care—it may be only a blind, " he warned. "They may come back at any moment. "

Jim's answer was to wriggle himself out of his narrow prison, slowly and painfully. He reached the floor, and stood stretching himself.

"If they come back, I'll meet them with my hands free, " he said. "Come on, old man; we're like rats in a trap if they catch us in those beastly tubs. At least, out here, we've our knives and our fists. Come out, and get the stiffness out of your limbs. "

"Well, I suppose we may as well go under fighting if we have to, " Desmond agreed.

Jim helped him out, and they stood looking at each other. They were a sorry-looking pair. Their clothes hung in rags about them; they were barefoot and hatless, and, beyond all belief, dirty. Thin to emaciation, their gaunt limbs and hollow cheeks spoke of terrible privations; but their sunken eyes burned fiercely, and there was grim purpose in their set lips.

"Well—we're out of the small traps, but it seems to me we're caught pretty securely in a big one, " Desmond said presently. "How on earth are we going to get out of this pepper-pot? "

"We'll explore, " Jim said. Suddenly his eye fell on a package lying on an empty box, and he sprang towards it, tearing it open with claw-like fingers.

"Oh, by Jove—*food!* " he said.

They fell upon it ravenously; coarse food left by one of the men, whose beer-drinking of the night before had perhaps been too heavy to leave him with much appetite next day. But, coarse as it was, it was life to the two men who devoured it.

It was nearly six weeks since the night when their tunnel had taken them into the world outside the barbed wire of their prison; six weeks during which it had seemed, in Desmond's phrase, as though they had escaped from a small trap to find themselves caught within a big one. They had been weeks of dodging and hiding; travelling by night, trusting to map and compass and the stars; lying by day in woods, in ditches, under haystacks—in any hole or corner that should shelter them in a world that seemed full of cruel eyes looking ceaselessly for them. Backwards and forwards they had been driven; making a few miles, and then forced to retreat for many; thrown out of their course, often lost hopelessly, falling from one danger into another. They had never known what it was to sleep peacefully; their food had been chiefly turnips, stolen from the fields, and eaten raw.

Three times they had reached the frontier; only to be seen by the guards, fired upon—a bullet had clipped Jim's ear—and forced to turn back as the only alternative to capture. What that turning-back had meant no one but the men who endured it could ever know. Each time swift pursuit had nearly discovered them; they had once saved themselves by lying for a whole day and part of a night in a pond, with only their faces above water in a clump of reeds.

They had long abandoned their original objective; the point they had aimed at on the frontier was far too strongly guarded, and after two attempts to get through, they had given it up as hopeless, and had struck towards the Rhine, in faint expectation of finding a boat, and perhaps being able to slip through the sentries. They had reached the river two nights before, but only to realize that their hope was vain; no boats were to be seen, and the frowning blockhouses barred the way relentlessly. So they had struck north, again trying to pierce the frontier; and the night before had encountered sentries—not men alone, but bloodhounds. The guards had contented themselves with firing a few volleys—the dogs had pursued them savagely. One Jim had succeeded in killing with his knife, the other, thrown off the trail for a little by a stream down which they had waded, had tracked them down, until, almost exhausted, they had dashed in through the open door of the old mill—for once careless as to any human beings who might be there.

The bloodhound had come, too, and in the mill, lit by shafts of moonlight through the narrow windows, they had turned to bay. The fight had not lasted long; they were quick and desperate, and the dog had paid the penalty of his sins—or of the sins of the human brutes who had trained him. Then they had looked for concealment, finding none in the mill—the floors were bare, except for the great barrels, half-full of a brown liquid that they could not define.

"Well, there's nothing for it, " Jim had said. "There's not an inch of cover outside, and daylight will soon be here. We must empty two of these things and get inside. "

"And the dog? " Desmond had asked.

"Oh, we'll pickle Ponto. "

Together they had managed it, though the barrels taxed all their strength to move. The body of the bloodhound had been lowered into the brown liquid; two of the others had been gradually emptied upon the earthen floor. With the daylight they had crawled in, drawing the sacking over them, to crouch, half-stifled through the long day, trembling when a step came near, clenching their knives with a sick resolve to sell their freedom dearly. It seemed incredible that they had not been discovered; and now the package of food was the last stroke of good luck.

"Well, blessings on Emil, or Fritz, or Ludwig, or whoever he was, " Jim said, eating luxuriously. "This is the best blow-out I've had since—well, there isn't any since, there never was anything so good before! "

"Never, " agreed Desmond. "By George, I thought we were done when that energetic gentleman wanted to begin overhauling the casks. "

"Me too, " said Jim. "Emil saved us there—good luck to him! "

They finished the last tiny crumb, and stood up.

"I'm a different man, " Desmond said. "If I have to run to-night, then the man that tries to catch me will have to do it with a bullet! "

"That's likely enough, " Jim said, laughing. "Well, come and see how we're going to get out. "

There seemed little enough chance, as they searched from floor to floor. The great door was strong enough to resist ten men; the windows were only slits, far too narrow to allow them to pass through, even had they dared risk the noise of breaking their thick glass. Up and up they went, their hearts sinking as their bodies mounted; seeing no possible way of leaving their round prison.

"Rats in a trap! " said Desmond. "There's nothing for it but those beastly barrels again—and to watch our chance of settling Emil and his pal when they come to-morrow. "

"Let's look out here, " Jim said.

They were at the top of the mill, in a little circular place, barely large enough for them to stand upright. A low door opened upon a tiny platform with a railing, from which the great sails could be worked; they were back now, but the wind was rising, and they creaked and strained at their mooring rope. Far below the silver sheet of the Rhine moved sluggishly, gleaming in the moonlight. The blockhouses stood out sharply on either bank.

"Wonder if they can see us as plainly as we see them, " Jim said.

"We'll have callers here presently if they can, " Desmond said. "That, at least, is certain. Better come in, Jim. "

Jim was looking at the great sails, and then at the rope that moored them.

"Wait half a minute, " he said.

He dived into the mill, and returned almost instantly with a small coil of rope.

"I noticed this when we came up, " he said. "It didn't seem long enough to be any use by itself, but if we tie it to this mooring-rope it might be long enough. "

"To reach the ground from here? " Desmond asked him in astonishment. "Never! You're dreaming, Jim. "

"Not from here, of course, " Jim said. "But from the end of the sail. "

"The sail! " Desmond echoed.

"If we tie it to the end of the sail's rope, and let the mill go, we can swing out one at a time, " Jim said. "Bit of a drop at the bottom, of course, but I don't think it would be too much, if we wait till our sail points straight down. "

"But——" Desmond hesitated. "The sail may not bear any weight—neither may the rope itself. "

"The ropes seem good enough—they're light, but strong, " Jim said. "As for the sail—well, it looks pretty tough; the framework is iron. We can haul on it and test it a bit. I'd sooner risk it than be caught here, old man. "

"Well—I'm going first, " Desmond said.

"That you're not—it's my own little patent idea, " Jim retorted. "Just you play fair, you old reprobate. Look—they keep a sort of boathook thing here, to catch the rope when the arm is turning—very thoughtful and handy. You'll easily get it back with that. "

He was knotting the two ropes as he spoke, testing them with all his strength.

"There—that will hold, " he said. "Now we'll let her go. "

He untied the mooring-rope, and very slowly the great sails began to revolve. They tugged violently as the arm bearing the rope mounted, and drew it back; it creaked and groaned, but the rope held, and nothing gave way. Jim turned his face to Desmond on the narrow platform.

"I'm off! " he said. "No end of a jolly lark, isn't it? Hold her till I get on the railing. "

"Jim—if it's too short! "

"Well, I'll know all about that in a minute, " said Jim with a short laugh. "So long, old chap: I'll be waiting below, to catch you when you bounce! "

He flung his legs over the railing, sitting upon it for an instant while he gripped the rope, twining his legs round it. Then he dropped off, sliding quickly down. Sick with suspense, Desmond leaned over to watch him.

Down—down he went. The mill-arms rose for a moment, and then checked as his weight came on them—and slowly—slowly, the great sail from which he dangled came back until it pointed straight downwards, with the clinging figure hanging far below. Down, until the man above could scarcely see him—and then the rope, released, suddenly sprang into the air, and the sails mounted, revolving as if to make up for lost time. On the grass below a figure capered madly. A low, triumphant whistle came up.

"Oh, thank God! " said Desmond. He clutched the boathook and leaned out, finding that his hands trembled so that the sails went round three times before he managed to catch the dangling rope. Then it was only a moment before he was on the grass beside Jim. They grinned at each other.

"You all right? " Jim asked.

"Oh, yes. It was pretty beastly seeing you go, though. "

"It was only a ten-foot drop at the end, " said Jim, casting his eye up at the creaking sails. "But it certainly was a nasty moment while one wondered if the old affair would hold. I don't believe it ever was made in Germany—it's too well done! "

"Well, praise the pigs we haven't got to tackle those barrels again! " Desmond said. "Come along—we'll try and find a hole in the old fence. "

They came out of the friendly shadow of the mill and trotted northwards, bending low as they ran; there was no cover on the flats, and the moonlight was all too clear, although friendly clouds darkened it from time to time. It was a windy night, with promise of rain before morning.

"Halt! Who goes there? "

The sharp German words rang out suddenly. Before them three soldiers seemed to have risen from the ground with levelled rifles.

Jim and Desmond gave a despairing gasp, and turned, ducking and twisting as they fled. Bullets whistled past them.

"Are you hit? " Jim called.

"No. Are you? "

"No. There's nothing but the river. "

They raced on madly, their bare feet making no sound. Behind them the pursuit thudded, and occasionally a rifle cracked; not so much in the hope of hitting the twisting fugitives, as to warn the river sentries of their coming. The Germans were not hurrying; there was no escape, they knew! Father Rhine and his guardians would take care of their quarry.

Jim jogged up beside Desmond.

"We've just a chance, " he said—"if we ever get to the river. You can swim under water? "

"Oh yes. "

"Then keep as close to the bank as you can—the shots may go over you. We'll get as near the blockhouses as we dare before we dive. Keep close. "

He was the better runner, and he drew ahead, Desmond hard at his heels. The broad river gleamed in front—there were men with rifles silhouetted against its silver. Then a merciful cloud-bank drifted across the moon, and the shots whistled harmlessly in the sudden darkness. Jim felt the edge of the bank under his feet.

"Dive! " he called softly.

He went in gently and Desmond followed with a splash. The sluggish water was like velvet; the tide took them gently on, while they swam madly below the surface.

Shouts ran up and down the banks. Searchlights from the blockhouses lit the river, and the water was churned under a hail of machine-gun bullets, with every guard letting off his rifle into the stream in the hope of hitting something. The bombardment lasted for five minutes, and then the officer in command gave the signal to cease fire.

"The pity is, " he observed, "that we never get the bodies; the current sees to that. But the swine will hardly float back to their England! " He shrugged his shoulders. "That being settled, suppose we return to supper? "

It might have hindered the worthy captain's enjoyment had he been able to see a mud-bank fifty yards below the frontier, where two dripping men looked at each other, and laughed, and cried, and wrung each other's hands, and, in general, behaved like people bereft of reason.

"Haven't got a scratch, have you, you old blighter? " asked Jim ecstatically.

"Not one. Rotten machine-gun practice, wasn't it? Sure you're all right? "

"Rather! Do you realize you're in Holland? "

"Do you realize that no beastly Hun can come up out of nowhere and take pot-shots at you? "

"It's not their pot-shots I minded so much, " said Jim. "But to go back to a prison-camp—well, shooting would be a joke to that. Oh, by Jove, isn't it gorgeous! " They pumped hands again.

"Now, look here—we've got to be sober, " Desmond said presently. "Holland is all very well; I've heard it's a nice place for skating. But neither of us has any wish to get interned here. "

"Rather not! " said Jim. "I want to go home and get into uniform again, and go hunting for Huns. "

"Same here, " said Desmond. "Therefore we will sneak along this river until we find a boat. Go steady now, young Linton, and don't turn hand springs! "

Within the Dutch frontier the Rhine breaks up into a delta of navigable streams, on which little brown-sailed cargo-boats ply perpetually; and the skipper of a Dutch cargo-boat will do anything for money. A couple of hours' hard walking brought Jim and Desmond to a village with a little pier near which half a dozen boats were moored. A light showed in a port-hole, and they went softly on deck, and found their way below into a tiny and malodorous cabin. A stout man sprang to his feet at sight of the dripping scarecrows who invaded his privacy.

South Africa had taught Desmond sufficient Dutch to enable him to make himself intelligible. He explained the position briefly to the mariner, and they talked at length.

"Wants a stiff figure, " he said finally, turning to Jim. "But he says 'can do. ' He'll get us some clothes and drop down the river with us to Rotterdam, and find a skipper who'll get us across to Harwich— the German navy permitting, of course! "

"The German navy! " said Jim scornfully. "But they're asleep! " He yawned hugely. "I'm going to sleep, too, if I have to camp on the gentleman's table. Tell him to call me when it's time to change for Blighty! "

CHAPTER XIX

REVEILLE

It was not yet dawn when David Linton, fully dressed, came into the cottage garden. The door stood open, and he kicked off his shoes and crept into the house.

Eva sat on the floor of the passage with her head in her hands. She looked up with a start as the big man came in, and scrambled to her feet; a queer dishevelled figure with her tousled head and crumpled cap and apron. A wave of dismay swept over Mr. Linton.

"Is he— —? " he whispered, and stopped.

The girl beckoned him into the sitting-room.

"'E's never stirred all night, " she whispered. "I dunno if 'e isn't dead; I never see any one lie so still. The nurse wouldn't sit there like a wooden image if 'e was dead, would she, sir? "

"Surely not, " said David Linton. "Where is Miss Norah? "

"Kneelin' alongside of 'im, same like she was when you was here. She ain't never stirred, neither. An' I'll bet a dollar she must be stiff!"

"And Mrs. Hunt? "

"She's in there, wiv 'em. She 'ad a little sleep; not much. No one's said one word in this 'ouse all night. "

"Why didn't you go to bed? " David Linton said, looking down at the pinched old face and the stooping shoulders. He had never noticed Eva very much; now he felt a sudden wave of pity for the little London servant. She loved Geoffrey too in her queer way.

"Not me! " said Eva defiantly. "And 'im very near dyin'. I been boilin' the kettle every hour or so, but none of 'em came out for tea. Will *you* 'ave a cup, sir? "

A refusal was on his lips, but he changed his mind.

"Thank you, " he said gently. "And have one yourself, Eva. "

"My word, I'll be glad of it, " she said. "It's bitter cold, sittin' out there. " She tip-toed off to the kitchen. Mr. Linton stood, hesitating, for a moment, and then went along the passage. A screen blocked Geoffrey's doorway, and he peeped over it.

As he did so, Mrs. Hunt moved to the end of the bed. Geoffrey lay exactly as he had been on the night before; so utterly still that it was impossible to say whether he were alive or dead. Norah crouched beside him, her hand still against his face.

Then, very slowly, Geoffrey turned, and opened his eyes.

"Mother! " he said. "Mother, I'm so thirsty! "

Mrs. Hunt was beside him as his eyelids had lifted. The nurse, moving swiftly, handed her a little cup.

"Drink this, sweetheart. " The mother raised his head, and Geoffrey drank eagerly.

"That's awful nice, " he said. "May I have some more? "

They gave him more, and put him back on the pillow. He looked at Norah, who knelt by him silently.

"Wake up, old Norah—it's Reveille! " he said.

She smiled at him, and put her face on his, but she did not stir. Suddenly the nurse saw Mr. Linton, and beckoned to him.

"Carry her—she can't move. "

Norah felt her father's arm about her.

"Hold round my neck, dear, " he said.

The nurse was at her other side. They raised her slowly, while she clenched her teeth to keep back any sound that should tell of the agony of moving—still smiling with her eyes on Geoffrey's sleepy face. Then, suddenly, she grew limp in her father's arm.

"Fainted, " murmured the nurse. "And a very good thing. " She put her arm round her, and they carried her out between them, and put her on a sofa.

"I must go back to Geoffrey, " the nurse said. "Rub her—rub her knees hard, before she comes to. It's going to hurt her, poor child! " She hurried away.

Geoffrey was lying quietly, his mother's head close to him. The nurse put her hand on his brow.

"Nice and cool, " she said. "You're a very good boy, Geoff; we'll think about some breakfast for you presently. " Mrs. Hunt raised her white face, and the nurse's professional calmness wavered a little. She patted her shoulder.

"There—there, my dear! " she said. "He's going to do very well. Don't you worry. He'll be teaching me to ride that pony before we know where we are. " She busied herself about the boy with deft touches. "Now just keep very quiet—put Mother to sleep, if you like, for she's a tired old mother. " She hastened back to Norah.

"Is she all right? " David Linton's voice was sharp with anxiety. "She has never moved. "

"The best thing for her, " said the nurse, putting him aside and beginning to massage this new patient. "If I can rub some of the stiffness away before she becomes conscious it will save her a lot. Run away, there's a dear man, and tell that poor soul in the kitchen that the child is all right. "

"He will live? "

"Rather! That sleep has taken every trace of the fever away. He's weak, of course, but we can deal with that when there's no temperature. Tell Eva to make tea—lots of it. We all want it. "

"Thus it was that presently might have been seen the astounding spectacle of a grizzled Australian squatter and a little Cockney serving-maid holding each other's hands in a back kitchen.

"I knew it was orright when I 'eard you comin' down the 'all, " said Eva tearfully. "No one's 'ad that sort of a step in this 'ouse since Master Geoff went sick. The dear lamb! Won't it be 'evinly to see 'is muddy boot-marks on me clean floor agin! An' him comin' to me kitching window an' askin' me for grub! I'll 'ave tea in a jiffy, sir. An' please 'scuse me for ketchin' old of you like that, but I'd 'ave bust if I 'adn't 'eld on to somefink! "

Geoffrey dropped off to sleep again, presently, and Mrs. Hunt came to Norah, who was conscious, and extremely stiff, but otherwise too happy to care for aches and pains. They did not speak at first, those two had gone down to the borderland of Death to bring back little, wandering feet; only they looked at each other, and clung together, still trembling, though only the shadow of fear remained.

After that Geoffrey mended rapidly, and, having been saintlike when very ill, became just an ordinary little sinner in his convalescence, and taxed every one's patience to keep him amused. Alison and Michael, who were anxiously watched for developing symptoms, refused to develop anything at all, remaining in the rudest health; so that they were presently given the run of all Homewood, and assisted greatly in preventing any of the Tired People from feeling dull.

Norah remained at the cottage, which was placed strictly in quarantine, and played with Geoffrey through the slow days of weakness that the little fellow found so hard to understand. Aids to convalescence came from every quarter. Major Hunt, unable to leave France, sent parcels of such toys and books as could still be bought in half-ruined towns. Wally, who had been given four days' leave in Paris—which bored him to death—sent truly amazing packages, and the Tired People vied with David Linton in ransacking London for gifts for the sick-room. Geoffrey thought them all very kind, and would have given everything for one hour on Brecon beside Mr. Linton.

"You'll be able to ride soon, old chap, " Norah said, on his first afternoon out of bed.

"Will I? " The boy looked scornfully at his thin legs. "Look at them—they're like silly sticks! "

"Yes, but Brecon won't mind that. And they'll get quite fat again. Well, not fat—" as Geoffrey showed symptoms of horror—"but hard and fit, like they were before. Quite useful. "

"I do hope so, " Geoffrey said. "I want them to be all right before Father comes—and Wally. Will Wally come soon, do you think? "

"I'm afraid not: you see, he has been to Paris. There's hardly any leave to England now. "

"'Praps leave will be open by Christmas, " Geoffrey suggested hopefully. "Wouldn't it be a lovely Christmas if Father and Wally both came? "

"Wouldn't it just? " Norah smiled at him; but the smile faded in a moment, and she walked to the window and stood looking out. Christmas had always been such a perfect time in their lives: she looked back to years when it had always meant a season of welcoming Jim back; when every day for weeks beforehand had been gay with preparations for his return from school. Jim would arrive with his trunks bulging with surprises for Christmas morning; Wally would be with him, both keen and eager for every detail in the life of the homestead, just as ready to work as to play. All Billabong, from the Chinese gardener to Mr. Linton, hummed with the joy of their coming. Now, for the first time, Christmas would bring them nothing of Jim.

She felt suddenly old and tired; and the feeling grew in the weeks that followed, while Geoffrey gradually came back to strength and merriment, and the cottage, after a strenuous period of disinfecting, emerged from the ban of quarantine. Alison and Michael had a rapturous reunion with their mother and Geoffrey, and Homewood grew strangely quiet without the patter of their feet. Norah returned to her post as housekeeper, to find little to do; the house seemed to run on oiled wheels, and Miss de Lisle and the servants united in trying to save her trouble.

"I dunno is it the fever she have on her, " said Katty in the kitchen one evening. "She's that quiet and pale-looking you wouldn't know her for the same gerrl. "

"Oh, there's no fear of fever now, " said Miss de Lisle.

"Well, she is not right. Is it fretting she is, after Masther Jim? She was that brave at first, you'd not have said there was any one dead at all."

"I think she's tired out, " said Miss de Lisle. "She has been under great strain ever since the news of Mr. Jim came. And she is only a child. She can't go through all that and finish up by nursing a fever patient—and then avoid paying for it. "

"She cannot, indeed, " said Katty. "Why wouldn't the Masther take her away for a change? Indeed, it's himself looks bad enough these times, as well. We'll have the two of them ill on us if they don't take care. "

"They might go, " said Miss de Lisle thoughtfully. "I'll suggest it to Mr. Linton. "

David Linton, indeed, would have done anything to bring back the colour to Norah's cheeks and the light into her eyes. But when he suggested going away she shrank from it pitifully.

"Ah, no, Daddy. I'm quite well, truly. "

"Indeed you're not, " he said. "Look at the way you never eat anything! "

"Oh, I'll eat ever so much, " said Norah eagerly. "Only don't go away: we have work here, and we wouldn't know what to do with ourselves anywhere else. Perhaps some time, when Wally comes home, if he cares to go we might think about it. But not now, Daddy. " She hesitated. "Unless, of course, you want to very much. "

"Not unless you do, " he said. "Only get well, my girl. "

"I'm quite all right, " protested Norah. "It was only Geoff's illness that made me a bit slack. And we've had a busy summer, haven't we? I think our little war-job hasn't turned out too badly, Dad. "

"Not too badly at all—if it hasn't been too much for my housekeeper, " he said, looking at her keenly. "Remember, I won't have her knocked up. "

"I won't be, Daddy dear—I promise, " Norah said.

She made a brave effort to keep his mind at ease as the days went on; riding and walking with him, forcing herself to sing as she went about the house—she had her reward in the look in the silent man's eyes when he first heard a song on her lips—and entering with a good imitation of her old energy into the plans for the next year on the farm. But it was all imitation, and in his heart David Linton knew it. The old Norah was gone. He could only pity her with all his big heart, and help her in her struggle—knowing well that it was for his sake. In his mind he began to plan their return to Australia, in the hope that Billabong would prove a tonic to her tired mind and body. And yet—how could they face Billabong, without Jim?

He came out on the terrace one evening with a letter in his hand.

"Norah, " he said. "I've good news for you—Wally is coming home."

"Is he, Dad? On leave? "

"Well—he has been wounded, but not seriously. They have been nursing him in a hospital at Boulogne and he writes that he is better, but he is to have a fortnight's leave. "

"It will be lovely to have him, " Norah said. "May I see the letter, Dad? "

"Of course. " He gave it to her. "Poor old Wally! We must give him a good time, Norah. "

"It's a pity Harry's leave didn't happen at the same time, " said Norah. "However, Phil will be a mate for him; they like each other awfully. "

"Yes, " agreed her father. "Still, I don't think Wally wants any other mate when you are about. "

"They were always astonishingly good in the way they overlooked my bad taste in being a girl! " said Norah, with a laugh. She was running her eye over the letter. "Oh—hit in the shoulder. I do hope it wasn't a very painful wound—poor old boy. I wonder will he be able to ride, Dad? "

"He says he's very well. But then, he would, " Mr. Linton said. "Since we first knew him Wally would never admit so much as a finger-ache if he could possibly avoid it. I expect he'll ride if it's humanly possible! "

Allenby came out.

"Hawkins would like to see you, sir. "

"Very well, " said his master. "By the way, Allenby, Mr. Wally is coming back on leave. "

The butler's face brightened.

"Is he indeed, sir! That's good news. "

"Yes—he has been wounded, but he's all right. "

"Miss de Lisle will certainly invent a new dish in his honour, sir, " said Allenby, laughing. "Is he coming soon? "

"This week, he says. Well, I mustn't keep Hawkins waiting. " He went into the house, with Allenby at his heels. It was evident that the kitchen would hear the news as quickly as the ex-sergeant could get there.

Norah read the letter over again, slowly, and folded it up. Then she turned from the house, and went slowly across the lawn. At the sweep of the drive there was a path that made a short cut across the park to a stile, and her feet turned into it half-unconsciously.

The dull apathy that had clogged her brain for weeks was suddenly gone. She felt no pleasure in the prospect that would once have been so joyful, of seeing Wally. Instead her whole being was seething with a wild revolt. Wally's coming had always meant Jim. Now he would come alone, and Jim could never come again.

"It isn't fair! " she said to herself, over and over. "It isn't fair! "

She came to the stile, and paused, looking over it into a quiet lane. All her passionate hunger for Jim rose within her, choking her. She had kept him close to her at first; lately he had slipped away so that she had no longer the dear comfort of his unseen presence that had helped her through the summer. And she wanted him—wanted him. Her tired mind and body cried for him; always chum and mate and brother in one. She put her head down on the railing with a dry sob.

A quick step brushed through the crisp leaves carpeting the lane. She looked up. A man in rough clothes was coming towards her.

Norah drew back, wishing she had brought the dogs with her; the place was lonely, and the evening was closing in. She turned to go; and as she did so the man broke into a clear whistle that made her pause, catching her breath. It was the marching tune of Jim's regiment; but beyond the tune itself there was something familiar in the whistle—something that brought her back to the stile, panting, catching at the rail with her hands. Was there any one else in the world with that whistle—with that long, free stride?

He came nearer, and saw her for the first time—a white-faced girl who stood and stared at him with eyes that dared not believe—with lips that tried to speak his name, and could not. It was Jim who sobbed as he spoke.

"Norah! Norah! "

He flung himself over the stile and caught her to him.

"Old mate! " he said. "Dear little old mate! "

They clung together like children. Presently Norah put up her hand, feeling the rough serge of his coat.

"It isn't a dream, " she said. "Tell me it isn't, Jimmy-boy. Don't let me wake up. "

Jim's laugh was very tender.

"I'm no dream, " he said. "All these months have been the dream— and you can wake up now. "

She shivered, putting her face against him.

"Oh—it's been so long! "

Then, suddenly, she caught his hand.

"Come! " she said breathlessly. "Come quickly—to Dad! "

They ran across the park, hand in hand. Near the house Jim paused.

"I say, old chap, we can't take him by surprise, " he said. "I was going to sneak in by the back door, and get hold of Miss de Lisle and Allenby, to tell you. Hadn't you better go and prepare him a bit? "

"Yes, of course, " Norah said. "There's a light in the study: he's always there at this time. Come in and I'll hide you in Allenby's pantry until I ring. "

They crept in by a side door, and immediately ran into the butler.

"How are you, Allenby? " Jim inquired pleasantly.

Allenby staggered back.

"It's Mr. Jim! " he gasped, turning white.

"It is, " said Jim, laughing. He found the butler's hand, and shook it. Norah left them, and went swiftly to her father's study. She opened the door softly.

David Linton was sitting in a big armchair by the fire, bending forward and looking into the red coals. The light fell on his face, and showed it old and sad with a depth of sadness that even Norah had hardly seen. He raised his head as the door opened.

"Hallo, my girl, " he said, forcing a smile. "I was just beginning to wonder where you were. "

"I went across the park, " Norah said nervously. Something in her voice made her father look sharply at her.

"Is anything the matter, Norah? "

"No, " she said quickly. She came close to him and put her hand on his shoulder.

"You look as if you had seen a ghost, " he said. "What is it, Norah? "

"I—I thought I had, too, " she stammered. "But it was better than a ghost. Daddy—Daddy! " she broke down, clinging to him, laughing and crying.

"What is it? " cried David Linton. "For God's sake tell me, Norah! " He sprang to his feet, shaking.

"He's here, " she said. "He isn't dead. " Suddenly she broke from him and ran to the bell. "Jim, " she said; "Jim has come back to us, Daddy. "

The door was flung open, and Jim came in, with great strides.

"Dad! "

"My boy! " said his father. They gripped each other's hands; and Norah clung to them both, and sobbed and laughed all at once.

"Let me sit down, children, " said David Linton presently; and they saw that he was trembling. "I'm getting an old man, Jim; I didn't know how old I was, until we lost you. "

"You couldn't get old if you tried, " said Jim proudly. "And you can't lose me either—can he, Norah? " They drew together again; it seemed complete happiness just to touch each other—not to speak;

to be together. Afterwards there would be explanations; but they seemed the last thing that mattered now.

They did not hear the hoot of a motor in the drive or a ring at the front door. Allenby answered it, and admitted a tall subaltern.

"Mr. Wally! "

"Evening, Allenby, " said Wally. "I believe I'm a bit ahead of time—I didn't expect to get here so soon. Do you think they'll have a corner for me? "

Allenby laughed—a rather quavering laugh.

"I think you'll always find your room ready, sir, " he said. "You—I suppose you 'aven't 'eard our good news, sir? "

"I never hear good news, " said Wally shortly. "What is it? "

Allenby eyed him doubtfully.

"I don't know as I oughtn't to break it to you a bit, sir, " he said. "You can't be over-strong yet, and you wounded, and all; and never 'aving rightly got over losing Mr. Jim, and— —"

Wally shuddered.

"For Heaven's sake, man, stop breaking it gently! " he said. "What is it? " In his voice was the crisp tone of the officer; and the ex-sergeant came to attention smartly.

"It's Mr. Jim, sir, " he said. "'E's 'ome. "

For a long moment Wally stared at him.

"You're not mad, I suppose? " he said slowly. "Or perhaps I am. Do you mean— —"

"Them 'Uns couldn't kill him, sir! " Allenby's voice rose on a note of triumph. "Let me take your coat, sir—'e's in the study. And you coming just puts the top on everything, sir! "

He reached up for Wally's coat. But the boy broke from him and ran blindly to the study, bursting in upon the group by the fire. There he stopped dead, and stared at them.

"Old chap! " said Jim. He sprang to him, and flung an arm round his shoulders. Then he gave a great sigh of utter contentment, and echoed Allenby unconsciously.

"Well, if that doesn't make everything just perfect! " he said.

CHAPTER XX

ALL CLEAR

"Kiddie, are you awake? "

"Come in, Jimmy. "

Norah sat up in bed and felt for the electric switch. The room sprang into light as Jim came in.

"I had to come and bring your stocking, " he said. "Merry Christmas, little chap. "

"Merry Christmas, Jimmy dear. " Norah looked at the bulging stocking on her bed, and broke into laughter. "And you a full-blown Captain! Oh, Jimmy, are you ever going to grow up? "

"I trust not, " said Jim comfortably—"if it means getting any bigger than I am. But you're not, either, so it doesn't matter. Do you remember all the Christmases at Billabong when I had to bring you your stocking? "

"Do I remember! " echoed Norah scornfully. "But at Billabong it was daylight at four o'clock in the morning, and extremely hot— probably with a bush-fire or two thrown in. You'll be frozen to death here. Turn on the electric stove, and we'll be comfy. "

"That's a brain-wave, " said Jim, complying. "I must admit I prefer an open fireplace and three-foot logs—but in a hurry those little contraptions of stoves are handy. Hold on now—I'll get you something to put over your shoulders. "

"There's a woolly jacket over there, " Norah said. "Let me have my property—I'm excited. " She possessed herself of the stocking and fished for its contents. "Chocolates! —and in war-time! Aren't you ashamed? "

"Not much, " said Jim calmly, extracting a huge chocolate from the box. "I lived on swede turnips for six weeks, so I think the family deserves a few extras. Fish some more. "

251

Norah obeyed, and brought to light articles of a varied nature; a pair of silk stockings, a book on *Housekeeping as a Science*, a large turnip, artistically carved, a box of French candied fruit, a mob-cap and a pair of housemaids' gloves, and, lastly, the cap of a shell, neatly made into a pin-tray.

"I did that in camp in Germany, " said Jim. "And I swore I'd put it into your Christmas stocking. Which I have done. "

"Bless you, " said Norah. "I would rather lose a good many of my possessions than that. " They smiled at each other; and, being an undemonstrative pair, the smile was a caress.

"Isn't this going to be a Christmas! " Norah said. "I've been lying awake for ever so long, trying to realize it. You alive again——"

"I never was dead, " said Jim indignantly.

"It was a horribly good imitation. And Wally here, and even Harry; and Major Hunt home; and Geoff getting stronger every day. And Dad grown twenty years younger. "

"And you too, I guess—judging by what you looked like the night I came home. "

"Oh, I've got turned and made up to look like new, " said Norah. She faltered a little. "Jimmy, I've been saying my prayers—*hard*. "

"I've done that, too, " said Jim. There was a long, contented silence.

"And somehow, now, I know you'll be all right—both of you, " Norah said. "I just feel certain about it. Before—ever since the war began—I was always horribly afraid, but now I'm not afraid any more. It can't last for ever; and some day we'll all go back. "

"And that will be the best thing in the world, " said Jim.

"The very best, " she said.

Some one tapped at the door.

"May I come in? " asked Miss de Lisle's voice. She entered, bearing a little tray.

"You! " said Norah. "But you shouldn't. "

"Bride and Katty have gone to church, so I thought I'd bring you some tea and wish you a merry Christmas, " said Miss de Lisle. "But I didn't expect to find the Captain here. " She did not wait for their greetings, but vanished with the elephantine swiftness peculiar to her; returning in a few moments with a second tray.

"And toast! " said Jim. "But where's your own, Miss de Lisle? "

"Never mind mine—I'll have it in the kitchen, " said the cook-lady.

"Indeed, you will not. Sit down. " He marched off, unheeding her protests. When he returned, he bore a large kitchen tray, with the teapot.

"It seemed simpler, " he said. "And I couldn't find anything smaller. This cup is large, Miss de Lisle, but then you won't want it filled so often. Have some of my toast—I couldn't possibly eat all this. "

"Well, it's very pleasant here, " said the cook-lady, yielding meekly. "I took some to Mr. Wally, but he merely said, 'Get out, Judkins; I'm not on duty! ' and rolled over. So I concluded, in Katty's words, that 'his resht was more to him, ' and came away. "

"He'll wake up presently and be very pleased to find it; it won't matter to him at all if it's stone-cold, " said Jim. "Queer chap, Wal. I prefer tea with the chill off it, myself. Judkins has hard times getting him up in time for early parade. Luckily Judkins is an old regular soldier, and has a stern, calm way with a young officer. "

"Who bullies *you* into getting up, may I ask? " demanded Miss de Lisle.

"I used to be bullied by a gentleman called Wilkes, in the grey days when I was a subaltern, " said Jim sadly. "Now, alas, I am a responsible and dignified person, and I have to set an example. " He sighed. "It's awful to be a captain! "

"It's so extraordinary, " said his sister, "that I never get used to it. "

"But you never had any respect for age, " said Jim, removing her tray and putting a pillow on her head. "Every one finished? then I'll clear away the wreck and go and dress. " He piled the three trays on top of each other and goose-stepped from the room solemnly—his long legs in pyjamas, under a military great coat, ending a curious effect to the spectacle. Miss de Lisle and Norah laughed helplessly.

"And a captain! " said the cook-lady, wiping her eyes. "Now I really must run, or there will be no breakfast in this house. "

Breakfast was a movable feast in the Home for Tired People, who wandered in and out just as they felt inclined. Hot dishes sat on a hot-water plate and a little aluminium-topped table; such matters as ham and brawn lurked on a sideboard; and Allenby came in from time to time to replenish tea and coffee. Norah and her father rarely encountered any one but Phil Hardress at this meal, since theirs was generally over long before most of their guests had decided to get up. On this morning, however, every one was equally late, and food did not seem to matter; the table was "snowed under" with masses of letters and Christmas parcels, and as every one opened these and talked all at once, mingling greetings with exclamations over the contents of the packages, Miss de Lisle's efforts had been in vain.

"I pitied your post-lady, " said Mrs. Aikman, the wife of a wounded colonel. "She staggered to the door under an enormous mail-bag, looking as though Christmas were anything but merry. However, I saw her departing, after an interval, with quite a sprightly step. "

"Allenby had orders to look after her, " Norah said, smiling. "Poor soul—she begins her round at some unearthly hour and she's hungry and tired by the time she gets here. "

"One of the remarkable things about this country of yours, " said Mr. Linton, "is the way you have continued to deliver parcels and letters as though there were no war. Strange females or gaunt children bring them to one's door, but the main point is that they do come. In Australia, even without a war, the post-office scorns to deliver a parcel; if any one is rash enough to send you one the post-office puts it in a cupboard and sends you a cold postcard to tell you to come and take it away. If you don't come soon, they send you a threatening card. "

"And if you don't obey that? "

"I never dared to risk a third, " said Mr. Linton, laughing. "I am a man of peace. "

"But what a horrible system! " said Mrs. Aikman. "Doesn't it interfere with business? "

"Oh yes, greatly, " said her host. "But I suppose we shall learn, in time. "

"I'm going over to the cottage, " Norah whispered to Jim. "Do come—Geoff won't think it's Christmas if you don't. "

They went out into the hall. Flying feet came down the stairs, and Wally was upon them.

"Merry Christmas, Norah! " He seized both her hands and pranced her down the hall. "Always begin Christmas with a turkey-trot! " he chanted.

"Begin, indeed! " said Norah, with a fine contempt. "I began mine hours ago. Where have you been? "

"I have been—contemplating, " said Wally, his brown eyes twinkling. "No one called me. "

"There's evidence to the contrary, " Jim said, grinning. "It has been stated that you called a perfectly blameless lady Judkins, and said awful things to her. "

"My Aunt! " said Wally. "I hope not—unless you talk pretty straight to Judkins he doesn't notice you. That accounts for the frozen tea and toast I found; I thought Father Christmas had put 'em there. "

"Did you eat them? "

"Oh, yes—you should never snub a saint! " said Wally. "So now I don't want any breakfast. Where are you two going? "

"To the cottage. Come along—but really, I do think you should eat a decent breakfast, Wally. "

"It will be dinner-time before we know where we are—and I feel that Miss de Lisle's dinner will be no joke, " said Wally. "So come along, old house mother, and don't worry your ancient head about me. " Each boy seized one of Norah's hands and they raced across the lawn. David Linton, looking at them from the dining-room window, laughed a little.

"Bless them—they're all babies again! " he thought.

The cottage was echoing with strange sounds; it might be inferred that the stockings of the young Hunts had contained only bugles, trumpets and drums. Eva, sweeping the porch, greeted the newcomers with a friendly grin.

"Merry Christmas, Eva! "

"The sime to you, " said Eva. "Ain't it a real cold morning? The frorst's got me fingers a fair treat. "

"No one minds frost on Christmas Day—it's the proper thing in this queer country! " said Wally. "Was Father Christmas good to you, Eva? "

"Wasn't 'e! Not 'arf! " said Eva. "The children wouldn't 'ear of anyfink but 'angin' up a stockin' for me—and I'm blowed if it wasn't bang full this mornin'. And a post-card from me young man from the Front; it's that saucy I wonder 'ow it ever passed the sentry! Well, I do say as 'ow this place ain't brought us nuffink but luck! "

Geoffrey dashed out, equipped with a miniature Sam Brown belt with a sword, and waving a bugle.

"Look! Father Christmas brought them! Merry Christmas, everybody. " He flung himself at Norah, with a mighty hug.

"And where's my Michael—and that Alison? " Norah asked. "Oh, Michael, darling, aren't you the lucky one! " as he appeared crowned with a paper cap and drawing a wooden engine. "Where's Alison? "

"It's no good ever *speaking* to Alison, " Geoffrey said, with scorn. "She got a silly doll in her stocking, and all she'll do is to sit on the floor and take off its clothes. Girls are stupid—all 'cept you, Norah! "

"Keep up that belief, my son, and you'll be spared a heap of trouble, " said Major Hunt, coming out. "Unfortunately, you're bound to change your mind. How are you all? We've had an awful morning! "

"It began at half-past four, " Mrs. Hunt added. "At that hour Michael discovered a trumpet; and no one has been asleep since. "

"They talk of noise at the Front! " said her husband. "Possibly I've got used to artillery preparation; anyhow, it strikes me as a small thing compared to my trio when they get going with assorted musical instruments. How is your small family, Miss Norah? "

"Not quite so noisy as yours—but still, you would notice they were there! " Norah answered, laughing. "They were all at breakfast when I left, and it seemed likely that breakfast would run on to dinner, unless they remembered that church is at eleven. I must run home; we just came to wish you all a merry Christmas. Dinner at half-past one, remember! "

"We won't forget, " Mrs. Hunt said.

Every one was dining at Homewood, and dinner, for the sake of the children, was in the middle of the day. The house was full of guests; they trooped back from church across the park, where the ground rang hard as iron underfoot, for it was a frosty Christmas. Homewood glowed with colour and life—with big fires blazing everywhere, and holly and ivy scarlet and green against the dark oaken panelling of the walls. And if the Australians sent thoughts overseas to a red homestead—Billabong, nestling in its green of orchard and garden, with scorched yellow paddocks stretching away for miles around it—they were not homesick thoughts to-day. For home was in their hearts, and they were together once more.

The dinner was a simple one—Miss de Lisle had reserved her finest inspirations for the evening meal, regarding Christmas dinner as a mere affair of turkey and blazing plum-pudding, which, except in the matter of sauces, might be managed by any one. "It needs no soul! " she said. But no one found any fault, and at the end Colonel Aikman made a little speech of thanks to their hosts. "We all know they hate speeches made at them, " he finished. "But Homewood is a blessed word to-day to fighting men. "

"And their wives, " said Mrs. Aikman.

"Yes—to people who came to it tired beyond expression; and went back forgetting weariness. In their names—in the names of all of us—we want to say 'Thank you. '"

David Linton stood up, looking down the long room, and last, at his son.

"We, who are the most thankful people in the world, I think, to-day, " he said, "do not feel that you owe us any gratitude. Rather we owe it to all our Tired People—who helped us through our own share of what war can mean. And, apart from that, we never feel that the work is ours. We carry on for the sake of a dead man—a man who loved his country so keenly that to die for it was his highest happiness. We are only tools, glad of war-work so easy and pleasant as our guests make our job. But the work is John O'Neill's. So far as we can, we mean to make it live to his memory. "

He paused. Norah, looking up at him, saw him through misty eyes.

"So—we know you'll think of us kindly after we have gone back to Australia, " the deep voice went on. "There will be a welcome there, too, for any of you who come to see us. But when you remember Homewood, please do not think of it as ours. If that brave soul can look back—as he said he would, and as we are sure he does—then he is happy over every tired fighter who goes, rested, from his house. His only grief was that he could not fight himself. But his work in the war goes on; and as for us, we simply consider ourselves very lucky to be his instruments. "

Again he paused.

"I don't think this is a day for drinking toasts, " he said. "When we have won we can do that—but we have not won yet. But I will ask you all to drink to a brave man's memory—to John O'Neill. "

The short afternoon drew quickly to dusk, and lights flashed out—to be discreetly veiled, lest wandering German aircraft should wish to drop bombs as Christmas presents. Norah and the boys had disappeared mysteriously after dinner, vanishing into the study. Presently Geoffrey came flying to his mother, with eager eyes.

"Mother! Father Christmas is here! "

"You don't say so! " said Mrs. Hunt, affecting extreme astonishment. "Where? "

"I saw him run along the hall and go into the study. He was real, Mother! "

"Of course he's real, " Major Hunt said. "Do you think he's gone up the study chimney? "

Wally appeared in the doorway.

"Will the ladies and gentlemen kindly walk into the study? " he said solemnly. "We have a distinguished guest. "

"There! I *told* you, " said Geoffrey ecstatically. He tugged at his father's hand, capering.

In the study a great fir-tree towered to the ceiling; a Christmas-tree of the most beautiful description, gay with shining coloured globes and wax lights and paper lanterns; laden with mysterious packages in white paper, tied with ribbon of red, white and blue, and with other things about which there was no mystery—clockwork toys, field guns and ambulance wagons, and a big, splendid Red Cross nurse, difficult to consider a mere doll. Never was seen such a laden tree; it's branches groaned under the weight they bore. And beside it, who but Father Christmas, bowing and smiling with his eyes twinkling under bushy white eyebrows.

"Walk in, ladies and gentleman, walk in! " he said invitingly.

Wally frowned at him.

"That's not the way to talk, " he said. "You aren't a shop-walker! " He inflicted a surreptitious kick upon the elderly saint.

"Hi, you blighter, that's my shin! " said Father Christmas wrathfully; a remark luckily unheard by the guests in the excitement of the moment.

All the household was there; Miss de Lisle beaming at Wally and very stately and handsome in blue silk; the servants, led by Allenby, with Con and Katty and Bride giggling with astonishment at a tree the like of which did not grow in Donegal.

"All mustered? " said Father Christmas. "Right oh! I mean, that is well. As you see, I've had no end of a time labouring in your behalf. But I love hard work! " (Interruption from Mr. Meadows, sounding like "I *don't* think! ") "Being tired, I shall depute to my dear young friend here the task of removing the parcels from the tree. " He tapped Wally severely on the head with his knuckles, and that hapless youth ejaculated, "Beast! ". "You'll get thrown out, if you don't watch it! " said the saint severely. "Now—ladies first! "

He detached the Red Cross nurse from her bough and placed her in Alison's arms; and Alison, who had glued her eyes to her from the moment of entering the room, uttered a gasp, sat promptly upon the floor, and began an exhaustive examination of her charms, unheeding any further gifts. Under the onslaught of Wally and Harry the tree speedily became stripped of its burden; Father Christmas directing their labours in a voice that plainly had its training on the barrack-square. Eva watched him admiringly.

"Ain't the Captin a trick! " she murmured, hugging her parcels to her.

The last package came down, and Father Christmas slipped away, disappearing behind a screen with a flourish that revealed an immaculate brown leather gaiter under the cotton-wool snow bordering his red cloak; and presently Jim sauntered out, slightly flushed.

"Oh, you silly! " said Geoffrey. "Where *ever* have you been? You've missed ole Father Christmas! "

"I never did have any luck, " Jim said dolefully.

"Never mind—he's left heaps and heaps of parcels for you. I'll help you open them, " said Geoffrey kindly.

The gong summoned them to tea; and afterwards it was time to take the children home, happy and sleepy. Jim tossed Alison up on his shoulder, and, with Geoffrey clinging to his other hand, and Michael riding Wally pick-a-back, Norah and the boys escorted the Hunts back to the cottage.

"You're coming over again, of course? " Jim said. "We're going to dance to-night. "

"Oh yes; we're getting a terribly frivolous old couple, " said Mrs. Hunt, laughing. "But Christmas leave only comes once a year, especially when there's a war on! "

"I think she needs a rest-cure! " said her husband, knitting his brows over this remarkable statement. "Come in and lie down for awhile, or you won't be coherent at all by to-night; Eva and I will put the babies to bed. "

"Can't I help? " Norah asked.

"No—you're off duty to-night. You've really no idea how handy I am! " said Major Hunt modestly.

"Then we'll see you later on, " Norah said, disentangling Michael from her neck. "Good-night, Michael, darling; and all of you. "

"We've had a lovely time! " Geoffrey said.

"I'm so glad, " Norah said, smiling at him. The cottage-door closed, and they turned back.

"I've had a lovely time, too! " she said. "There never was such a Christmas! "

"Never! " Jim said. "I believe that five months in Germany was worth it. "

"No! " said Wally sharply.

"No, it wasn't, " Norah agreed. "But now—it helps one to forget. "

They came slowly across the frozen lawn. Before them Homewood loomed up, little beams of warm light coming from its shuttered windows. Then the door opened wide, letting out a flood of radiance; and in it stood David Linton, looking out for them. They came into the path of light; Norah between the two tall lads. His voice was tender as he looked down at their glowing faces.

"It's cold, " he said. "Come in to the fire, children. "

Lightning Source UK Ltd.
Milton Keynes UK
06 August 2010
158025UK00001B/73/P